^{The} Lilac House

The Lilac House

BARBARA JOSSELSOHN

Bookouture

Published by Bookouture in 2020

An imprint of Storyfire Ltd.
Carmelite House
50 Victoria Embankment
London EC4Y 0DZ

www.bookouture.com

ISBN: 978-1-83888-158-0
eBook ISBN: 978-1-83888-157-3

CHAPTER ONE

Anna mixed the pancake batter and thought about Greg's summer smell.

That's what she'd called it, his summer smell. It would return as if by magic every June, when the kids were finishing up school, and the azaleas under the front window were bursting out red. She remembered breathing it on him a year ago, when he'd come back so early from his run, wearing that old Binghamton University tee shirt he loved. He'd run out of steam, he'd explained—he hadn't slept well last night in anticipation of the five-hour drive to Lilac House. She'd poured him some ice water and followed him to the table, where she'd stretched her pajama-clad legs onto his bare knees. He'd kneaded her toes for a few luscious minutes, and then gone upstairs to take a shower and rouse the kids, shouting, "Last one to breakfast gets the pancake that fell on the floor!"

God, how she missed that smell. It was warm, kind of like sandalwood. A little citrusy. A little cinnamon. Less apparent in the morning when the scent of body wash prevailed. Stronger after he'd exercised, or in the evening, when the kids were asleep and she'd curl up by his side on the sofa, the two of them lit only by the glow of the TV…

"Mommy?"

Anna started. "What? *What?*" she blurted out.

Evie stood in the kitchen doorway, her hands grasping the hem of her green "Lake Summers Day Camp" tee shirt. Her copper hair was neatly parted in the middle and pulled back into a low, sensible ponytail.

"I just wanted to show you I'm ready," she said, her ten-year-old voice apologetic. "You told us to come down when we were dressed."

"Yes, of course I did, and look at that—you found last year's camp shirt!" Anna forced herself back into the present. "You know, you'll get a new one this year. Blue, I think."

"Blue's good. But I like the green. But I like blue, too. I'll like them both, right, Mom?"

"Of course you will," Anna said, walking over to her daughter and stroking her cheek. "They're both great colors. You'll be very happy with the new shirt, I promise. Okay?" She smiled when Evie nodded. "Okay! Now, would you do me a favor, and see if your brother's dressed? Tell him it's time for breakfast. And make sure you've put everything you want in your duffel."

Evie went back upstairs, and Anna heated the griddle. She hadn't meant to be staring off into space like that. There was still a lot to be done. She and Greg had instinctively divided the final chores each June, with her packing up the last-minute items and him preparing the house to be empty all summer. They'd been such a great team, working in tandem without saying a word. Now he was gone, and it was all on her, and she felt ashamed for taking his role for granted. She tried to visualize what he might have been doing last year in these final hours. Tying up and taking out the last bag of trash, no doubt. Setting the timer on the hall light. Turning up the thermostat so the air conditioning wouldn't kick in. Turning off the valve to the outdoor waterspout—no, he did that when they went away in the winter, so the pipe wouldn't freeze. Or did he do it in the summer, too?

She poured the batter, and went to the hall closet to see if anything more came to mind. The top shelf was lined with assorted household necessities: light bulbs, duct tape, a hammer, a screwdriver, and the big yellow flashlight. She figured Greg had probably kept a supply of such things at Lilac House, but wondered if she should take the flashlight just in case. No, she thought. She could always buy one up there. The one here was old, and the switch always stuck. Greg had used it so much last year, always checking that it was working so they'd be ready if a storm blew in and the power went out. He wanted to be certain that they'd be safe, come what may. She knew that was why he chose to drive home during last fall's rainstorm. How she wished he'd stayed put and waited in the hotel until morning.

"Zac and Evie!" she called as she returned to the kitchen. "Come on, breakfast."

Evie came downstairs and laid out the plates, forks, and glasses, while Anna finished the pancakes and put a stack of three on each child's plate. Zac appeared a few moments later and dropped into a chair.

"Good morning, honey," Anna said.

He speared a pancake.

"How'd you sleep?" she said, taking off his Silver Plains Middle School cap and stroking his hair. She loved the color—kind of neutral, the color of twigs and tree trunks, until you looked closer and saw the touches of auburn and dark caramel. Greg's hair had been the same, although strands of gray had been working their way through.

"Did you remember to pack your headphones?" she said. "Because if you can't fall asleep at first—"

"Oh *God*, why do you *do* that?" he said, yelled, jerking his head away. "I *hate* when you remind me. Now I have to go check, I have to make sure—"

"I'm sorry, honey, I was only trying to help…" But he was already gone. She looked at his still-full plate. "Terrific," she murmured. "He didn't even eat anything."

"Don't worry, Mom, it's not your fault," Evie said. "And anyway I packed some granola bars. And Aunt Hope has food in her new store, probably. Healthy snacks, because it's a dance store, right, Mom?"

Anna watched her daughter examine a syrup-covered triangle of pancake atop her fork, her feet in their flip-flops swinging beneath her chair. She planted a kiss on the top of Evie's head.

"Yes, honey, but we don't have to wait until we get to Aunt Hope's to eat," she said. "We'll stop on the way to Lake Summers for lunch. You both like Big A's Diner on the highway, right?"

Evie tilted her head as though giving the matter great thought, and then nodded. "And then Zac won't be hungry," she said. "So don't worry about it. We're fine, Mom, right?"

"Yes, of course," she said, as Evie ate the last of her pancake, then slid off her chair and headed upstairs. It had to be the third or fourth time this morning that Evie had ended a sentence with "Right?" and Anna knew there'd be more. Her daughter was always looking for reassurance. The therapist last winter said the kids were doing well, considering that they had lost their father just a couple of months earlier. But she knew her kids, and she knew in her heart that they were struggling. She stood in the silent kitchen, then took a bite of pancake from Zac's plate as she carried it toward the sink, listening to the soft, thick sound of her chewing. Quietness was familiar to her now. But the helplessness she felt when she tried to read her kids—that was a feeling she'd never get used to.

She washed the dishes by hand so they wouldn't sit in the dishwasher all summer, and then dried and put them away. The cabinet still held Tupperware and Pyrex containers from all the casseroles and fruit salads she'd received last fall when the news about Greg got around. There'd been so many, she wasn't even sure whose they were.

Then she went to her bedroom and fetched the two empty suitcases from her closet, so she could load them in the car before the kids came back down. She didn't want to have to explain that she planned to clean out Lilac House. Greg's brother had stressed after the funeral that she should sell it—she shouldn't be carrying two mortgages and keeping up two homes. It was the only advice she remembered from his dizzying set of financial recommendations, none of which made sense. Yes, they'd spent down their savings on Greg's last political campaign, but there was the brokerage account with Greg's share of the inheritance his grandfather left. Why was money an immediate concern? She hadn't asked the question, though, because ultimately it didn't matter. She *wanted* to sell Lilac House. She and the kids couldn't keep returning each summer to that idyllic place, now that Greg was gone. It would be like reopening a wound, over and over and over again. They would have this summer to reinforce their memories, and to say goodbye. And then they would move on.

Still, she wasn't going to tell the kids right now about selling, because she didn't want to make them face yet another sudden loss. They needed time to adjust. She'd play it by ear. Probably they'd decide on their own that Lilac House belonged in the past.

Rolling the bags onto the front step, she paused before popping the trunk of the car. A year ago, she and Greg had emerged to find a horde of reporters and photographers at the foot of the driveway. Greg had taken off his sunglasses and hooked them on the placket of his polo shirt, and then winked at her so she'd do the same. He thought that people who wore sunglasses in front of the press looked like they were hiding something. She'd nodded and removed hers, too, and then smoothed her hair along her neck in preparation for being photographed.

Then he put his arm around her shoulder, and she wrapped hers around his waist, and they walked down the front steps so Greg could talk to the reporters. Their questions that morning were all about Willow Center, the proposed mental health facility slated for downtown Silver Plains. Greg told them that he wasn't worried about the pockets of opposition because he knew the local residents would put aside their fears once they understood the facts. She'd marveled at how optimistic he sounded. He was boyish that way. Always expecting things would turn out right.

Now the block was empty, except for a small red Civic parked across the street. The young woman inside waved a large envelope. Anna forced herself to smile and wave back. It was her own fault—if she'd responded to Crystal's emails or texts last week, then Crystal wouldn't have felt compelled to come over this morning. But the accident was just last fall. Couldn't they give her a little more time?

Crystal ran over, her speed impeded by her pencil skirt and heels. "Hi, Anna, I know you're getting ready to go, but I wanted to make sure you got my messages. It was so unlike you not to call back—"

"I did get them, Crystal. I'm sorry."

Crystal smiled sheepishly and raised the envelope. "Well, it's all here. I'll go over a few things, real quick—we received the list of approved trees for the memorial along the highway, and we need your choice so we can get it planted. And Dan Groner from the *Inquirer* wants to visit you in a few weeks, to interview you for a story to run right before the city council meeting in August. And the monument—it will say 'In memory of State Senator Greg Harris,' but is there a quote he liked, or a poem, a song lyric…?"

Anna put a hand to her mouth. How was it that these conversations could still make her sad? Greg hadn't been a scholar, he didn't read poetry or quote famous people. That was part of his charm. He liked regular things. Action movies. Baseball. A Big Mac and large fries every once in a while. The song lyrics he liked were from Disney movies he watched over and over with the kids when they were little: *Frozen, The Lion King, Aladdin*. He made them laugh when they got older because he still remembered all the words.

Crystal gasped. "Oh God, Anna, I didn't mean to upset you," she said. "Oh, shit, now I'm going to cry." She took a couple of breaths and waved her hands in front of her face, as though to fan her eyes dry. "Okay, I'm okay. I feel horrible, bothering you. But I needed to touch base on these things. And we're worried about the Willow Center project, too. I can't stop thinking of how hard Greg worked on it, and how tired he looked. We'll all feel horrible if it fails. And you're the closest thing we have to him…"

Anna took the envelope from Crystal and wrapped her in a hug. Greg's staff had been young and passionate, and they'd idolized him. They'd all landed on their feet, thanks to Crystal, who had kept her job as communications director with the new state senator and brought the rest of the gang with her. But the loss of Greg hit them hard. Anna had realized at the funeral that many of them had never had anyone close to them die, except maybe an elderly grandparent. They'd all looked so shell-shocked. She'd made time at the reception to listen to their stories about Greg. She'd tried to reassure them that they'd be okay.

"You were right to stop by, Crystal," she said. "I'm on this, I promise."

Crystal brushed the bottom of her nose with her fingertips. "Thanks, and again, I'm sorry I made you sad. Have a good trip, okay?"

Anna nodded and waved as Crystal took off. She liked Crystal—in fact, she'd liked all of Greg's staff. Being a kind of mother figure to them had been something she'd enjoyed. But playing that role now was like trying to hold onto a snowflake. The role had dissolved when Greg died, and as long as she kept performing it, she'd never stop thinking about how wonderful her old life had been and how much she missed it. She unzipped one of the suitcases to push the envelope inside, telling herself she would deal with Crystal's questions once she got upstate. Although it wasn't going to be easy to find the time. She had to start clearing out the house. And see if the winter had caused damage that should be repaired. And then find a handyman, and a realtor, and maybe a home stager, too…

But at least she would have Hope, her father's younger sister, to help. Anna had barely known her aunt when she was growing up—Hope had been in Europe back then, touring as a principal dancer with the Hamburg Ballet Theatre. She hadn't even come home that awful summer Anna's father died. But Anna knew it wasn't Hope's fault—she'd been traveling from city to city, sometimes jumping onto a train only a couple of hours after completing a performance. Anna had wanted to find Hope and ask her to come home, but didn't know exactly where Hope was or how best to leave a message. And in retrospect, Anna was glad her phone calls and letters never reached their target. Hope was pursuing her dreams, dancing her heart out in gorgeous theaters and in front of adoring crowds. Anna would have deeply regretted it if she had pulled Hope away from her soaring career to help with the funeral.

Anna put the empty suitcases into the trunk and then went back toward the house. Evie was sitting on the front step and looking out onto the street, her elbows on her knees and her chin in her hands, her duffel next to her and her backpack strapped over shoulders. She hoped Evie hadn't been there for the conversation with Crystal. She tried so hard not to cry in front of the kids.

"You okay, honey?" she said.

Evie nodded.

"Where's your brother?"

"He said he had to check something."

"Again?" Anna looked skyward, as though hoping for some insight. Zac was often checking locks and lights and faucets now, just as Greg used to do. It was almost as if he didn't trust that she could keep them safe on her own. Her heart ached for him, and the way he thought he had to carry all that responsibility on his thirteen-year-old shoulders.

"That's what he told me," Evie said. "Do you want me to get him?"

"No, honey, I'll do it," Anna said, but before she could get to the door, Zac came out of the house, his expression still strained. He brought his duffel to the driveway, and Evie followed with hers, as Anna went inside for her packed suitcase and other bags. Then she locked the front door and worked with the kids to finish loading the trunk.

She stepped back to survey the baggage. It wasn't as neat as when Greg used to load the car—the bags would look like pieces in a finished jigsaw puzzle when he was through—but at least everything fit, and nothing stuck up so high that her view would be blocked.

Zac got into the front passenger seat, and Evie climbed into the back. Anna got behind the wheel.

"Goodbye, house," Evie said. "Goodbye, trees. Goodbye, grass."

"Oh, *God!*" Zac groaned. "What's *wrong* with you? You don't say goodbye to a house."

Evie didn't respond, but just lowered her voice. "Goodbye, house," she whispered. "Don't change while we're gone. Right, Mom? You want it to stay the same, right?"

Anna nodded as she backed out of the driveway. But the truth wasn't that simple. On the one hand, she agreed with Evie—there had been way too many changes in their lives these last nine months. And yet she hoped that some things would change while they were away. She hoped the kids would accept her decision to sell Lilac House. She hoped she'd prove strong enough to face the things Greg had left there last summer, fully intending to return with them now. She hoped she'd be able to offer up the house, and to leave it with no regrets, resolved to let a new family make wonderful memories there.

She hoped that when the three of them came back in September, it would be to a life that was beginning to feel normal.

"Mom, what are you most excited about for Lake Summers?" Evie asked as they took off down the street.

That was an easy one. "Being with Aunt Hope and seeing her new store."

It was the only thing giving her strength—the knowledge that Hope was waiting for them. Hope was bold and independent and daring—all the things Anna wasn't but wished she was. Just the way Hope had found out about the abandoned building on Main Street last summer, and then envisioned her own dance store and made it all happen—Anna was in awe of that. She couldn't wait to see the store. She and Greg had planned to be there for the grand opening last month, but she hadn't felt strong enough to go alone.

But now… now was when she needed to be with Hope. Maybe her aunt could help her rediscover her spark, her love of life, which surely was buried deep inside her. After all, Hope had always believed that Anna had the talent to be a world-class ballerina, too—even at times when Anna was sure she'd never live up to her father's expectations. "You have the strongest feet of any dancer I know," Hope would tell her. "And the most engaging smile—that's a dancer's most important feature, you know." That's what had given Anna the courage to keep persevering all those years ago: knowing her Aunt Hope believed in her with all her heart.

Hope was her only living relative, the only person in the world who had known her before she'd married Greg. Anna needed Hope to remind her of the person she used to be.

CHAPTER TWO

Hope transferred the fresh packages of dance tights from the shipping carton to the wicker basket, and then carried the basket to the stand near the window. Retracing her steps, she picked up the packages that had slid to the floor and balanced them on top of the pile. She knew they'd probably slide right off again the moment a customer dug in, but she didn't care; she'd pick up the strays as often as she needed.

She loved the look of a well-stocked store, with tops and bottoms bursting from the racks and sparkly jewelry, key chains and picture frames adorning the glass display case. It made her feel secure, like that old picture book she used to love, about the magic pot that wouldn't stop making porridge. There was something so exciting about knowing there was *more*. That you could dig and dig through the bins, and never come up short.

Sure, the overflowing merchandise was not there by magic, like the porridge. The abundance was due entirely to the orders she'd placed, and the invoices would need to be paid. But that didn't matter. In fact, it *was* a little like magic, the transformation that had happened in one short year. Finally she had a place she could call her own, and things she could control. She was the owner of The Lilac Pointe, the most beautiful dance shop on the planet. She had found the perfect location—a short drive from Jayson College, a small liberal arts school with a popular dance major. And she had named it after one of the most glorious solos in classical ballet, the Lilac Variation from *The Sleeping Beauty*. It was her debut solo, the one she'd danced in Hamburg. The one she'd taught Anna that first summer she returned to New York to visit, when Anna was only eight years old. The solo that made Anna fall in love with ballet, too.

Hope took a sip of hot coffee, then put the cup back on the counter and brought the emptied merchandise carton outside. It was quiet on Main Street this early in the morning—not a regular quiet, but a loaded, anticipatory quiet, the kind that only a downtown merchant could feel and appreciate. There was a promise of discovery and activity in the warm June breeze that bathed her bare arms and played with the hair that had come loose from her long ponytail. She put the carton by the side of the building and then came back around. Tucking a wayward section of hair behind her ear, she waved to Stan, who was sweeping the walk in front of his smoothie shop next door.

"Hi, Hope," he called, resting his chin on his broom, so his bushy salt-and-pepper beard spilled over the handle. His raspberry-colored "Smoothie Dudes" apron stretched wide over his large belly. "You're getting an early start."

"I wanted to do a little extra straightening up," she said as she walked toward him. "My niece and her two kids get back into town today."

Stan shook his head. "How is it that you have a grown-up niece with kids of her own? You look like a kid, yourself!"

Hope playfully punched his elbow. "I think your eyes need checking. Trust me. I'm plenty old."

"I'm telling you, I don't believe it… hey, wait," he said, his expression turning serious. "Is this the niece you went to see last fall? The one with the husband…?"

Hope nodded. "I went there for the funeral."

"God, that's a sad story. Trey and I googled them while you were away, did we tell you? We recognized the family from the pictures—they used to come in for smoothies. We had no idea he was so important. He seemed like a regular guy."

"He liked to lay low up here," Hope said. "So Anna and the kids could have a break." She folded her arms over her chest and looked down along Main Street. She didn't want to think about Greg, not with Anna coming so soon. She didn't want to relive the talk she'd had with him last summer, and the way she'd agreed to keep his secret.

"Well, I'm sure she's looking forward to being with you," Stan said. "Family is important at times like this, you know?"

The word "family" stung Hope like a bug bite, but she kept her composure and nodded. Anna meant so much to her. She'd adored her niece as a little girl, and had come to love her even more as an adult. It filled her with pride to see how Anna, whose mother had died when she was a baby, had grown up to be such a wonderful mother herself. And Hope loved the rest of the family, too. Greg had been empathetic and charismatic, if sometimes a little moody, and Zac was a mirror image of Greg. Evie, on the other hand, was more like Anna's side of the family—observant and analytical. She was similar in that way to Anna's father, David—Hope's only sibling. Hope was so glad Anna had decided to come to Lilac House this summer. She wanted to make this a healing time for Anna and the kids. She only wished that Anna would still love her, too, and want her as family when all was said and done.

She lifted her head when Stan called out. "Say, Hope, can you come by later to taste our July Fourth flavor?" he said.

She hesitated. Stan and his husband, Trey, fancied themselves the Ben & Jerry's of the smoothie business, but they weren't quite as skillful in inventing flavors. The Red-Hot Flag Day smoothie she'd tried two weeks ago had made her throat burn all afternoon.

"Okay, as long as there's no hot sauce in this one," she said.

"And no horseradish, either! Don't worry, we learned our lesson!"

He waved, and she watched him return to sweeping, tenderly addressing the last-minute chores he had before opening time. As was she. She climbed the front steps to the porch, stopping for a moment to massage the sides of her bad knee with the pads of her fingers. Stan might think she looked young, but she owed that to good genes, an arsenal of makeup tricks gleaned from a life on stage, and Bethany, the talented colorist in the hair salon across the street. The truth was, she was almost sixty—and worse yet, she had the joints of an eighty-year-old. That's what years of leaping and landing and twirling in pointe shoes could do to a body. She'd refused to acknowledge the growing damage while she was dancing, convincing herself that ice and Advil and athletic tape when needed could make her good as new. But eventually she had to face the truth. Everything you did in life had consequences.

Reaching the veranda, she straightened the gray-blue cushions on the wicker sofa, and fluffed the throw pillows on the rocker. That's when she noticed a large figure in her peripheral vision, walking her way from the direction of Village Hall.

Oh no, she thought. *Aidan*. Pretending not to see him, she went inside. She felt bad ignoring him, because he was very nice. But she suspected he was coming to give her more advice, and if she was doing something wrong, she wasn't in a mood to hear it.

Picking up the final, heaviest carton from yesterday's shipment, she walked down the small hallway behind the jewelry counter. This was the part of the store she loved the most—the dance studio. She took off her sandals and stood on the threshold, taking it all in, as she did at least once every day. The view was breathtaking. The floor was a gleaming blond wood that matched the double row of wooden barres circling the room. The walls were covered in floor-to-ceiling mirrors, and the steepled ceiling had wooden beams and three tilted, rectangular skylights that filled the space with natural light. In one corner was a smoky glass case that housed a sound system; the lights on the equipment flickered a cool blue. Small speakers were mounted discreetly where the walls met the ceiling.

Hope carried the carton across the studio floor to the storage closet. The studio was not only beautiful, but also incredibly functional. She had invested in the highest-quality mirrors so there'd be no distortion, and installed a combination of overhead recessed lighting and strategically placed wall sconces to eliminate glare. The hardwood floor, in combination with a floating, shock-absorbing subfloor, had the perfect amount of give to launch dancers skyward when they leaped, and to cushion them as she imagined a cloud would when they landed. She planned to teach a range of ballet classes, starting with children as young as three or four. She couldn't wait to introduce a whole generation of local kids to dance, helping them grow strong and confident as they explored the thrill and power of music and movement. She envisioned older kids rushing to the studio after school, pushing their backpacks into the dressing room cubbies and descending onto the dance floor, proud of their progress and eager to master new skills.

Reaching up, she slid the carton onto the top shelf. Designing the studio and then tenderly taking care of it—damp-mopping the floor and wiping down the barre with a soft cloth and homemade vinegar-and-water mix each evening—was the most satisfying thing she'd done since she'd returned for good from Europe. It had dissolved so much of the hurt she'd brought back with her. And the bits of hurt that remained—they somehow had become far less painful as the studio came together. Every time Hope set foot in this room, she felt like a new person, almost like a better version of herself, refreshed and reinvented. She liked herself better, she appreciated herself more, when she was in the studio. She hoped Anna would feel the magic, too.

Walking back into the studio, she ran her palm along the barre, thinking about the last time she'd visited David and Anna in the old New York City apartment. She'd just completed her sixth season with the Hamburg Ballet Theatre. Anna was fourteen at the time, and had pictures of Hope from *Dance Magazine* plastered all over the walls of her bedroom. She'd listened, spellbound, to Hope's stories about performing on grand stages across Europe. As did David, even though he knew very little about the ballet. He was just so proud of her success. It was on the last day of her week-long visit that Hope decided she couldn't admit what had happened to her in Paris, even though she'd planned to tell David and ask for his help. He and Anna admired her so much, and she was just so ashamed. She'd decided instead to leave for good and not say a word.

Holding back her tears, she'd wrapped her niece in a hug. "Keeping dancing, Anna," she'd said.

The chime on the front door of the shop rang out, the tone mingling with the almost equally high-pitched sound of children giggling. She slipped on her sandals and went back to the sales floor. Two young moms in sundresses and two little girls who looked about five or six were surveying all the merchandise.

"Hi, are you the owner?" one of the moms said.

"Yes, I'm Hope Burns." Hope nodded.

"I'm Dana Silver and this is my friend, Karen. And these are our girls, Olive and Emma. They just graduated from kindergarten yesterday."

"My goodness, congratulations!" Hope said, bending down so she was eye level with them. "Moving up to first grade, that's quite an achievement!"

"We said they could visit the new dance store to celebrate," Dana told her.

"I'm honored," Hope said. "Olive and Emma, do you like ballet?"

The girls looked at each other and both raised their shoulders at the same time. Then they burst out laughing.

"I think they honestly don't know," Karen said. "There's never been a dance school anywhere close before. But Dana and I took ballet classes together when we were little. Remember, Dana? This place reminds me so much of the dance store near us when we were little."

"Would you like to see the studio?" Hope said. "The children's classes start next week, and I can give you a schedule—"

Just then the door chime sounded again, and this time three teenage girls strode in. They were dressed in black leggings and drapey black tops, and had tightly coiled buns planted on the tops of their heads.

One of the little girls looked up at Hope. "Are those *real* dancers?" she whispered.

"They're dance students right now, but one day they might be professional dancers," Hope said. "They're studying dance at Jayson College, over in Ayelin Point."

"Wow, you have students coming here from Jayson?" Dana said. "That's on the other side of the lake."

"I was lucky. One of the girls there, Melanie"—Hope pointed to the smallest of the three—"was driving through town on her way to school, and she stopped in. She loved the store, and has been bringing all her classmates here."

"Hope?" the teenager named Melanie called over. "We need you for shoes!"

"Well, we won't keep you," Dana said. "We just wanted to stop in for a minute and take a look."

Hope reached for two schedules from the pile on the top of the jewelry case. "I hope you'll come back to see the studio, and maybe even sign the girls up for a class," Hope said, handing a schedule to each of the moms. "And congratulations, again, Olive and Emma!"

"Girls, say thank you!" Karen said, and the girls happily obeyed. "I don't know about dance classes this summer—the girls go to day camp," she added. "But maybe in the fall. So nice meeting you!"

Hope nodded and walked them to the door, then turned her attention to the teenagers, who were sprawled on the quilted lavender ottomans in the shoe corners. "Hi, girls," she said. "How are finals going?"

"It's so annoying that Jayson has finals in June when every other college in the world finished up in May," Melanie complained. Hope smiled. She had a soft spot in her heart for Melanie, since she had been short for a dancer, too, and had to fight against teachers who thought that would hinder her abilities.

"And why do they make freshmen take math anyway?" one of the other girls said. "We're dance majors."

"How about me? I overslept and missed the friggin' test," the third girl put in. "Now I have to make an appointment with the dean."

"Dean Carter?" Melanie said. "He's not so bad."

"Yeah, but he's all about that thing, personal responsibility. He's going to go crazy on me."

"And he never stops talking," the second girl said. "You'll be there all day. I'd take the F!"

Hope watched the girls carry on. For a moment she yearned to be in their place, to know what it felt like when even the most vehement frustrations weren't so bad, when an infraction that seemed serious could earn you nothing worse than a session with a long-winded academic official, and when there were always friends around to complain to. She had never experienced what they were going through, because her mother homeschooled her so she could spend more time in dance class. And she'd never finished college. She'd never had a best friend, or even a group of close friends, and she envied these girls their easy camaraderie with one another. She even felt a twinge of sadness when her thoughts settled for a moment on the two young moms she had just met. How lucky they were to have been friends as children, and now to be raising their daughters to be friends, too! Sometimes she wished she could go back in time and change her childhood—even for a day, a moment—just to see how it felt.

Melanie sauntered over to the leotards and pulled out a black style with lacey arms. "This is *so* pretty," she said. She took it across the floor to a fitting booth.

"Oh, and that's Abby and Kristin," she called over her shoulder. "They want to see some pointe shoes."

"We're both size eight, sometimes eight and a half," Kristin said.

Hope nodded and went to the large pine shoe armoire against the wall. She opened the doors and pulled a half-dozen clear drawstring sacks from the countless tiny cubbies inside. The girls took off their street shoes and pulled on the nylon half-socks and gel toe pads that Hope kept in a basket for try-ons. They loosened the drawstrings and poured all the shoes into a big pile on the floor.

Abby slipped her feet into a pair and examined them in the full-length mirror. "They're pretty, but jeez, they hurt," she whined.

Hope kneeled to assess the fit. "Well, they're Grishkos—they tend to be a little hard." She pressed and poked the toe and arch portions of each shoe. "They will soften up over time," she added. "But if you want something softer to begin with, I have some new Mirella styles that may work. They're downstairs, I'll go get them."

She went behind the leotards and downstairs to the basement, and then over to the shoe cartons she hadn't gotten around to unloading yet, wondering if she should add another shoe armoire to fit all the new styles. She was determined to have the largest pointe shoe assortment in the region, maybe even in the whole state. Finding the Mirellas, she pulled out two pairs in the right style and size, then turned off the lights and climbed back up. She reached the sales floor just as two women in running clothes left the store and started toward the sidewalk.

"Did they want something?" she asked the girls.

Kristin raised her shoulders and let them drop. "We said you were downstairs."

"Did you say I'd be right up?"

"They said they'd come back."

Hope watched through the window as the women finished stretching and began their run. They looked like they spent money on good fitness apparel. She regretted missing them. That was the advice Aidan had given her—not to ignore the potential customer pool right here in town and devote too much of her attention to the dance students from Jayson. She supposed he was right. Still, there was nothing she could do about it now. At least she had spent some time with those nice young moms and their daughters. Next time she had to run downstairs, she'd tell the college girls to ask other customers to wait.

She handed the Mirellas to Abby and Kristin as Melanie walked back over, the new leotard squished into a ball in her hands.

"It looked better on the hanger," she said as she handed it to Hope. She turned to her friends. "So, which did you like?"

Hope went to the dressing room to retrieve the leotard's hanger. When she came back, the three girls were tucking away their phones.

"What do you think about the shoes?" she asked.

"I like the Mirellas best," Abby said. "But I'm going to think about it."

"Yeah, we're both going to think about it." Kristin stood up. "Look, guys, I need to go back and try to find Dean Carter."

"Yeah, we all better get back," Melanie said. "Thanks, Hope, see you soon—"

"No, wait!" Hope followed them toward the door. "Did any of you get a chance to look at the class schedule? To supplement your Jayson classes? Mel, did you show them? Maybe when you come back with a decision about the shoes, you can sign up for—"

"We'll look at it. See ya, Hope!" Melanie called as the girls sprinted down the walk. The screen door slammed behind them, and Hope cringed, hoping the wood wouldn't splinter. Maybe it was too much to expect teenage girls to be more careful. She wouldn't know—she'd never had kids of her own.

Hanging the leotard back up, she thought about the way the girls had pulled out their phones when she went to get the hanger. She tried to tell herself that they were probably just texting other friends. But she knew that wasn't the case. Last week, she had seen Melanie and another girl reading the product codes off the shoe bags when they thought Hope wasn't looking. That's when she figured out that they were taking down style numbers so they could find a cheaper price online, after they had tried them on here and decided which ones fit them best.

And now it seemed maybe Melanie was pulling the same stunt with the leotard she'd tried on.

Hope kneeled and began sorting the shoes and slipping them into their proper sacks. She didn't blame the girls for wanting to find a good deal. After all, they were students. But she felt miffed that Melanie, in particular, would take advantage of her. Melanie had been her first customer, rushing in that day to get a black leotard for class. But it had turned out that she'd forgotten her wallet. She didn't have time before class to go back to the dorm and get it, so she'd begged Hope to let her return the next day to pay. She'd sounded desperate and scattered, and Hope warmed to her. Almost as if she were a daughter or a niece, or a version of Anna, the version Hope had missed knowing all those years ago. She'd given Melanie the leotard as a grand opening gift.

But now, perhaps Melanie and her friends were using her, treating her like a clueless old woman, and her store like their complimentary sampling space. She didn't want to let this happen. But she didn't know what to do about it. She didn't want to confront the girls, because then they'd never come back. And she needed the Jayson College students to come here, to buy their dance gear here, and to take classes here, to supplement those they took at Jayson. She needed lots of customers, and lots of sales.

Because that's what she'd been hoping to report to Anna when today finally arrived—that the store was on a course to success. She'd envisioned showing Anna a store crowded with dancers. A class schedule with full rosters, and waiting lists. Spreadsheets that could barely contain the steadily growing sales figures.

Walking across the quiet sales floor, she looked out the window at the curb where Anna's car would soon roll up. She could see Dana, Karen and their girls emerge from the smoothie shop, all holding tall paper cups with bright blue straws. She knew Trey and Stan must have enjoyed serving this delightful bunch. Oh, how she loved this town! People were so happy to connect and bask in one another's company. It was wonderful, how the two moms this morning had introduced themselves and their daughters to Hope, rather than just stopping in and walking right off. Even her frustration with the teenagers couldn't dissuade her from feeling that Lake Summers was exactly where she wanted to spend the rest of her life.

But how would she even broach the subject with Anna, of how she had gotten the money to buy the store—and how deeply involved Anna was? Things had looked so promising last summer, and if Greg hadn't died, they might be promising still. But now everything had changed, and she couldn't help but fear that the news she had to give Anna was going to end up as yet another burden on her poor niece's already weighted-down shoulders.

She was Anna's aunt, and she was supposed to be helping her, guiding her, sharing her own experience and wisdom. She wanted to make up for all those years she was away, especially now, when Anna was struggling to get through so much heartbreak. But the piece of news she had to deliver, the news that was supposed to be a great surprise, was going to be a big blow instead. Delivering big blows—that wasn't something real aunts did.

She could only hope Anna would think about how far they'd come ever since Hope had returned. That she could make Anna understand—and that they could find a way out of this impossible situation without losing all they'd gained.

CHAPTER THREE

"Dad? Hey, Dad!"

"In here, bud," Aidan called, turning from the stove at the sound of Liam barreling into the house, the living room furniture shifting noisily as his feet rocked the uneven floor. The thin swinging door to the kitchen groaned as Liam pushed it forward, and Aidan caught it before it could snap off the hinge. "What's up?"

"I made the team," Liam said, with a shake of his head and a laugh. "Can you believe it? I definitely don't."

Aidan smiled at his instinctive humility. Emilia had been that way, too—like mother, like son. He clapped Liam on the shoulder. "Good for you. Good for you!"

"I didn't think it was going to happen. I didn't even swim my best. Hey, is that dinner?"

"Spaghetti à la Dad."

"Sweet, I'm starved. I'll go put my stuff down and be right back." He swung his backpack over on his shoulders and pushed the door.

Aidan caught it again, and stood on the threshold, watching Liam take off for the narrow staircase, a fresh scent of chlorine floating in the air behind him. He really was like Emilia, Aidan thought. Not in obvious ways. His hair was the color of sand, while hers had been more like light maple syrup. His was cut short and kind of choppy, and she'd worn hers long and smooth. But they'd shared that same ability to be happily surprised when the world was kind enough to throw them a bone. And then there was that upper lip they had in common. Thicker than the bottom one—not by much, but it was noticeable. Aidan had always connected Emilia's swelled upper lip with her softness. Vulnerability. Although it was sensual, too. He'd loved the way her upper lip felt when he pressed it against his own.

Stepping back into the kitchen, he ladled sauce onto the spaghetti and used the dishtowel on his shoulder to clean up the drips. *Proud beyond words.* He could almost hear Emilia saying that, as though she'd been there in the kitchen with the two of them, stirring her homemade sauce. She'd have dropped the spoon and rushed over to hold Liam's cheeks in her hands. She'd have kissed each cheek and told him she was proud beyond words. And he'd have twisted away like any fifteen-year-old boy, rolling his eyes and muttering, "Mom, *stop*." But not really fighting all that hard.

He put the empty Prego jar into the sink to rinse out and carried the platter to the small table on one end of the living room. He went back into the kitchen for the canister of grated cheese and the Italian bread.

Liam came downstairs in a fresh blue tee shirt and his gray shorts.

"Looking sharp," Aidan said. "You going back out?"

Liam shrugged as he sat down. "Just meeting some of the team later. They hang out by the green. Jeez, I'm hungry."

He planted two tongs' worth of spaghetti onto his plate, and then scooped up a mouthful with his fork. "So anyway, the team's great, Dad. They're almost all gonna be seniors this fall." He leaned over the table to eat. The ends of the spaghetti rose up rhythmically, as he sucked in a couple of inches more after every swallow.

"And get this," he added, after the last of the strands disappeared into his mouth, the sauce from the ends splashing onto his chin. "I'm the only one who's a sophomore!"

Aidan took some spaghetti for himself. What would Emilia have said about the way Liam was holding his fork, wrapping his fingers around the handle and using it like a shovel? Or how he'd be hanging out tonight with boys who were all mostly seniors? It was approaching two years since Emilia had died, and Aidan still didn't know when to speak up and when to keep quiet. How had Emilia always known just what to say, how to make her point without ruining the moment?

He wasn't going to chance it. He hadn't seen Liam this happy since they moved here in January. He thought for a moment about how great it would be if he could bottle this enthusiasm and take it out whenever Liam was down. Or even better, if he didn't need to bottle it. If this was finally the tipping point, and things would be good from here on out.

He handed Liam his napkin and asked when practice started.

"Next week," Liam told him, swiping the napkin across his chin. "Monday and Thursday afternoons, and Saturday mornings."

"No kidding? In the summer?"

"They don't usually start now, but the coach has us going to this national competition in Atlanta in August. ESPN's actually gonna stream it on their website. Not all of us, he's only taking seniors, but he wants us all to be at the practices. He's a great guy. He spoke to us for like a half hour after the tryouts. Really into nutrition and stuff. He'd lose it if he saw this dinner."

Aidan pretended to take offense. "It's a perfectly balanced meal. You got your carbs…" He lifted the cheese canister. "You got your protein… and see the parsley in the sauce? You got your vegetables."

"Yeah, right." Liam rolled his eyes. "Some of the guys have been talking about trying to go vegetarian. But the coach isn't into it. He says we need meat, like red meat."

"Guy after my own heart."

"But he was pushing organic, too. The guys were ragging on him because that's such a California thing. This guy Bryce was like, 'Hey, Coach—pesticides are good for you, they build up the immune system.' It was hysterical."

Aidan flinched. "He's from California?" he said, trying to keep his voice even.

Liam tore off a piece of bread and pushed it in the sauce on his plate. "Yeah, he swam on the USC team. He actually was talking about Mickey's on Long Beach, the place with the burgers and the big awning. I couldn't believe he knew it."

It was too dangerous to let the matter slide. Aidan put his elbows on the table and clasped his hands in front of his face. "You didn't say you knew it, too, did you?" he asked.

"No, not at all."

"Because you can't say you were there." Aidan made his voice low and stern, just like Emilia had done when Liam was six and ran out into the street: *You must never do that, ever again, understand?* She'd let it sink in before she'd hugged him and given back his ball. She'd said you needed to be tough when he did something unsafe.

"I know, Dad. I know."

"You have to say you moved here from Rochester—and only if he asks. You never went to Mickey's. You've never even been to California."

Liam threw the chunk of bread onto his plate and pushed back his chair. "I'm getting some more water," he muttered, and grabbed his glass.

Aidan reached out to save the chair from toppling. "I just want us to be clear," he said.

"Do we have to talk about this all the time?" Liam shouted from the kitchen.

"I need to be sure that you won't slip."

"I'm sick of talking about it all the time."

"Not all the time. Just when we have to."

Liam pressed open the kitchen door. "What do you want, Dad? You don't want me to be on the team? Because if you don't want me to do it, I won't."

"No, bud. I don't want that." Aidan hoped his quiet tone would calm Liam down. "I want you to do this. I'm proud of you."

"Then why are you trying to ruin it?"

"I'm not. Look, come sit down. I'm sorry if I bring this up too much. Come on and tell me more about the coach."

"I'm done—"

"You were still eating—"

"I'm done, I said. I'm going to meet the guys."

Aidan got up from the table. "Okay, but look, don't stay out too late. You're opening at Pearl's tomorrow."

"I know, okay? I know that, *too*." Liam pulled his sweatshirt off the hook in the hallway and opened the wooden screen door. "I don't know what you're so worked up about," he called as he walked out. "*I'd* be the one who'd get the worst of it, not you."

Aidan threw his napkin onto his plate and rubbed the fingers of one hand against his forehead. No, that was wrong—Liam wouldn't get the worst of it. *He* would. Because if his in-laws had their way, then he'd lose Liam. And nothing could be worse than that.

He went to the front window and watched his son march toward town, until he couldn't see him anymore. Then he sighed and went back to clear off the table. He was mad at himself for destroying Liam's first good moment since they'd arrived in Lake Summers. The past few months had been so tough on him, having to move so suddenly, and right in the middle of his freshman year—a southern California kid who didn't ski or skate but had to pretend he'd lived around snow all his life. The guys at the high school had mostly grown up together and knew one another from as far back as preschool—just as Liam had known his own friends back home. And now he couldn't even stay in touch with those guys.

Aidan's neck muscles tightened when he thought about them—all the things Liam had to do that no kid his age should ever have to do.

Carrying the dishes to the sink, he thought about the Atlanta competition Liam had mentioned. It was a relief that only seniors were going. At least that was one thing he wouldn't be forced to deny his son. Because there was no way he could let Liam go, even if he were a senior. Who knew who he might run into, if there were teams from across the country coming? Who knew who might recognize his face, if it were splashed on the ESPN website?

In the kitchen, he dipped a paper towel under the faucet and went to clean up the tomato sauce that had splattered when Liam got up from the table.

Liam liked to be happy. It was in his nature. These last few months had made him different from the person he was meant to be. Squatting to wipe the floor, Aidan remembered his son as a toddler the first time he walked on the beach. Leaped is more like it—he'd leaped from one chubby leg to the other, laughing and dancing in circles as the tips of the waves touched his toes and then slid away. He'd had this all-out laugh—not a titter or a giggle but a real guffaw that started in his belly and took over his body. Aidan and Emilia would always try to elicit more of those amazing belly laughs. Emilia would succeed by throwing her head back and letting loose one of her giant, endless, pretend sneezes.

He loaded the dishwasher, then tied up the trash and took it to the can at the side of the house. Coming back, he placed a key under the front mat, where Liam would know to get it if he'd left without remembering his. He walked inside, and even though it was still dusk, he put on the outside light. He didn't expect to be going downstairs again tonight, and he assumed Liam would be getting home after dark.

His phone buzzed, and he picked it up from the kitchen counter. It was a text from Pamela, one of three receptionists who ran the Visitor's Desk in Village Hall.

A few of us are going to the place by the lake to see Carl's brother's band. You should come!

He smiled. Pamela was cute, with those big, round glasses of hers, and kind of clever, good at small talk. She'd told him that she moved to town a few weeks ago after finalizing her divorce, and was living with her parents until she could afford to buy a small place for her and her kid. He knew she was hoping to go out with him. And he was tempted. He was lonely. But he wasn't going to bring anyone new into this mess he had made. It wouldn't be fair to her, and it wouldn't be fair to Liam, who needed and deserved all his attention. He could handle being alone. He'd never been a party guy anyway. He'd been in love once, with Emilia, and he had a son. He was lucky. Some people didn't even get that much.

No, but thanks, he texted back. *Have fun.*

He dimmed the kitchen light and paused at the foot of the staircase. The last time he'd stood by a darkened staircase was the final night Emilia spent at home. He'd listened, his head against their bedroom wall, his chest aching, as she explained to Liam what a hospice was. He'd heard the two of them gasping and sniffling, and he'd waited, wanting to make everything better for them, but knowing the best thing he could do was let Liam have this time with his mom.

It was good that Liam was out this evening, he told himself as he went upstairs. It was good that he was making friends. And hopefully the two of them would quickly get past the spat they had tonight. He wanted to watch Liam compete, to clap him on the shoulder when he won, to sit with him and console him when he lost. He wanted to teach him to drive, and to rent him a tuxedo and see him leave to pick up his prom date. He wanted to be the one Liam talked to the first time he had his heart broken.

Upstairs, he passed his room and Liam's room, and went into the third, smallest bedroom. Sitting down at the white particleboard desk, he took out his pliers, his wire cutter, and his roll of copper wire. His father had dabbled in jewelry-making over the years, and when Aidan was a kid, he'd loved to watch him. These days he had no stomach for jewelry, but he'd seen the copper wire at the hardware store when they first moved to town, and had decided on a whim to buy it. He liked working with his hands. Even though his fingers were short and thick, they were flexible and capable.

He looked over at the windowsill, where his finished pieces were lined up, each on a short wooden pedestal. They formed a series, each one depicting a different sports mishap. He didn't know where that idea had come from, but it felt like something that suited him. He'd made a tennis player who had a hole in his racquet—he'd made the strings of the racquet from wire mesh. He'd made a baseball player loading up at home plate with a feather instead of a bat. He'd made a basketball forward trying to shoot into a hoop that was sealed off at the bottom. Now he needed his next idea. Something with swimming, maybe? A race. He wondered what kind of a mishap there could be. Maybe a swimmer with no lane?

It would be the most complicated sculpture he'd done. He'd need to make maybe four swimmers total. Three would be on their blocks, about to dive. And the fourth would be standing off to the side, alone. Because he had no lane.

He put on the spare pair of glasses he kept up here for close work, and then unrolled two feet of wire. He curled and twisted it to make the head, the arms, and the body of the first swimmer.

He knew the project would keep him busy, which was good. He didn't want to worry about Liam being angry, about Liam maybe saying something to the guys tonight that he shouldn't. He didn't want to think about their life, his and Liam's. How tenuous it was, how unreliable.

How unlike the metal wire he was shaping with his hands.

CHAPTER FOUR

It was after four when Anna drove across the drawbridge and into Lake Summers, the tiny resort town tucked away in the southwestern corner of the Adirondack Mountains. The lake below sparkled from the angled orange sun. She kept her eyes focused ahead, so she wouldn't have to look at the castle-like Lake Summers Resort to her right, but just knowing it was there made her breath jagged. She and Greg had met on one of the hiking trails behind the resort.

In the back seat, Evie snored gently. Zac was asleep, too, his chin lifted and his forehead smooth. It was rare to see him so peaceful. She longed for the days when she had the words or the touch that could make him break out in a smile. Looking at him now, she remembered how anxious and restless Greg had been, too—a little bit last summer, and even more so when they got back to Silver Plains. He'd had Willow Center on his mind, he'd said, and would often wander the house at two or three in the morning. Like father, like son. Zac also had trouble falling asleep.

She continued onto Main Street, the gently sloping road lined with oak trees. She'd always loved the old clapboard houses that had been restored and transformed into appealing shops and eateries, such as Pearl's, the coffee place where Greg would stop after his morning run, and the Ice Creamery, with its small takeout window, where kids were gathered now to place their orders. Even without Greg beside her, the town still felt familiar and welcoming, and the bustle of people dressed in their breezy summer clothes made her smile. On her right was the village green, with its romantic gazebo in the center, where Greg had proposed to her. And across the street was Summers Playground, teeming with young moms spotting toddlers atop the jungle gym—a structure the community had funded and built two years ago under the supervision of local contractors. She, Greg, and the kids had been so excited to pack up all the tools in the house and head downtown to pitch in.

With Zac and Evie still asleep, Anna decided to stop by Lilac House before heading over to Hope's store. It was going to be a shock to see the house for the first time since Greg died, and she thought it might be best to get through that moment alone, before the kids woke up. She turned left past the village green, and after a few gradual curves, she steered the car around one longer bend and to the end of the cul-de-sac that fronted the woods.

And there it was, the enchanting two-story Colonial she had fallen in love with the moment Greg brought her there on their first wedding anniversary. The house was a pale golden tan, the color of summer wheat, rich and gorgeous in its subtlety, and it was bordered on the sides with tall trees and wild grass. There was a line of windows along the top floor and a line of taller ones on the first, each window framed by white wooden shutters. The long front porch was shaded by an overhang and encircled by a white railing with slender spindles. A dormer roof jutted majestically from the center of the second story, below which was a grand front door, painted a delicate cornflower blue.

Anna slowly circled the end of the cul-de-sac and took another look at the house. In a strange way, it looked slightly unfamiliar to her, as though the color were a little off, or the shape of the porch had changed. But no, she realized—it wasn't Lilac House that had changed. Just her.

Back on Main Street, she passed the Grill, where they usually went for burgers on their first night back in town. She wondered which would make the kids feel worse today—going there for dinner or not going there. Before she could decide, she came upon the spot where the boarded-up building once was. In its place was a brand-new store, fronted by a cozy veranda and a white sign just below the roofline with violet lettering: *The Lilac Pointe*.

She parked and took in the words. There were so many layers of meaning in that name. Lilac House was, of course, the name of Anna and Greg's house, which Hope had come to love as well. She'd visited them every summer from the time Zac was a baby, and fallen so much in love with the house and the town that she'd decided to move to Lake Summers for good. And the Lilac Variation was the first solo Hope had danced after she joined the Hamburg Ballet Theatre. Hope taught Anna the solo during one of her brief visits back to New York, and Anna had intended to make Hope proud by dancing it in her own professional debut, with the Soho Dance Collective. But everything changed when Anna fell during the final dress rehearsal. She'd shattered her ankle, and that was the end of her dream to follow in Hope's footsteps.

She gently jiggled Zac's shoulder and reached to nudge Evie's knee. That's when she heard the screen door of the shop creak open. Looking through Zac's window, she saw Hope coming down the steps. She waved and then got out of the car and circled to the curb.

"Hey, you're finally here," Hope said, enveloping her in a hug. "Oh, Anna! I'm so glad to see you."

"Aunt Hope," Anna said, and she melted into her aunt's arms. It had taken her a long time to be able to say *Aunt* Hope. Partly it was because Hope wasn't much older than she was. But mostly it was because Hope hadn't felt like her aunt for a long time. Anna had grown up desperately wanting Hope around. Sometimes when she was in a dance school recital, she would imagine that Hope had come back from Europe to surprise her, and was out there in the darkened auditorium, glowing with pride. Sometimes she would even pretend that Hope was right next to her, in her room or waiting for her outside school to take her to a movie or shopping at Bloomingdale's. Sometimes at night she would scrunch over to the edge of her bed, pretending that Hope was in the next room and would soon come in and snuggle with her until she fell asleep.

But when Hope finally retired from dance and showed up again in Anna's life, shortly after Zac was born, it was as though she'd never left. The essence of Anna's father suffused Hope's whole being, so having Hope around felt a lot like having a piece of her father back again. Not that they were entirely alike—her father had been restrained, while Hope could be impulsive. But they both had those dark eyes that crinkled when they laughed, and those long, graceful arms, and minds that were always generating ideas.

Hope squeezed Anna's hands and then peered into the car windows. "So, where are those little creatures of yours?" she teased. She opened the back door, and when Evie scrambled out, she picked her up and twirled her around. Meanwhile, Zac pushed his door open and dragged himself out of the car, leaning one hip against the front end. Hope mussed his hair and kissed his cheek, and didn't seem to mind when he groaned and rolled his eyes.

She took Anna's hand again and led them all up the walk to the porch. "I'm so glad to finally show you this place," she said. "Believe it or not, you guys, I *moved* here—well, not exactly in the store, more like over it. My apartment is upstairs, you can see the entrance around the side. But I barely have much furniture yet. I've been working all year… on this."

She opened the screen door, and Anna gasped as she stepped inside. It was a dancer's wonderland, just as Hope had described it last summer when she first laid out her vision: clean and well organized, bursting with exciting arrays of merchandise, and finished with tender, sensual details, like the silvery sound of the door chime and the subtle scent of lilac in the air.

Anna turned to look at her aunt, feeling like she was seeing a new side of her. Yes, Hope was beautiful as always, in her sleeveless gray jersey dress that showed off those toned shoulders. Her long hair was still the color of honey, and her heart-shaped face still had those dark eyes that had seemed to pop right out of the pages of the dance magazines Anna used to collect. But there was also a kind of maturity in her face, the way her cheekbones had become more prominent, and the tiny lines around her eyes were a touch deeper than Anna remembered from last summer. The changes didn't make her look old—only more serious and approachable. Hope looked exactly like… well, maybe not a motherly figure, but like a woman who knew that life could pack a punch and was stronger for it. Someone who could help Anna stand again on her own two feet.

"Oh, Aunt Hope," Anna said, "it's magnificent. You kept saying last summer that you wanted to plant some roots and build something real, and here it is—"

The front door slammed, making the two of them jump. Zac had walked out of the store, and Anna could see him through the screen, plopping down on the wicker sofa, and then stretching out his legs and resting his dirty sneakers on the glass-topped coffee table.

"Zac, please!" she said. He threw his head back and slowly took his feet down, one at a time, as though they weighed a million pounds.

She looked at Hope. "I'm sorry. He's tired from the drive."

Hope shook her head. "Don't be silly, you must be exhausted. Why don't you go on to the house? I can show you all this another time—"

"But what about the studio? That's what I really want to see."

"Are you sure? The kids will be okay for a few more minutes?"

Anna looked over at Evie, who was examining the charms on the jewelry counter. She seemed content for the moment, as was

Zac, who was now occupied with his phone. Her kids, and even Greg, had never had all that much interest in her very abbreviated dance career. Her aunt was the only person who understood the strange way a rehearsal hall or a dance studio or a theater stage could sometimes make you feel even more at home than a kitchen table or a hand-stitched quilt. Last summer when Hope described her plans, Anna had surprised herself by feeling so excited at the prospect of setting foot on a real dance floor once again.

She nodded, following Hope behind the jewelry counter, past a small office, and on down the hall. She paused when she got to the threshold of the studio.

"Wow," she whispered. The room was so beautiful, it seemed almost sacred. She removed her shoes and tiptoed into the center. The floor felt smooth under her bare feet. It had a pleasing sense of give when she pressed down on the ball of her right foot. She pressed down gently on her left, feeling only the tiniest twinge around her heel and ankle. It was a testament to the quality of the construction. A harder floor would still have caused a jolt of pain to shoot up through her leg.

Hope came up behind her and wrapped her arms around Anna's shoulders. "Oh, Anna, it's good that you're here this summer," she said. "This place can work wonders for a person, believe me. Just wait until you put on some of the beautiful dance clothes up front. This floor, it's a dream to dance on—"

"I can't dance on this ankle, you know that."

"Then you'll do whatever feels right, and… and it will all get better." She walked around to face Anna. "Oh, sweetheart, I can only imagine how hard it must be for you. Greg was an amazing person. Everyone adored him. I know I did."

Anna nodded. "He loved you, too. He felt like you were his aunt as much as mine." She chuckled. "He loved meeting you at Pearl's for coffee in the mornings after he finished his run. He said that you would probe the deepest mysteries of the universe together."

"Well, he was a philosopher at heart, wasn't he?" Hope said. "He had such strong convictions about how life should be lived, and what made a life worth living. And he'd talk about you. Did you know that when he was stressed about work and couldn't sleep at night, he'd sometimes sit and watch you sleep? He said it helped him relax, to see you so snug and still."

Anna looked down at her hands. She'd actually been awake many times when Greg was sitting and watching her. She'd let him think she was asleep, because she knew he'd feel bad if he thought he'd awoken her.

"But we also talked about fun things," Hope continued, and Anna lifted her eyes. "Like those oversized blueberry cheesecake muffins he'd bring home from Pearl's. He said that even though you complained about the calories, you still couldn't resist them."

"*He* was the one who couldn't resist them," Anna said. "He only pretended he brought them home for me."

"Could be," Hope said with a laugh. "He truly had a soft spot for those homemade muffins. Sometimes he'd order a chocolate chip one to have with his coffee, and he'd swear me to secrecy. He said if you knew he'd wolfed down a muffin, you wouldn't let him have any pancakes when he got home."

"Although I always knew," Anna said. "I could tell from the speck of powdered sugar on his chin. I think he kept it there on purpose. He wanted to get caught."

"I think you're right," Hope said. "He never could keep a secret from you. And he knew I'd never want to keep one either…"

She paused and Anna saw her smile disappear. "But surprises are different," Hope said. "Surprises aren't secrets, right? Oh, I know it can feel the same now, but that's why… I mean, if I knew how things would go, I never would have…" She left the rest of the sentence hanging.

"Would have what?" Anna said. "You never would have—"

Suddenly Evie appeared at the door. "Mommy?" she said. "Zac says he's leaving if you don't come out right now."

Anna looked at her daughter, not knowing what to do. Wherever Hope was going with this conversation, it sounded serious, and Anna's guard was up. Even now, she still didn't know everything there was to know about her aunt. She didn't know what had driven her to stay away so long; she didn't know why Hope had stopped visiting or answering her letters; why she'd only come back into Anna's life after Zac was born. For a moment Anna wondered if this talk about secrets was Hope's way of slowly breaking the news that she was leaving. Maybe she was planning to return to Europe. Anna prayed that wasn't what her aunt was about to say, not when the kids still had to face the memories waiting at Lilac House. Hope was in their lives now. The joyfulness she'd always brought to the stage—she brought it here, too, even when she was doing something ordinary, like collecting rocks with Evie near the lake, or playing chess with Zac at the dining room table. What if Hope were leaving? Could Anna be happy for her? Or was she selfish enough to tell her not to abandon her again?

Evie knocked on the studio wall. She looked on the verge of tears. "Mommy, I'm so sorry, but Zac is getting madder…"

Anna looked at the doorway. She didn't want to let this go. But she didn't feel she could leave Zac alone any longer—or Evie, too, for that matter. She didn't know how being here would affect them, and she knew she should stick close to them.

"Okay," she said. "I have to get going."

Her aunt nodded. "I close up in another hour or so—how about I take you all out to dinner? We can meet at the Grill, or I can bring over some pizza and salad. Give me a call when you decide which you'd like." She went to the doorway and slipped on her sandals, then took Evie's hand. "Okay, peanut. Did you see any bracelet you liked?" she said as the two of them headed back to the sales floor.

Anna started to follow them, but then her eyes found the mirror on the front wall of the studio. The politician's wife who met her gaze was small and sad. She studied the image, and then watched as the woman's tailored blouse and capri pants melted away, replaced by an exquisite lilac-and-gold dance costume from the past. As she stood there on the blond wood dance floor, with mirrors all around, she suddenly felt at home. And deep within her, she heard a voice asking why she'd stayed away so long.

Anna steeled herself for what was to come. It felt strange to be driving to the house from Main Street, since they had mostly walked to and from town. They generally all piled into the car only when they were going to or coming from the lake. She had always loved that ten-minute drive in the late afternoon, how the air would be cooling down and the shady patches on the roads would stretch wide. They'd all be nicely tired, their skin warm and bristly from baked-on sand, their hair stiff and tangled from sweat, wind and water. She'd loved the delicious anticipation of what would come next—cool showers for all, then a glass of white wine on the sun porch for her while Greg stretched out on the other chaise lounge, and the kids dozed inside on the soft armchairs in front of the TV, their washed hair still wet, their limbs clean and glistening.

She reached the house again, and this time pulled into the driveway and put the car into park. Sliding her fingers to the top of the steering wheel, she rested the side of her head on her knuckles. How naive she had once been to assume that nothing would vary from summer to summer other than the kids outgrowing bikes and clothes. Right now, she thought, Greg should be pulling the bikes off the hitch with his long, skinny arms, and then opening up the trunk to get the luggage and shouting with the kids:

Who belongs to the green bag?
That's mine!

Here, catch! Throw it to Evie! Now take the orange one. Assembly line!

Passersby would often stop and watch their unloading antics, which at one time made her self-conscious. Greg always seemed to be staging impromptu events, turning mundane tasks like hauling luggage into public extravaganzas. One time he half-jokingly proposed climbing up the big crabapple tree on the side of the house and tossing the duffels directly into Zac's window, which was only a few feet away from one of the thickest branches. And when she'd told him that was crazy, he implored some neighbors who were watching to come take his side. But whenever she caught herself feeling embarrassed, she'd look at her kids' faces. They loved when he played like that, and the people watching did as well. Greg was born to be the main event, and his delight in that role was contagious.

She picked up her head from the steering wheel and looked at her kids. Zac was sunk low in his seat, his shoulders hunched and his head down, his face expressionless. Then she looked up, and her eyes met Evie's in the rear-view mirror. Evie's eyes questioned her: *Are you okay? Can you do this?*

She cleared her throat. It wasn't doing anyone any good to just sit here in the car. She had to be strong for her kids—wasn't that what everyone told her? That her kids needed to know they could fall apart because she'd be there to catch them?

"Okay, guys, let's go," she said. "Take your stuff and let's unpack a little before dinner."

She got out of the car and pulled her suitcases from the trunk. She told Zac to remember to close it when he and Evie got their bags out, and then walked toward the front door. But she felt her resolve weaken as she heard the unfamiliar sound of her suitcase's metal wheels rolling on stone, a sound that used to be drowned out by her family's escapades: Evie calling out "Echooo!" to see if her voice would reverberate in the woods surrounding the house;

Zac kicking his dad's butt and then scuttling away, shouting "Yes!" at the top of his lungs, Greg dropping his bags on the lawn and charging after Zac; her calling to Greg to please stop goofing around, he had the house key and her arms were breaking under the weight of the duffels…

She pulled the key out of her bag and unlocked the door. Because of the slight downhill slope of the house, it fell open. She took a breath and stepped inside.

The house was dark and cool, as it usually was in the early evening. The floor creaked under her weight, same as always. There was a familiar, early-summer scent of lemon furniture polish, which meant the cleaning service had been there as usual, the third week each June. The furniture was the same—the storage bench in the entranceway, the oversized almond-colored sofa in the living room at the end of the hallway, the lamp tables with the family photos, the writing desk with the desktop computer against the far wall. But the atmosphere was different. Where was the fun, the energy, the silliness? She turned to the staircase. Zac and Evie had come in and were wordlessly lugging their bags. Evie's body was slanted as she balanced her duffel on her left hip, holding the strap with both hands and heaving it rhythmically with each step. Where was Greg to run up behind her, scooping her up with one hand and her bag with the other?

She turned back. Across the living room, she saw the tiny plastic Sleeping Beauty she had put there on the windowsill many years ago. She pressed her lips together and waited until the kids were all the way upstairs before she sniffled and let out a ragged sigh. Then she walked over and picked the doll up, touching the red smudges on top of her head where Evie had once tried to draw a rose tiara.

"Okay, I'm embarrassed," Greg said, looking up from the tree stump he was sitting on, a hamburger in one hand and an envelope of French fries balanced on his knee. "I didn't expect to run into anyone here. What can I say? I like McDonald's."

Her eyes dropped to the cardboard box on the ground beside him. "Yeah, it gets worse," he said, his brown curls dancing as he shook his head. "I guess it would be better if I were eating something manly like a Big Mac. But the smaller size feels less unhealthy. So, here I am, a twenty-six-year-old guy with a Happy Meal"—he lifted the box, and the toy inside fell onto his lap—"and a Cinderella."

"That's not Cinderella," she'd told him, thinking it was kind of cute, that he was sitting here in gym shorts, eating a burger. So many of the MBAs she'd met last night had seemed full of themselves, commenting on the caviar as though they were trained food critics. He was one of those MBAs, too. But he didn't seem that way at all.

"It's Aurora," she said. "Sleeping Beauty."

He let his jaw drop. "Don't tell me you like Happy Meals too."

She smiled, thinking how her father would roll over in his grave at the thought of a McDonald's burger in her hand. "I recognize her from the ballet. I'm… I used to be a dancer."

"Used to be?" he said, sliding along the tree trunk so she'd have room.

She went to sit down, drawn to his adorable smile. "I stopped dancing last summer," she said…

Anna put the doll back down and brought her suitcase upstairs to her bedroom. She hoisted it onto the bed, then circled back to the hallway to see how the kids were doing. Peeking into Evie's room, she saw her daughter methodically unpacking, just as she'd been told to do, folding her underwear and bathing suits and bringing them to the dresser. Then she moved onto her shirts. She looked over her shoulder and noticed Anna. "See, Mom? I'm doing a good job, right?"

Anna nodded—"Yes, of course"—and peeked in on Zac. As she suspected, Zac was lying on the bed, playing with his phone. His duffel was the floor, untouched.

She went into his room. "What's going on, honey?" she said.

He shrugged and kept tapping. She took his phone from his hands and put it on his nightstand.

"Hey!" he said.

"Hey, nothing. It's time to unpack."

"Oh, God," he groaned. "What's the difference if my clothes are here or there?"

"There's a big difference," she said. "You can't live out of your duffel all summer."

"But I don't know where everything goes."

"Just organize it like at home."

"But at home has five drawers and this is four."

"So combine some things—"

"I cannot *do* this, okay?" His voice got harsh and his face grew red. "What the *fuck* does it matter?"

Stunned, Anna stared at him, and then left the room and started down the stairs, not even feeling the wood beneath her. What on earth had set him off? She'd never heard him talk like that. She knew she could go upstairs again and tell him to never, *ever* speak that way again. She could threaten punishments worse than the loss of his phone if he didn't apologize and start unpacking *this minute*. Or she could just leave him alone. Maybe he was right, what difference did it make if his clothes stayed in his duffel all summer? But she also knew this was about so much more than clothes. Something was twisting deep inside him, keeping him from sleeping at night, making him lash out. His moodiness wasn't easing up, as the time since Greg died grew longer. If anything, it was getting worse.

She hated herself at moments like this, when she didn't know what to do. So much was at stake—two little lives she loved more than anything. She hated herself because she was their mom, and she was failing. She wanted to love them and be happy with them. But sometimes watching her kids was so painful.

She sat down on the bottom step and clasped her hands between her knees. It was always right around this time every year—a half hour or so after they arrived at the house—that she'd call up to the kids to drop what they were doing so they could all head to Penny Treats near the green for candy. How had she forgotten that? She supposed she'd been too preoccupied with how hard it would be to enter the house this year. But now she remembered how Greg would always tease her—"You just told them to unpack, and now you're telling them to stop? This time you said you'd stick to your guns! You're crazy, you know that, right?" She'd laugh and shrug and shoo him away. It was true; she always intended to have them unpack right away, and she always changed her mind just after they got started. She couldn't have them spend their first moments in Lake Summers doing chores. There were too many places to revisit, too many people to see and memories to recall and new memories to be made. She'd tell the kids that there was a candy emergency, the candy drawer in the kitchen was empty, and it needed to be refilled before the house would truly be ready for them. A second later, Zac and Evie would come flying downstairs and out the door.

She got up from the bottom step and went back upstairs. "Okay, you guys, we have an emergency," she said. "The candy drawer is empty. Come on, let's go to Penny Treats and get some reinforcements. Then we'll meet Aunt Hope at the Grill for burgers. Who's in?"

She watched her kids head obediently back down the stairs.

Later that night, Anna let Evie fall asleep next to her on the sofa, in front of the TV. It had been a busy evening. They'd met Hope at the Grill—Hope loved burgers and fries almost as much as the kids did—and afterward, she'd come back to the house and challenged Evie to a game of checkers and Zac to a game of chess, while they'd all sampled chocolates from Penny Treats. The competition had been fun, and the house had been lively, and although Anna wanted to ask Hope about the conversation they'd started in the studio, she hadn't wanted to ruin the mood. Still, the mood changed on its own when Hope had kissed them all goodnight and left for the evening. Anna felt a creeping sense of loneliness set in, and she suspected the kids must feel it, too.

Evie wriggled closer on the sofa and put her head on Anna's lap. Anna pulled out her ponytail and ran her fingers through the soft, wavy strands that framed her daughter's face. She remembered how lonely she had often been as a ten-year-old, with no mother and a father who worked long hours at an accounting firm during the day and took shifts as a waiter at a fancy restaurant at night to make ends meet. She knew he loved her and raised her as best he could, but he struggled to balance his work with parenting, and she often spent her evenings doing homework in the homes of neighbors who'd agreed to watch her. One of the things she'd loved about Greg was that he'd grown up in a regular family. She was sure he would know how to raise a regular family, as well. Never in a million years would she have wanted her kids to have the sad childhood she did. But now, with Greg gone, that seemed exactly what they were headed for.

She nudged Evie awake and walked her upstairs to brush her teeth. In the bathroom, she noticed four bath towels on the floor by the sink. She sighed. Why had Zac needed so many towels, and why did he have to leave them like that? If he had hung at least one up, then he could use it tomorrow. He did this kind of thing sometimes at home, too, but it was different there—she had a lot of towels and a nice, big washer that could handle them. But she didn't have an endless supply of towels in this house, and the washer was smaller. She picked up the towels and threw them in the hamper. She'd have to talk to him about it.

She tucked Evie in bed and then hesitated outside Zac's closed door. He often got angry when he was doing something and she interrupted him, but she wanted to make sure he knew she wasn't mad about the way he had spoken to her earlier. She didn't want him to stay up all night feeling guilty. She wanted him to be able to sleep. Greg had often told her not to worry about his sleep—that some people just didn't sleep well. In fact, Zac and Greg would often meet up in the hallway in the middle of the night. Greg used to say that he and Zac had some of their best heart-to-hearts—about the Yankees, politics, pretty girls at school—over peanut butter sandwiches at two o'clock in the morning. But now Greg wasn't there to reassure him. When she heard Zac up at night and went to ask if he wanted a sandwich, he would tell her he was fine, and she should go back to sleep.

She knocked on his door. "Knock, knock," she said as she opened it.

He was sitting on his bed, studying his phone. "Why do you say 'knock, knock' if you're knocking anyway?" he asked.

She gave a small laugh. "I don't know," she said. "I honestly don't know why I do that." She walked over and sat on the edge of his bed. His legs were under the covers and he didn't move them to make room for her, so she just sat there on the end, more like squatting than sitting. She didn't mind. She just wanted to be next to him for a moment.

"So, how are you doing?" she asked. She lifted her arm to stroke his hair. He pulled his head back so fiercely that it made her flinch.

"Sorry," he said. "I'm fine."

"It's pretty early for you to be in bed. Do you feel okay? Just tired?"

He nodded. She knew he wanted her out, but she couldn't help thinking that if she just kept making conversation with him, saying different things to comfort him or make him smile, maybe she could push past the wall he had put up. All she wanted was to see a smile on his face. Even a little one. She loved his smile so much, the way it spread so wide and showed off his dimple and made sweet crinkles form at the sides of his eyes.

"You know, you can sleep in tomorrow," she said. "But then it's up and out early on Monday, mister. The counselor-in-training meetings are eight thirty. So I'll probably get you up at seven thirty to have a good breakfast." She raised her eyebrows, to ask if he was good with that. He shrugged and looked away.

"I think you'll like being a C.I.T.," she said. "It's more fun than being a camper."

She watched him run his tongue over his teeth. She had seen him do that before when he seemed stressed.

"What is it, honey?" she said. "Are you missing Dad? Because we don't have to stay here all summer. We can leave. We don't ever have to come back."

He looked away.

"Do you want to talk about Dad?" she asked.

He shook his head.

"Do you want to, maybe, start seeing the psychologist again?"

He closed his eyes.

"Honey, I'm just trying to help. What would you like me to do?"

He rubbed his eyes with the heels of his hands, as though trying to make her disappear. "Can you just stop asking questions, Mom?" he said, almost in a whimper. "Can we just stop talking?"

She nodded, feeling the tears coming but wanting to hold them back. She'd seen him angry before, but she'd never seen him withdraw like that, rubbing his eyes as if he wanted her and the rest of the world to disappear. If he knew he made her cry, then there was no chance he'd be able to sleep at all tonight. She knew how he was.

She nodded. "You're right. I am talking way too much. Just one last thing—if you have any trouble sleeping tonight, you can come get me. Or if you don't want to do that, you can listen to a little music. You have your headphones, don't you? I mean, I know you packed them. I know you were on top of that."

He pointed toward the duffel and she got up and dug around until she found them. She didn't say anything about the fact that it was still mostly full.

"Here, I'll leave them right next to your phone so you don't even have to get up," she said, putting the headphones on the night table. "Just don't look at the phone too much, because looking at screens at night can make it even harder to fall to sleep. Just listen to the music if you want to, okay?"

He nodded.

"Do you want me to turn off the light?"

"I'll do it."

"Door open or closed?"

"Closed."

"Okay, honey. Goodnight," she said, leaning over to kiss his forehead. "Sleep well, see you in the morning."

She left his room and started downstairs, then sank on the steps and leaned her head against the bannister. This wasn't going to work, she thought. Zac was feeling worse, not better—how else to explain that rather than getting angry just now, the way he often did, he had tried to withdraw and block her out instead? Bringing them all back was a mistake. None of them belonged here anymore, not even for this one last summer. The camp program started Monday, the day after tomorrow, and as soon as she sent them off, she'd get started. She'd line up a broker and put the house on the market, and then start to clean it out. Maybe she could get things organized in a couple of weeks, maybe even less if Hope could help her. At least that way if Hope *was* going to go back to Europe, she and the kids wouldn't be in town without her. And once she had the ball rolling, she'd talk to the kids. They'd agree it was best to go home. They'd find something else to do for the rest of the summer.

The sooner they were out of Lilac House, the better.

CHAPTER FIVE

"Maybe I won't go." Evie looked up, the heart-shaped lenses of her plastic sunglasses glinting in the sun. "Maybe I'll stay home with you."

Anna squeezed her daughter's hand. "No, Evie, go. You love camp."

"But what will you do?"

"Just chores around the house."

"I can help."

"Honey, you'll be bored."

"But I like the house."

"You'll be there all evening."

"But what if you're lonely?"

"I have Aunt Hope to keep me company."

"She's not there anymore. She left when we did."

"I know, but maybe I'll stop by her store later to say hello. I'll be fine—and you will, too, honey. I promise. Better get going—the groups will be lining up soon."

Anna pointed to the bottom of the slope, where dozens of kids were converging in a fluid blob, the boys chasing one another or leaping high and propelling themselves forward into chest bumps, the girls standing back-to-back to see who was taller or attempting cartwheels in the soft sand near the lake. Teenagers with clipboards and blue tee shirts emblazoned with COUNSELOR across the back were holding up flags heralding group names. Parents—mostly moms, some dads—stood near

Anna and Evie on the sidewalk, watching the action below. Anna recognized the faces from past summers.

Evie fingered her sunglasses. "None of the girls are wearing any," she said.

"You can wear them anyway. It doesn't matter about the other girls."

"But I look so different."

"Then take them off. Daddy wouldn't mind."

"I guess they're babyish."

"It's up to you. Do you want me to bring them home to keep them safe?"

"No, I'll keep them." She slithered out of her backpack, and Anna thought her heart would break as she watched her daughter's short fingers work the zipper and then tuck the sunglasses deep inside. Greg had taken Evie to the drugstore on Main Street to buy them when she was six and starting camp for the first time. He'd told her the heart-shaped lenses were to remind her how much he and Mommy loved her. She hadn't used them for a couple of years, but had come downstairs wearing them this morning.

Now the kids were starting to form lines. Anna ached to keep hold of Evie's hand and bring her to her counselor, but the routine was for parents to stay back. She didn't think it would be good for Evie to be the only kid whose mom went down by the lake. She wrapped her arm around Evie's shoulder and gave her a squeeze and a kiss on the check.

"Go ahead now," she said. "You don't want to miss check-in. Go find your group and have fun, okay? I'll be right here to get you at four o'clock."

With her eyes on the activity below, Evie took a deep breath and started toward the crowd. Her feet slid on the sandy slope. Anna nodded each time she looked back.

"First days can be hard, no matter how old they get, right?" one of the moms nearby said to her. "But in two seconds they're fine and want you nowhere around."

Anna smiled, although she wasn't convinced Evie would get settled nearly that quickly.

"Did you have a nice winter?" the woman asked.

She hesitated. She didn't know this woman, other than to smile and say hi, and she didn't want to burden her with the truth. And she also didn't want to face the kind of pitying look she'd become used to in Silver Plains. Their life had been so public there, with Greg's constituents approaching them at the mall, at school events, and even in restaurants to shake Greg's hand and launch into whatever was on their minds—a local intersection that could use a traffic light, or an increase in parking fees that felt excessive. They acted like Greg was a longtime pal, which she knew spoke volumes about him. The complaints had congealed last fall around Willow Center, with many people arguing that a mental health support facility right downtown was bad for the town. They insisted it would bring too many strangers into the community, and would lead to more noise, more trash, and more traffic. Greg always followed the same routine, tilting his ear toward the person speaking and nodding thoughtfully before offering a vision of a modern, welcoming institution that would elevate the entire community. Often he'd discreetly catch the server's eye, so his plate could be brought back to the kitchen and kept warm. He'd nod at Anna and the kids to eat without him.

"A little rough, but we're good now," Anna answered. "And you?"

The woman commented on how unusually cold it had been, and they both went back to looking toward the lake. Anna had never been upset about those dinnertime interruptions. She was proud of Greg, how well he could handle even the most blustery constituent. Still, she'd been so grateful for the anonymity that

Greg allowed them in Lake Summers. She'd protected their privacy, avoiding making plans or having anyone come over other than Hope. And last summer had felt especially sweet, since she'd suspected their days of flying under the radar were numbered. Support was building for Greg to run for governor in two years, and Crystal was pushing him to introduce himself to local officials and start to build a following upstate. Anna had accepted the coming change the same way she accepted the end of a beautiful summer day, regretful to see the sun sink low even though a starry night sky could be lovely, too. Sometimes she'd catch Greg staring over the lake, and a tiny piece of her wondered if he actually wanted to be governor. But his expression was hard to interpret—fear? agitation? weariness?—and disappeared so quickly. Sitting on the blanket alongside him, she'd assumed the ambivalence wasn't his, but hers. Being governor was a big job. He'd be even busier, and away from home more. He'd be under even more stress.

Evie turned around one last time, and Anna gave her a thumbs up, then watched as the little girl dropped her chin and got on line, looking like she was at the doctor's office for a flu shot. She wished she knew for sure what was going on in that little head. Did Evie really want to stay at the house all day? Or did she feel guilty having fun without Greg around? Had finding those sunglasses triggered all this? What did she need that Anna wasn't providing?

Scanning the area, Anna spotted Zac, who had left earlier that morning. He was sitting behind a table with a few other boys his age, handing out blue tee shirts to the campers. At least *he* looked okay. Wasn't that always the way, she thought—if one kid was happy, the other was sure to be miserable? The day Evie earned a badge with her Brownie troop, Zac got cut from travel basketball. When Zac got into Honors Math, Evie was passed over for a speaking role in the school play.

And yet those ups and downs felt so small now. Her kids' feelings since Greg died had become so much more complicated, so much more unknowable, so much more potentially damaging. Who was suffering today, who would suffer tomorrow? Whose breath was jagged in bed in the dark because of a sudden, unexpected memory of Daddy saying goodnight? Whose chest hurt more at breakfast in the morning, because of the inevitable emptiness left by a tickle that didn't come, a silly joke that was never made? Greg's favorite observation about human nature was that attitude followed behavior—that people had to put an idea into action before they would perceive its benefits. But how long would she have to go on pretending that life was normal, and acting like life was normal, before they would all believe it *was* normal? Was parenting children who'd lost their father an impossible task—or just impossible for her?

The sandy area by the lake was emptying now. Anna saw Evie marching with her line toward the ball field, while Zac and the other boys broke down the folding table and boxed up the leftover shirts. Starting the walk home, she noticed the flat spot on the sand where she used to go for sunrise yoga classes on Sunday mornings, the one day of the week that Greg allowed himself to sleep in. It had felt good to get up at dawn and stretch out while the rest of the family was still asleep, while the warmth of Greg's sleeping body still lingered on her skin. Ahead was the green, where they used to have picnic dinners on Wednesday evenings and listen to big band music under the stars. And Pearl's Café, with those delicious muffins Greg couldn't resist. Every space of this town had been part of the life she and Greg had woven together. Now they were just loose, dangling scraps of fabric.

Back at the house, Anna stepped into the front hallway. Evie had been right—it felt lonely. And it unsettled her. Not because she was by herself; she'd often been the only adult here, when Greg had to travel for a couple of nights at a time for meetings at the state capital in Albany, or back to his office in Silver Plains. But even when he was gone, the house had seemed to anticipate his return. Now it just screamed of loss. She remembered how Greg would talk about his grandparents' bungalow where he'd spent his summers as a kid, along with his parents, his brother, and a range of aunts, uncles, and cousins. He'd describe family Olympics games and camp-outs in the backyards, and Sunday afternoons when his grandfather would bring all the cousins to McDonald's for lunch. His grandfather had sold the bungalow right after his grandmother died—despite the objections of the rest of the family—because he couldn't bear not having her there.

"We'll have to die of old age together," Greg had said the evening they'd closed on Lilac House. "So neither one of us will ever have to face this place without the other."

In the bedroom, she opened Greg's closet. They hadn't kept much here year-round in the way of clothing, and all she found was a sweatshirt, some tee shirts, a couple of pairs of shorts, and a pair of sandals. And a tuxedo, covered in plastic. He'd kept it here for the one or two times each summer they'd had a formal affair to go to. Like last summer, when they'd gone to the gala for the new mental health center in Syracuse, the model for Willow Center. Anna pulled up the plastic and lifted the jacket sleeve to her cheek. The fabric felt substantial, like it still had plenty of wear left. But it didn't have Greg's summer smell. It barely had a smell at all.

Across the room were the empty suitcases she'd brought from Silver Plains, and inside one, she found the envelope Crystal had given her. She pulled it out and walked through the living room and out the French doors to the section of the porch that wrapped around the back. They'd installed a porch swing out there last year, where she and Greg would sit after the kids were asleep and watch the stars come out atop the woods behind their yard. The crickets would sing as Greg wrapped his arm around her and pulled her close to him, and the sounds of his heart beating drew her into a delicious trance that she never wanted to end. Now she sat down on the swing by herself. The woods didn't look as enchanted as they had on those nights with Greg, and the crickets weren't singing. But the trees were still tall and fragrant, the canopies of leaves thick and green, and the thought of how many decades, or even centuries, the woods had existed made her feel peaceful nonetheless.

Sitting sideways on the swing, she stretched out her legs, and emptied the contents of the envelope onto her lap. The top sheet had photos of trees the highway department had approved for Greg's memorial alongside the stretch of road where he crashed. She had hated the idea of the memorial from the start: why would any driver want to be reminded of the place where Greg's life essentially came to an end? What was healing about that? Greg wasn't a hero because he skidded off the road, flipped over, and slammed headlong into the embankment; he was a hero because he cared about making people's lives better, making the city he served a more caring place. But she hadn't argued. Greg's staff and the city officials were committed to the project, and they all thought it a wonderful and meaningful tribute.

So which tree would he have liked? A sycamore? A maple? A crabapple, like the one right outside Zac's window, which was bursting with cheery pink blossoms when they arrived in town each June? Anna bent her knees and looked outside. All she knew about trees was that she loved all the ones that circled Lilac House, especially those that stretched into the woods. She remembered how they'd looked when she and Greg came back from the Syracuse gala last summer, how the light from the crescent moon that evening had filtered through the leaves, giving the backyard an inky, dreamy hue. The kids were with Hope for the night, and Greg had proposed that they open a bottle of wine and go out back. The air had been warm and breezy, and Greg looked so handsome and sweetly rumpled in his tux, and his summer smell was so warm and sexy, and before she knew it, they were in the woods, stripping off their fancy clothes with the single-minded passion of teenagers after senior prom.

But the ground had been bumpy and uneven, and the tree roots dug into their backs and legs, and then, unexpectedly, it had started to rain—not a gentle, cleansing shower, but buckets of fat, blinding raindrops. They'd scrambled back into their clothes—Greg refused to run naked across the lawn, just in case a neighbor happened to be looking out—and gone back to the house, where they'd wrapped themselves in towels and laughed hysterically and then found their way to their bedroom to finish what they'd started, under the cool white sheets.

It was probably the last time she'd been entirely, unabashedly happy. September had been especially difficult, the pressure on Greg from work making it hard for him to relax.

By October, he was dead.

Anna stuffed the papers back into Crystal's envelope. What she had to do—starting right now, right this very moment—was enlist her aunt's help and figure out a plan for getting away from Lilac House for good, notwithstanding whatever it was that Hope had to tell her. She understood how Greg's grandfather had felt; how he didn't want anything to do with that bungalow once he lost his love. She felt the same. She couldn't look at the backyard, couldn't look at the little Sleeping Beauty doll that sat on the lamp table; she didn't want to see the lake or the green anymore. Silver Plains was the place where she, Greg, and the kids had lived, but this was the place they'd loved. And that was why they had to go.

*

Hope was on her hands and knees alongside a teenage girl, checking the fit of a pair of pointe shoes, when Anna walked into the store a short time later. The floor around her was a sea of pointe shoes and empty plastic sacs.

"I think they're good—do a couple of pliés and relevés, and see how they feel," Hope said. She turned to the girl's friend. "Now, let's get started with you. Why don't you try on the Capezios, and we'll take it from there?"

Anna gave a quick wave to her aunt and went over to the opened shoe armoire to wait. She read the shelf labels: Grishko. Capezio. Freed. Mirella. Sansha. Repetto. Chacott. How romantic dancewear brands used to sound to her ears! How romantic they still sounded. She found a Chacott style in her size, and pulled out the sac, then loosened the drawstring to let the shoes slip out. It was the shade of pink she'd always loved—soft and muted, bordering on beige. She'd never been one for shiny styles or flashy, attention-grabbing pinks.

With Hope still involved with the girls, Anna wandered down the hallway toward the studio, imagining herself stitching on some ribbons and elastics and taking the shoes for a spin. Stepping into the center of the studio and rising to the sky on her toes. She could almost feel the ground underneath her feet, the lengthening of her rib cage, that gorgeous contrast between rooting down and pulling up, which was the very essence of dance. Then she heard the door chime. Assuming the customers had left, she went back to the sales floor.

Hope was alone now, sorting the shoes on the floor. Anna bent down to help.

"Look at these beauties," she said. "So which did they buy?"

Hope shook her head. "They didn't," she muttered. "They want to think about it."

"They didn't buy *anything?* They looked like such serious dancers."

"Yeah, but they're also college girls. They can be difficult."

Anna nodded. "I guess that's part of retailing—the customer's always right, right?" She picked up a shoe. "So which were they leaning toward? These Grishkos?"

Hope pulled herself up to her feet and gave Anna an amused scowl. "*You're* the only one who ever liked those shoes. If I remember correctly, your father said hard shoes were the only kind you'd wear."

"I loved how much work it took to break them in," Anna said. "It felt like such an accomplishment just to get up on my toes. But I don't know… if I were still dancing today, I think I'd choose these." She lifted the pair she'd taken from the armoire.

"The Chacotts?" Hope said, sitting on an ottoman and massaging her bad knee. "With your strong feet? You'd dance right through them. You'd have to buy a new pair every week."

Anna stroked the silky toe box. "No, I'm not that strong anymore. I wouldn't want to do that now, duke it out with my shoes until they surrendered. I'd want shoes that are soft. That give."

"Oh?" Hope said. "So why don't you try them? Let's go into the studio."

"I was just thinking about that… but I don't think so."

"Come on, sweetheart, you look like you want to. Go play a little, why not? Look how you're holding that shoe, like it's a baby or something. You were such a beautiful dancer when you were growing up."

"That was before I fell."

"That was a long time ago. Your ankle's healed."

Anna shook her head, but her aunt persisted.

"Nobody's around," she said. "I don't even have to come if you don't want me to. What's there to be scared of?"

"I don't want to do it, okay? Let's just drop it." She carried an armful of sacs to the armoire, then sighed and turned back around. "I'm sorry, Aunt Hope. I don't mean to snap at you. Thanks so much for stopping by this morning for breakfast. It made everything easier having you there."

Hope gathered up the last few sacs. "Please, it was you who did the me the favor," she said. "The mornings can be pretty lonely when you live by yourself. I was glad for the company. I intend to make this a regular event."

She pulled herself up, and Anna saw her wince and rub her knee before bringing the sacs to the armoire. "The kids looked excited for camp," she said. "Evie was adorable, with that big backpack and those sunglasses Greg gave her. How did they do?"

"Zac seemed okay. Evie had a little trouble, but she pulled herself together."

"And how about you, sweetheart?" Hope said. "How was it for you, being back in Lilac House last night?"

Anna looked down. "It was horrible after you left," she said. "Greg's all over that house. It's something so real that you can't breathe, and you can't even move without coming up against it all the time. The kids felt it, too." She turned away and began placing the sacs into their cubbies, needing something to do with her hands so she could get the next painful sentences out.

"I didn't want to say anything with the kids around this morning," she said. "But I've made a decision. I'm going to sell the house and go back home. It's too hard for us to be here anymore."

"You're… you're selling? Lilac House? Oh Anna, no…"

"I have to. I thought we could make it through this summer, but we can't." She turned back to face Hope. "And I came here to ask you to help me, so I can get out of here sooner. I need you."

Hope paused and brought her hands in front of her waist, kneading her fingers. "But Anna… you haven't even given yourself a chance here yet. You just arrived."

"But I can tell it's not going to work. So why drag this out? We miss him way too much to be back here without him."

"But he wanted you to be here," Hope said. She pushed her hair away from her forehead. "He loved it here, and he meant for you to have this house forever… you and the kids, all of you—"

"But he didn't want the kids to suffer." She raised her palms upward, confused by her aunt's nervous energy. "I thought you'd understand. I thought I could count on you. I know you don't want the kids to suffer, either."

"No, no of course not." Hope turned around and walked toward the window, fingering the seam of her collar. "I love them, and I love you."

"So what's the problem? You're leaving too, right?"

Hope turned back. "*Me* leaving? What are you talking about?"

"The thing you were starting to tell me the other day. When we were in the studio and Evie came in." Anna put the remaining sacs on the counter and walked closer to Hope. "You're leaving, too, aren't you? That's what you wanted to tell me, isn't it?"

Hope shook her head. "No, not at all. That isn't at all what I was going to say."

"Then what was it? What did you have to tell me?"

Hope reached out and took Anna by the shoulders. "Sweetheart, I wish I didn't have to spring it on you like this," she said. "But you can't leave Lake Summers. Because you're tied to this place. Not just your feelings. You're tied here for real.

"Oh, Anna," she said. "You *own* this store."

CHAPTER SIX

"I... *what?*" Anna stood unmoving, as though stillness could compel her aunt to revise the crazy thing she'd just said.

But there was no revision. "He planned this all for you," Hope said. "He never got to tell you—"

"Who? Greg?"

"He came over last summer and said you told him what I was doing, and he wanted to go in halves. He wanted to surprise you."

Anna sank against the wall. That sounded like Greg—he loved planning surprises. He'd surprised her when he'd brought her to Lake Summers on their first anniversary and shown her the cashed check for a down payment on the house. She'd had no idea he'd been researching listings and talking with realtors. She'd thought he was bringing her there to introduce her to an old work friend. But when she saw the engraved slate plaque near the front door, "Lilac House," she knew the home was meant to be theirs. Greg had called it fate, and she'd joked that it was *bashert*, the term her father would use when he was feeling particularly Jewish. And they continued to believe that the house was where they belonged even after they learned that the lilac bushes along the front walk bloomed in May, and the lilacs were long gone by the time they arrived each year in June. In fact, Anna came to love the house even more for that. There was something poetic and poignant in the timing.

Still, Greg's purchase of the house had been different from what he did with the store, Anna now thought. After all, she and he had spoken often about how they eventually wanted a summer home for their family, like Greg's grandparents had had. And they'd both been in love with Lake Summers from the time they'd met on that trail behind the resort. Why would he buy her a store, of all things? And why choose one here, when they were only in town for eight weeks a year?

She stood and breathed out, trying to calm down so she could get a handle on things. "What... exactly did he buy?" she asked.

"Half of everything. Fifty-fifty."

"Half of what? Spell it out."

"Okay, first there's the building—"

"He bought half of the *building?*"

"It made more sense at the time than trying to rent a place. The building was for sale, and we both thought it was a good investment. And then there's the inventory and fixtures... and, of course, the construction costs..."

Anna lifted her hands, palms upturned. "But how? We don't have that kind of money."

Hope paused, pressing her lips together. "He said something about a brokerage account from his grandfather—"

Anna opened her mouth to protest more, then dropped onto an ottoman. The money he'd inherited when his grandfather died, the money that she'd thought was still there. The account had been in Greg's name only. They'd never bothered to change it, and he'd have been able to close it out without her ever knowing.

She cupped her forehead with the palm of one hand. "So... he took out all the money? Without even telling me?"

"Oh Anna, I know I should have said something to you right after Greg died. But I kept waiting for a good time." She squatted down next to her. "I wanted to tell you when I came down for the funeral, but you were already dealing with so much. And then I figured Greg's brother would have told you. He's your accountant, right? He must have shown you a list of assets—"

"Maybe he did, I don't know. Ivan was saying all these complicated things, and I couldn't make sense of it. And I didn't see the urgency of going through everything because I thought I had that money if I needed it. I told Ivan we'd go over everything again in the fall after he gets back from this India trip he's taking—"

"But I thought you knew, and weren't ready to talk about it. And then when I realized you probably didn't know, I was going to call you. But there were construction issues—nothing bad, just normal delays and stuff—and I wanted to get things on a sound footing first. And then the summer was coming, and I thought it would be better if we talked about it when you got here."

She stroked Anna's shoulder. "He was so excited to do this for you. He loved you so much."

Anna nodded, feeling the catch in her chest that always came just before the tears. She pressed her hand against her mouth because she didn't want to cry. She knew how thrilled Greg must have sounded when he proposed the idea to Hope. She could practically see how he must have looked, his eyes growing wide and his fists pumping as he worked through the details of the partnership. He was never so animated, so boyish and adorable, as when he was cooking up a new project that he thought would be a winner. Last fall when they returned home from Lake Summers, he'd suggested surprising the kids with a puppy. She'd thought it was a good idea, that it might help calm Zac down, give him something new and fun to turn his attention to. Greg had been so ecstatic that it was almost impossible for him not to spill the beans every night at dinner. They were planning to go to the Humane Society the weekend after he died.

Still, it was shocking to think that she'd owned half of this store for—what, almost a year now? It made her think of the night when the police chief showed up at her door to suggest that she call a neighbor to watch the kids and then come with him to the hospital. That was before she knew how serious the accident had been, before she knew Greg wasn't going to make it. All she knew was that something had happened that shouldn't have. It was like being outside of her own skin, watching someone who looked like her but wasn't her at all.

Because Greg had never shown any interest in dance, or even any interest in her life as a dancer, after that first conversation on the trail behind the Lake Summers Resort. The only time he'd ever attended a dance production was soon after they'd started dating, when he bought tickets to the ballet for her birthday. He'd been fidgety for the whole first half, and she'd found the performance hard to watch, too, because she was so attracted to him. When intermission came, they went out to the fountains on the Lincoln Center plaza. He held her hands and leaned over to kiss her, and she concentrated on the way her skin felt under his fingers, because she'd never known that hand-holding could feel so intimate. They kissed some more, the mist from the fountains floating over to coat her bare arms. They never returned to their seats.

"Did Greg say… *anything* else?" Anna said, grasping for more information. It was always hard to be without him, but ten times harder at a moment like this, when she needed to know what he was thinking. "It's so out of the blue."

Hope shook her head. "It wasn't a long conversation. We talked mostly about the money. And he looked… almost relieved, I guess, when I said I'd go along with it. Oh, Anna, there were times when we met for coffee and he looked so troubled. He said he had a lot of work pressure, and he was nervous about whether he'd make a good candidate for governor. But that moment we agreed to go halves on the store—it was like he had finally found an answer to some question that had been eating away at him."

Anna looked up and shook her head. "I can't even wrap my mind around this."

Hope sighed. "I'm sorry, Anna. I know now that I handled it all wrong. I should have insisted that we bring you into the conversation. But he felt so strongly about doing it his way—you know the way your husband was, it was hard not to get caught up when he felt he'd zeroed in on a great idea. And I thought you'd love owning the business with me. I didn't think for a minute that it would turn out..." She paused. "He just wanted to surprise you."

The door chime sounded, and a mother with two young daughters came inside. Hope rose to her feet, and Anna saw her wince and massage her knee for a moment before going over to help the woman. She took a deep breath. A piece of her wanted to accuse her aunt of being thoughtless and foolish, for accepting the money without her knowledge. It made her think about all those years that Hope stayed away, not even coming back in those weeks and months after her father's funeral. Shouldn't her aunt have thought through the possible repercussions, and tried to ensure she was doing the best for her niece way back then—and this time, too? Wasn't that what aunts were supposed to do, especially when there were no parents around?

But watching Hope walk so slowly, Anna knew she couldn't be mad at her. The past was the past—that's what she had decided when Hope came back into her life twelve years ago and asked for a fresh start. She'd made Anna promise never to ask her what happened that kept her away so long, and Anna had wanted her back in her life so badly that she'd agreed. And now... now she couldn't blame her either. She couldn't blame Hope for saying yes about the money, not when it had been Greg's idea. And even if Hope had had misgivings about hiding the truth, Greg would have convinced her to do it anyway. "Greg Harris, Greg Harris, and Greg Harris"—that's what one of the Silver Plains City Council members had said with a laugh when a reporter asked his top three reasons for supporting Willow Center. And it wasn't entirely a joke. Greg's enthusiasm was irresistible. No one was immune.

And even though Hope should have told her sooner, really, what difference did it make? Maybe it was better that she hadn't known before now, Anna thought. Maybe dealing with her kids and her grief was enough these last months. As her aunt had said, the information was right there in the list of assets Ivan showed her. But she hadn't wanted to look all that closely.

She couldn't blame Greg, either. If she'd objected years ago when he bought Lilac House for her as a surprise, maybe he'd have thought twice about the store. But she'd been thrilled when he'd put the canceled check in her hand. He knew about her childhood—how her mother had died, how her father had struggled to balance work and parenting, how she'd grown up a city kid who never learned to ride a bike, never toasted marshmallows over a campfire, never climbed a tree. So Lilac House hadn't merely been a piece of property; it had been Greg's invitation to summers like those of *his* childhood. Summers they could give to the children they'd someday have.

The mom and her kids left after buying a bag of hair clips, and Hope walked over and clasped her hands together, looking like she was waiting for a judge's decision. "So, what are you thinking?" she asked.

Anna shook her head. "I'm not mad—not at you, and not at him…"

"But?"

"But I'm scared. Because it's a lot of money that I thought I had, and now I don't."

"I know… I know…"

"And I can't even ask Ivan what it means until he comes back at the end of the summer. I just know that we went through so much of our other savings to pay for Greg's campaign, and Ivan seemed worried about my finances—I didn't understand it then, but I do now."

She stood and took her aunt's hand. "Oh, Aunt Hope. I know this store is your dream. I know how much you love it, and it *is* beautiful. But I don't think I can own this store with you."

Hope paused, her eyes wide. "Sweetheart, what are you saying?"

"I don't think… I don't see how I can keep all that money tied up like this. I have two mortgages to pay, and Zac will be going to college before I know it."

"Anna… you can't pull out."

"But I have to. Please understand."

"I can't give you the money back."

"But I need you to. I can't own a store now—"

"But you *do* own it, that's the point. I don't have the cash to give back to you. There's hardly any cash at all, it's all tied up in the business. The only thing of value now is the building."

"Then what can we do?"

"I don't know. If we close the store, that would mean defaulting on our bills and declaring bankruptcy. You'd never get all your money back—and you'd create a whole new set of financial problems for yourself."

"What if we sold the building, but kept the store?"

"And give some landlord the power to charge us a sky-high rent? Sweetheart, that's not going to get you your money back either."

"Then maybe I can find someone who wants to buy my half. There has to be someone in town who wants in on this beautiful store."

"I wish that were true, but the business isn't solvent yet. We're just getting started…"

Anna shook her head and walked toward the large picture window at the front of the store. Main Street glowed in the sun, and some purplish irises in a planter across the street were facing skyward to drink in the sunshine. A couple were just coming out of the smoothie shop, the young woman holding a baby, the man holding a large pink smoothie. The woman leaned down to gently place the baby in a nearby stroller, while the man steadied the stroller with one hand. Then he offered her the cup and she took it and kissed his cheek.

"It's so hard to believe," Anna said, almost in a whisper. "I always felt so at home in this town, as though I were meant to be here. And now I don't even know if I belong."

Hope walked up beside her. "Oh, Anna, of course you belong," she said. "I know this business about the store comes as a huge shock. But Lake Summers is a part of your life. You can't think it's some strange, unwelcoming place now. That's not going to help your kids—"

"But it's too hard here. We're surrounded by Greg, like I told you. I'll never find myself again if he's always around. I'll always feel like Greg's wife, and I can't be Greg's wife anymore, because that life is over."

"So you left Silver Plains because you thought you could get a fresh start here, and now you want to leave here and go back there?"

Anna shook her head and took a few steps away. "I don't know—maybe I just have to go somewhere completely new. Maybe I can find a small place in Connecticut. Or a little further north."

"Massachusetts, Maine, Canada? Don't you think he'd be there, too? Sweetheart, what you're running away from is not outside of you. It's inside. The Greg who lives in your head and your heart, and your kids' hearts, too—you can't run away from that. You have to make peace with it."

Anna looked out the window a moment longer, and then let out a breath. Greg would have teased her mercilessly for just standing around, feeling sorry for herself. *You need to do something*, he'd have said. *What's your plan?*

She turned back around. "Okay, here's my idea," she said. "We'll stay for the summer, and you and I will work together to make this store succeed. And in August, I'll find a way to sell my half, and you'll keep yours. Or we'll arrange for you to buy me out and own the whole thing. Whatever's best. But if everything goes well, you'll have your store, and I'll have my savings back again. What do you think?"

Hope let out a sigh that sounded as though she'd been holding her breath for days. "I think that sounds wonderful," she said.

A few minutes later the two of them were huddled close together in front of Hope's laptop on the top of the jewelry display case. Anna pressed her elbows onto the counter and rested her chin in her hands, while Hope scrolled through inventory records, merchandise orders, bills, and dance class schedules. She explained that she'd been open a month and was starting to get a sense of the store's strengths and challenges. On the plus side, she said, the townspeople were charmed by the store, thanks largely to its novelty; but on the minus side, the town had never had a dance store or studio before, so nobody felt compelled to shop or take classes there. It simply wasn't yet becoming a part of people's lives, and Hope didn't know how to make it one.

As for the Jayson dancers, Hope explained, those students *did* have a need for a well-stocked dance store, and The Lilac Pointe, they said, was the best-stocked store in the region. But she was pretty certain the students were taking advantage of her by checking out her merchandise before buying cheaper elsewhere—and she didn't know how to change that, because she thought that if she confronted the students, they'd never return.

Anna pressed herself up from the countertop. "So how do we fix all this?" she said.

Hope stood, too. "That's what I've been wrestling with."

"There should be something we can do," Anna said. "Isn't there someone around we can ask for advice? Maybe the Chamber of Commerce, or something?"

Hope shook her head. "Stan and Trey are smart, but they sell smoothies. And there's a consultant, Aidan something, who the town hired to revitalize Main Street. But I don't trust him. He wears a wedding ring, but no one ever sees his wife."

"You don't think he's worth even talking to?"

"He's tried to give me some advice, but he doesn't know anything about the dance business. I don't know how much he knows about any business, actually. He hasn't been in town all that long, and nobody knows much about him. They did a piece on him in the paper when he arrived, but he didn't talk at all about what he did before coming here."

Hope closed the documents on the computer, and Anna wandered from the jewelry counter over to the clothing racks. She ran her hand along the line of colorful leotards, listening to the staccato clacking of the plastic hangers gently colliding with one another. What unsettled her as much as the precarious state of the store was that she still couldn't make heads or tails of Greg's motives. She'd never given him any sign that she wanted to be a shopkeeper. She'd been happy working in his office as community service liaison, a volunteer job he'd invented that entailed finding ways to support local nonprofits. She'd helped a church group create an English-language program for Asian immigrants, and she'd loved the program so much that she'd taught three of the classes herself.

He looked so stressed, Hope had said. *That moment we agreed to go halves on the store—it was like he had finally found an answer to some question that had been eating away at him.* Anna thought back to the day late last summer when she told Greg about Hope's idea. He'd seemed way more interested than she expected, considering that the Yankees were on TV. Later that night in bed, he'd lain down alongside her and moved one arm beneath her, using the other hand to stroke her hair, her cheek, her collarbone. She slid her arms around his neck, waiting for the sense of belonging she always felt when they made love. It was then she'd realized that things between them were changing—and they continued to feel different in the fall, after they'd returned to Silver Plains. Something about how he held her was tentative. It was as though he was no longer offering security. It was as though he were asking for it.

"I think I need to clear my head," she said, looking over her shoulder at Hope. "I'm going over to Pearl's to get a coffee. Can I get you one?"

Hope shook her head no, and Anna left the store and started down Main Street. The town was crowded, even more so than when she'd arrived the other day. She looked over toward the entrance to Pearl's to see if there was a line outside. That's when she noticed a banner flying high above the converted Victorian residence that now housed Village Hall:

Better than a Sidewalk Sale!
SUMMERFEST
Wednesday, August 14
On the Grand Lawn of the Lake Summers Resort
Merchants: Space is Limited! Info and Applications Inside

SummerFest? Hope hadn't mentioned it at all, and Anna wondered if it was something they should know about. If space for merchants was limited, they should know sooner rather than later. Looking at her phone, she saw that she still had time before she had to get Evie. She crossed the street and entered Village Hall. There was a long wooden reception desk at the far end of the lobby. She asked the woman staffing it where she could get SummerFest information.

"Oh, our consultant is handling that, I'll get him," the woman said, and went through a doorway behind her. A moment later, a man in a black pullover shirt and gray slacks appeared. He had a subdued but awfully kind smile.

"I'm Aidan Lawrence," he said. "You were asking about SummerFest?"

CHAPTER SEVEN

Hope watched Anna go down the front steps to Main Street, feeling admiration and love. Her niece could have reacted very differently. She could have accused Hope of being selfish and thoughtless, for taking the money and not insisting that Greg okay it with her first. She could have brought up how Hope had disappeared for so many years, that Hope had waited all these months after Greg died before bringing the matter up: *How do you watch me lose my husband, and not feel compelled to say something? It's like you ran away all over again, Aunt Hope, like you abandoned me the same way you did when my father died. Why did I even let you back in my life? Why was I there for you, when you were never there for me—not back then when I needed you, and not now, either?*

She could have described scenarios where Hope's actions had put her family in danger. What if that brokerage account was the kids' college fund? What if the loss of those reserves meant Anna had to sell their Silver Plains home as well as Lilac House, just to meet expenses and start to save again for college? What if they had to move to a different town, and the kids had to change schools and leave their friends and their teachers so soon after losing their dad?

But Anna hadn't said any of those things. She'd acted with courage and calmness even as the news shot like an arrow straight into her chest, and she ultimately agreed to see things the way Hope suggested. And it was the thought of Anna's generous response that soured Hope's relief and left her with a heaviness deep in her stomach that made her want to fold in on herself and shrink away.

She knew what that feeling was. It was shame. And it wasn't the first time she'd felt that way. Not by a long shot.

Walking back from the window, she replaced some packages of tights that had slipped from the basket onto the floor. It had been a remarkable day, that day she'd first spotted the "For Sale" sign on the abandoned building. She'd been working in the back office of the Lake Summers Resort, trying to convince herself that she was content with her stable job and predictable daily life. But then she saw the sign, and she immediately knew she had to make that space her own. She wanted to create something tangible, something that could have a transformative effect on other people, something into which she could pour all her expertise and creativity and love. She'd thought that if she could pull that off, she could finally hold her head up. She could become someone she could like.

But two weeks later, sitting opposite Greg at Pearl's, she'd let her excitement get the better of her. She hadn't mentioned how tired he looked; she hadn't asked what was wrong; she hadn't taken out her phone to bring Anna into the conversation. She'd thought only about how grateful she was for Greg's vote of confidence, and how fun it would be to partner with Anna on this thrilling new project.

And instead of lashing out, Anna had agreed to partner with Hope, not because she wanted to, but because she loved her aunt too much to do anything else. Hope was so proud of her niece, which reinforced her resolve to make the store a resounding success. Anna had come through for her, and now Hope had to step up and be the kind of aunt that Anna truly needed.

The door chime sounded. "Hellooo?" said Trey, looking as slim and pulled together as always—the polar opposite of Stan. His short, blond hair rose artfully from his forehead before flipping neatly to the side. The only blemish to his appearance was his right ear, which was slightly misshapen after an aggressive melanoma. He usually placed his hand against the side of his face or tilted his head away when he talked to anyone besides Stan. Hope had almost cried a few months ago when Trey finally told her about the cancer, and he no longer made an effort to hide his ear from her.

"I think I have the recipe right this time," he said, holding out a small paper cup. "Can you give it a taste?"

She nodded, glad for the company, and took a sip. Tears sprang to her eyes. "Yikes. That's sour."

"For real? Too much?" He grimaced. "I want some drama, you know? Everything nice and sweet, and then suddenly, *bam!* Like fireworks in a cup, the tartness hits… you're not buying it, huh?"

"I'd tone it down a little," she said. "It's kind of painful with all that lemon."

"That's what Stan said," he told her. "But maybe it's our Fourth of July marketing hook—*only for the free and the brave!* Sure, it's a little startling at first, but we people need a jolt now and again, don't you think? We have to get this done, July Fourth is not that far away, and… what's the matter? Something wrong?"

Hope bent over and rubbed her knee. "No. I'm okay."

"You don't look okay. I thought you'd be happy, with your family back in town. Your knee must be hurting pretty bad."

"No worse than normal for this stupid old woman—"

"Stupid old woman? Now you're really scaring me."

"No, I'm okay. Really. It's just…" She walked behind the counter and leaned her elbows on the glass surface. "Trey, what do you do when you're scared you're going to let someone down? Someone you love more than anything in the world?"

He looked at the cup in her hand. "Ouch. Is that meant for us? Is this your way of saying we should find another line of work?"

She had to laugh. "No, this isn't about you at all. It's about me."

"How could you possibly hurt someone? You're not a mean person. Not by a long shot."

She shook her head. "Then what's wrong with me? Even when I think I'm handling something right, it turns out wrong."

He sighed and stepped closer to rub her shoulder. "Hey, everyone feels they've let someone down at one time or another," he said. "When my sister's kid came to visit last summer, he tried to make his own smoothie and sliced his finger with the blender blade. Needed eight stitches. I felt like shit about that. And you know the crazy thing? He still likes it here. He wants to visit again. Go figure."

He went to the front door. "I've got to get back to work. But we love you, Hope, you know we do. You're the best person that's moved onto this block in a long time. Don't ever forget that."

She waved back and threw the cup into the trash. It was nice to hear him say all that. But they didn't know her past; they had only met her last year. And anyway, Trey and Stan were like that—nice, generous people. And that was why they had each other, why they always would. They deserved to be loved. Trey had told her how Stan had kept his spirits up, kept him smiling and laughing, through the scary diagnosis and the disfiguring surgery and the flawed, painful recovery. He told her how Stan never stopped thinking he was beautiful. And that sustained him still, to this day.

But despite what Trey had said, it didn't erase the selfish, stupid way she'd messed up her life and hurt the people she cared about most. And the saddest part was that everything had started out so right, those many years ago. She'd felt so positive that summer when she left home, where she'd been studying dance at a local college, to move to New York and live with her brother, David, and his seven-year-old daughter, Anna. David's wife, Libby, had been killed in a freak accident when Anna was an infant—a taxi driver who had swerved to avoid a stopped garbage truck had lost control of the car and plowed into a group of pedestrians. Anna had been in the path of the taxi, and people said the last thing Libby did before being struck was to push her daughter's stroller out of the way. As a teenager, Hope couldn't stop thinking about Anna, who would never know the mother who'd saved her life. She was so glad when she finally stepped up to help her brother raise her young niece.

Life was wonderful in New York. Hope loved taking care of Anna, and she found stability and warmth in the sweet life the three of them shared—qualities that were lacking when she'd lived with her mother and stepfather. And David was a perfect older brother. He knew how much ballet meant to her, and how hard she'd worked to train for a career in dance. Thanks to a neighbor who worked in the theater, he was able to connect her with a renowned ballet coach, who helped improve her technique and secured multiple auditions for her. Ultimately, she landed a spot with the *corps* of the Hamburg Ballet Theatre in Germany.

Although she was sorry to leave New York, dancing in the ballet was a dream come true. Hope loved Europe and loved performing. She became the subject of photo spreads and newspaper features, and was often a guest at glamorous banquets and galas. Yes, she missed David and Anna, and their cozy life together, but she was delighted that Anna adored ballet, too, and wanted to follow in Hope's footsteps. She was certain that when it came time to wind down her career, she could be instrumental in helping Anna launch a dance career of her own.

Who would ever have believed that she had finally found her way, only to lose herself again? That at her happiest moment she'd end up making the worst decision of her life?

The door chime sounded, and a young mother with a little girl who looked about Evie's age came into the store. Hope introduced herself, grateful for the distraction.

The girl ran over to the apparel rack and pulled on the bottom of a coral-colored leotard. "Oh, Mom, this one!" she said.

"That's one of the new summer colors," Hope told them, taking the leotard off the rack. "The manufacturer just started making this fabric—it's soft it's soft and so lightweight. And the lace is very popular. Can I help you find the right size?"

The woman examined the price tag. "Very pretty," she said.

"Is your daughter interested in ballet?" Hope asked. "My summer session starts next week, and there's still time to sign up."

"She takes gymnastics," the woman told her.

"Ballet is a great foundation for gymnastics," she said. "It helps with balance and flexibility, and strength, too. Would you like to see the schedule—or maybe take a look at the studio in the back?"

The woman looked at the tag on the leotard again. "We'll think about this, honey," she said to her daughter. "We'll come back another time."

Hope watched the pair leave. She wished the woman had done even one thing that could be considered positive: taken a schedule, bought a hair ribbon, agreed to consider ballet classes for her daughter, or even just stated out loud that while the leotard was beautiful, the price seemed high. Maybe then Hope could have explained about the renovation and the expense of building a world-class studio. Maybe she could have informed her that the leotard was pricey because of the lace and innovative fabric. Or they could have agreed that a child that age didn't need such a high-quality leotard, since she'd probably grow out of it before it wore out. She might have been perfectly fine with one of the less expensive leotards over on the opposite rack, which were also quite pretty.

But the mom hadn't even given Hope a morsel to work with, except to say that her daughter took gymnastics. And what good did it do to know that? Hope couldn't teach gymnastics, and her studio wasn't built for it. There was no room for gymnastics equipment, even if she wanted to spend the money on it. And there was no way she could put balance beams and parallel bars on that delicate floor. Besides, the daughter was probably perfectly happy with the gymnastics classes she already attended.

Hope hung the leotard back on the rack, and then grabbed the duster from behind the counter. She brought it to the shoe armoire and ran it over the top, then opened the doors and brushed inside the rows of cubbies. The Grishkos and Mirellas that Melanie's friends had tried on were right there, and she recalled how the girls had left without buying, running from the store so that Kristin could meet with the dean about missing her final. She'd said she was in for a bad time—the dean was a stickler about respect and taking personal responsibility. It struck Hope as ironic that Kristin had been talking about personal responsibility at the very moment she was surreptitiously garnering style numbers so she could cheat Hope out of a sale she'd earned.

She closed the armoire doors and paused before taking the duster back. What might this stickler of a dean think about the girls benefiting from her time and expertise, and then buying their shoes online? She wondered if he'd believe it was as much a violation of personal responsibility as missing a test was. Would he find the girls' behavior disrespectful? Perhaps even more important, did he even know that The Lilac Pointe existed—and might he see value in having such a well-stocked store nearby? Maybe he'd be thrilled to know that she was open for business, and that some of his students had already found their way to her shop. Maybe there were ways she could help support the school's priorities and curriculum. After all, if the dean was so interested in his students' ethics, then surely he was also concerned about finding new ways to help them enrich their studies and move closer toward achieving their dreams.

She went to her computer at the far end of the countertop and pulled up the Jayson College website. What had the girls said his name was… something with a C? She found the administration page and scanned the deans' names. There it was… Carter. Keon Carter, Dean of Student Life. She thought about sending him an email, but changed her mind. College administrators probably got a ton of emails every day, and she didn't want hers to sit for weeks without being read. She wanted his input now.

She found his number, picked up her phone, and tapped the keys.

He answered right away. "Dean Carter speaking."

"Dean Carter? My name is Hope Burns," she said. "I own The Lilac Pointe, it's a dance store in Lake Summers. And some of your dance students have been coming by to get fitted for pointe shoes—"

"Hold a moment, would you?" he said. She could hear voices in the background. "Okay, I'm sorry," he said when he returned. "Who did you say you are?"

"I'm Hope Burns, and I own the new dance store in Lake Summers. I'm calling about your students, and what they need for class—"

"I'm sorry, we don't give out our students' email addresses," he said.

"What? But I—"

"Our policy is not to give contact information to telemarketers. You can place an ad in one of our student publications, or post a brochure in the student union."

"It's… no, it's—"

"I've got to get to a meeting. Sorry not to be more help. Good luck with your store, and thanks for your interest in our school."

She heard the click on his end, almost before she had registered what he'd said. Then she slapped her phone on the counter.

Was this the way a college dean was supposed to behave— especially one who aimed to promote respect and responsibility among his students?

She pressed her lips together and breathed in deeply, thinking how she'd been around men like this before—men who made her feel bad about herself, as though she didn't deserve a voice.

But things were different now. She had spent years pulling her life together and trusting her own judgment, and she finally had a lovely family and a beautiful store to show for it. And this phone call, she told herself, was not going to set her back. No; Dean Carter's self-absorbed behavior was only going to make her more determined than ever to succeed with the store—for Anna, for herself, for Lake Summers, and now also for the Jayson students, who were young and green and needed her, even if they weren't yet fully aware of just how much.

CHAPTER EIGHT

"I own the dance store up the hill." The words left a strange taste in Anna's mouth as she answered Aidan. It used to be so easy to walk into an office building and introduce herself. *I'm Anna Harris. That's right, Greg Harris's wife.*

"You own The Lilac Pointe?" he said. "Nice little shop. I stopped by a few weeks ago, right after you opened. I met… is she your co-owner?"

"Yes, my aunt. Hope Burns."

"That's right, Hope. I wanted to talk a little about strategy, but she said she was busy so I told her I'd come back another time." Aidan's mention of Hope rang a bell, and she realized that this was the consultant Hope had told her about.

As they stood by the front desk, Aidan explained to Anna that SummerFest was an event the town was hosting to help downtown merchants end the summer on a high note and get a jump-start on the fall. He spoke with a kind of authority that convinced her he was smart, but there was also a casualness in his tone that charmed her. She couldn't imagine why Hope had gotten such a bad impression of him. She felt he was someone whose advice they could use.

"It's meant to be like a block party," he said. "There's a nominal cost for merchants, to cover cleanup, security, and so on. But once you sign up, you can be as creative as you want. You can do merchandise sales, or giveaways, raffles—you can even set up a small stage and run a few sample dance classes…"

He stopped. "I'm sorry. You seem a little distracted. Am I going too fast?"

"What? No," she said. She'd only partially been listening. The words *block party* had reminded her of the one she'd organized two Novembers ago for the Silver Plains Library renovation. For refreshments, she'd brought in some farmers from Long Island, who served up cider and baked potatoes loaded with butter and cheese. She remembered watching Zac and Evie munching away, bundled up in hats, scarves and gloves. She hadn't been able to tell if their cheeks were bright red from the cold air or the piping-hot potatoes.

"It's not your fault," she added. "You're being very nice. It's just that owning a store is very new to me."

"Well, openings are always tough," he said. "You've got a short window of time to get the momentum going. Your aunt sounded like she had it all in hand. But if you ever want some ideas for building store traffic, I've got some strategies I'm happy to share."

She took in his words, remembering the consultants she'd interviewed to help her prepare for personal appearances during Greg's campaign. She'd always kept Greg's warning in mind: that the flamboyant ones often had the least talent—they used their personalities to mask how little they knew. Aidan wasn't flamboyant; he was serious, and he sounded capable. No matter what conclusions Hope had jumped to, Anna thought he could have something to offer.

"I know things didn't get off on the right foot with my aunt," she said. "But we could use some advice. Do you possibly have time? Or I can come back another day."

"I've got a few minutes right now," he said. "Want to sit down?"

He led her to a nook near the window of the lobby, and they sat on opposite sofas, facing each other. Aidan was a big man, strong and solid. His short, dark hair was parted on the side, and his eyes were dark, too—intense when he was talking, warm when he was smiling. His full face made him look gentle and approachable, and Anna found her eyes resting for a while on the layer of stubble around his jaw.

"So, tell me what's going on," he said.

"I've only been here a few days, so most of this information comes from Hope," she said. "Apparently we're not getting a lot of customers—and Hope says the ones that do come in are buying little things. Or not buying anything at all."

She went on to explain about the Jayson girls, and how much time Hope had spent fitting them. "The thing is, I'm only staying through the summer," she added. "So I want the store to be successful—or, at least, on the road to success before I leave."

He stroked his jaw. "Well, competing with online retailers is a part of the business these days," he said. "Everyone wants to pay less. But people shop for many reasons besides price. Otherwise there wouldn't be any bricks-and-mortar stores left at all.

"Let's step back," he said. "Why did you and Hope choose to open a store in the first place?"

She looked down at her hands. "I didn't choose to, actually. My husband bought it for me. I never even saw the store until last week."

"So you don't want to be there?"

"No, I do," she said. "It's a long story. But it's not that I don't like the store. I love the store. I loved it the moment I stepped inside."

"Yeah? Why?" he asked.

"Because it's a dance store. It's about making beauty from movement and space. There's nothing else in the world like that. And the shoes and the clothes and the accessories and the mirrors—they all add to the beauty you're creating."

"So I take it you're a dancer?"

"No... well, I once was," she said, remembering how it had ended so suddenly, with the news that her father was back in the hospital. She'd known that she couldn't concentrate when the final rehearsal began. But she hadn't expected to fall that badly.

Aidan leaned forward, his hands clasped. "Look, there's a lot of quick solutions I can suggest to get things moving," he said. "If fittings are an important service that your aunt provides, then charge a fee. Customers can apply the fee to their purchase, but if they don't buy from you, they're going to have to pay for the fitting. And I'm a big believer in grand opening promotions. Offer something for free, maybe a trial dance class, maybe some accessory if they spend a certain amount. Print up fliers—you can leave a stack here. And I would get a website up. It doesn't have to be fancy. My son has built a few for some local merchants—he can build yours, if you want."

His tone softened. "But what you said about dance—that's a vision for the long term. Creating beauty through movement, and feeling that excitement—who wouldn't want to spend every day in a place like that? The stores that succeed are the ones that help people love their lives a little more. Just focus on that, and you'll do fine."

She looked at him and smiled, moved by his enthusiasm and his confidence in her. He looked back at her, and their eyes met for a moment, until she turned away. He clapped his thighs and stood, and she wondered if he had felt the same way she had—unsettled by how nice it was to lock eyes with one another. Or maybe he'd sensed her discomfort and wanted to ease her tension.

"Enough lecturing for one day," he said. "I'll get you that SummerFest application, and you can be on your way."

She followed him back toward the desk, and he pulled a sheet from a nearby rack. "So, you said it was your husband's idea to buy the business?" he said. "Is he involved too, or is it just you and Hope?"

She couldn't avoid saying something, as she'd done with the woman at the lake. He'd asked directly, and she didn't want to lie.

"My husband passed away last fall," she said, then held her breath, waiting for the information to sink in. She hated this moment, when someone first learned the news. People were so thrown by it. They couldn't appreciate that time had passed, and the healing was underway; they reacted as though the accident had happened just a day ago. It felt right now the way it always did—as though she were playing a cruel joke: Aidan had tossed her a softball, and she'd whacked it right into his solar plexus. Next she'd have to watch him double over in pain, knowing she had caused it and trying to offer what little comfort she could—*Thank you. It's okay, we're getting through*—until he finally pulled himself upright again.

"I'm sorry," he said. "Although it doesn't help when people say that, does it? I know. My wife died almost two years ago."

His words stunned her. She guessed he was a little older than she was, maybe in his late forties. She didn't know anyone so close to her age who had also lost a spouse.

"I'm so sorry, too," she said, her surprise and sympathy for him taking precedence for the moment over her own situation. "You… you have a son, you said?"

He nodded. "He's fifteen."

"How's he doing?"

"It's very hard. He misses her so much. You? Kids?"

"I have two. Zac is thirteen, Evie is ten."

"And how are they?"

She shook her head. "I don't think I know for sure. Sometimes they seem to be adjusting, and sometimes it's like they're suffering as much as ever."

He put his hands in his pants pockets. "It's brutal to watch them, right? You want to fix everything, even though you know you can't. But I don't know what I'd do if it wasn't for Liam. He's the one thing that keeps me going."

"I know. They're everything. And the funny thing is, they each remind me of Greg, in their own way. Evie tries to make everything right, and Zac wrestles with himself inside. Always thinking he can do better."

She sighed. She wasn't usually comfortable discussing her kids and their loss, especially with someone new; but there was an energy, a welcome pull, in finally listening to and talking with a person who knew what she did.

"Sometimes it feels like my life is a long track that goes on forever," she added. "And before, it was both of us running. And now it's as though Greg stopped, and I have to keep going. And when I turn around, I can barely see him anymore, and when I need to ask him something, there's silence. All I have are questions with no answers. It's like he's just waiting for me to finally wave goodbye."

Aidan stroked the side of his jaw. "It gets a little easier after the first year," he said. "And maybe he's kind of protected, being back there. That's how I think of Emilia. There's something innocent about her now. I try to remind myself of that sometimes."

He handed her the sheet, and they walked to the door, weaving around people who were moving in and out of the building, too involved in their own business to pay them any mind. "I'd better get upstairs," he said, looking at the large clock above the reception desk. "I've got a meeting with the mayor and a reporter from the *Lake Summers Press*. But stop in again sometime. I'm usually somewhere in the building.

"And Anna?" he added as he opened the screen door. "I hope you enjoy your store. I owned a jewelry store with my dad before Liam and I moved here. I know it's not what you had planned, but you could build so many memories there."

She smiled, and as she walked back toward Main Street, she couldn't help but picture a small, welcoming jewelry store. Long windows and wood floors and pendant light fixtures suspended from the ceiling. Rustic display cases and cabinets, maybe made of distressed wood. A few antiques, such as old clocks and hand mirrors, displayed on the countertops. She thought of Aidan and his dad helping customers choose one-of-a-kind engagement rings or a vintage watch or set of cufflinks. She imagined the proposals and weddings and graduations and anniversary celebrations at which those beautiful presents would light up someone's heart.

Opening the door to Pearl's for her coffee, she thought about what Aidan had said, how she might see the dance store as inspiration for creating new memories. She had never connected her return to Lake Summers with new memories; she had only seen the town as a reminder of all she had lost.

But now she wondered if there could be great new memories to make. And she wondered if Aidan was looking to make new memories, too.

CHAPTER NINE

"So the July Fourth fireworks are going to be super, and right after that, we start the new family movie nights and our new jazz series on the green," the mayor said. "And then we finish up in August with SummerFest."

He took off his wire-rimmed glasses and rubbed the side of his balding head, where bristly gray hair sprouted. "What do you think, Aidan? Did I cover everything?"

Aidan looked away from the mayor and toward the earnest young reporter across the table, who slid her phone closer to him to record his response. "I think you did, Bill, as far as special events go," he said. "But did you want to tell Lacey about the street beautification project we're launching?"

"Yes, that's right," the mayor said, and as Lacey slid her phone back, he went on to talk about the additional workers the city had added for trash removal and street cleaning, and the new planters and streetlamps being installed on the central portion of Main Street. Aidan listened, his hands in prayer position, his fingertips lightly tapping together.

"So you're expecting a good summer?" Lacey asked. "No more store closings?"

"A superb summer," the mayor said. "Aidan can give you a few specifics."

Aidan pursed his lips. This was exactly what he'd been hoping to avoid. He didn't want to be quoted. "Well, Lonny's Hot Dogs bought the small shoe store next door and turned it into an outdoor deck that I think will become a great nighttime gathering spot. And that upscale dance store has just opened. Turnover is normal, and a strong downtown is built to survive the ebbs and flows, but we're looking very strong. Although there's no need to quote me. Bill's given you a lot of information about what we're doing downtown, and as for the retailers—I'm sure they'd rather speak for themselves."

"Okay, I'll get a few quotes from them, and then I'll wrap this all up," she said. "Front page of next week's issue. But I'll need a picture. How about the two of you outside the building?"

"No, just the mayor," Aidan said. "He's the guy who matters. You don't need me in there."

"Sure, we do," Bill said. "You're the one responsible for all the changes. SummerFest is your idea."

Aidan pulled at the front of his shirt. "No, I'm not even dressed right, I think this calls for a tie. And anyway, it's after five and I want to pick up a couple of those special sandwiches from the Grill before Liam finishes work. No problem, take the picture. I'll be in it next time."

Bill got up and pulled his pants higher around his large belly. "I don't get it, I thought consultants loved publicity. Fine, then, if that's what you want. Come on, Lacey, let's get you what you need."

Aidan walked the two of them outside and then started up Main Street, glad that he had dodged the coverage, especially the photo, without too much of a ruckus. He didn't know how he'd get out of being quoted or having his photo taken the next time—he didn't know how many times he could blame his clothing or insist that others be quoted instead. But hopefully he wouldn't have to deal with Lacey or any other reporter for a long while, now that the summer article was finished. He remembered how he and his dad used to love when local reporters came by, how they would spend hours cleaning the countertops and fixtures, how his dad would wear a crisp white shirt and his signature blue tie with little diamond rings in place of polka dots. They'd always make sure to have cookies or a cake at the ready. They'd always bring the reporter to the round table at the back of the store and offer fresh coffee or a cold drink. His dad had kept a scrapbook with all their press clippings.

He walked a few blocks to the Grill and climbed up the metal stairway to the covered deck. He took a seat at the bar and waved off the menu that Maxine offered.

"Same as always," he said with an embarrassed half-chuckle. "Two Chicken Cutlet Heroes to go."

"Your boy likes the smothered onions and cheese, right?" she asked.

"That's right. Put a little extra on, if you can."

"Marinara on yours, hot sauce on his?" He nodded. "Got it. I'll put that right in." She threaded her pencil into her hair and headed toward the kitchen.

The bartender wandered over. "Hey, Aidan. Scotch on the rocks?"

He nodded and folded his hands on the bar. He hadn't seen Liam since dinner last night, when he'd stormed out. He'd heard him come in around midnight, while he was still in the small bedroom, working with the wire.

"I'm back here, bud," he'd called. But Liam hadn't answered. Aidan had listened to him go into the bathroom and then into his bedroom, shutting the door hard behind him. He'd figured he'd give his son the night to cool off. He'd stayed up a few more hours, working on his swim sculpture, trying to figure out how to suspend three swimmers over the platform so it looked like they were mid-dive. He didn't want to have to anchor them to the rest of the sculpture; he wanted them free. It would be no problem to make the fourth swimmer. The one standing on the edge, without a baton. Just standing.

In the morning, Liam had gotten up and out without even saying goodbye. Aidan had stayed upstairs, waiting to see if his son would want to make contact. He didn't, so Aidan had decided to give him the day, and then sit down with him over sandwiches from the Grill in the evening to clear the air. On his way into work, he'd glanced into the window of Pearl's, to make sure Liam was okay. His son was there behind the counter, wearing his green Pearl's apron, pouring coffee and bagging muffins.

Aidan downed a mouthful of Scotch and then twirled the glass on its paper coaster. The sun was at an angle now, aiming its light beneath the overhang and onto the bar, and when he looked in its direction, he saw it sitting in the sky across the street, right above The Lilac Pointe. The sight of the storefront made him think of Anna. She was pretty, in a natural way. Brown hair that didn't look overly fixed or styled, but just swept behind her ears and down the back of her neck. The outer corners of her eyes dipped down and he wasn't sure if that was because she was sad, or just their normal shape. Her features were small and kind of jewel-like, but there was something rugged about her face, too—the straight line of her jaw, the prominent cheekbones. He could tell she was suffering, but he had a feeling she was tough enough to get through this bad time.

He thought about what she'd said, how her husband seemed so far behind her on that track she imagined. It was true, what he'd said to her—that if he had to lose Emilia, at least she was protected from the bad things. It would have devastated her—the loss of the jewelry store, the sudden move across the country, the secrets. Still, it was hard to imagine exactly what she'd have thought, what she'd have said. Anna was right; when people died, they just stopped. When he paused for a moment, he could remember the tone of Emilia's voice, the gentle curve of her shoulders, the swing of her maple-syrup ponytail when she went out for a run. But what he could never know was who she'd be now. How she would have changed, who she would have become, what they would have become together. The answers she would have had, the things she would have said that could make everything better. Living without her was like reading a book with a character missing, finishing a puzzle without all the pieces.

"Here you go," Maxine said, placing a plastic bag on the bar in front of him. "I wrapped the sandwiches good and tight so they'll be warm when you get home. And I threw in some of those brownies you both like. Say hello to your boy."

"I will. Thanks, Maxine," Aidan said, reaching for his wallet. He looked over the check and handed her the money, adding a few extra dollars above the normal tip. He didn't go overboard—he didn't want to embarrass her—but she'd mentioned last week that her car needed a new transmission. He drained his drink, paid the bar tab, and walked to the exit.

At the bottom of the restaurant's stairway, he looked across the street at the dance store. Through the window, he saw Hope standing behind the counter, her chin in her hand. He assumed the store was still open—most stores on Main Street didn't close during the week until seven—but there were no customers inside. He hadn't meant to put her off when he'd stopped in a few weeks ago, but he was concerned about how much she'd spent on the renovation—the fixtures, the lighting, and that fancy studio floor. He didn't understand why she was aiming to appeal only to serious ballet dancers. Why limit the store like that? Why not broaden the concept, and target the full range of customers in the community? He hoped she and Anna could make a go of things. He needed the store to succeed. Every retail space on Main Street was occupied now, but things could change on a dime. When one store closed, often that led to uncertainty and more closings, and that would reflect badly on him. He couldn't lose this job. He couldn't make Liam move again.

He started down Main Street toward Pearl's. What had Anna said—now all she had were questions with no answers? He felt the same way. Except his questions weren't only for Emilia. They were for his dad, too. People didn't have to die to be unreachable. Sometimes people could be right in front of you, sitting in a tall-backed, vinyl-upholstered chair in the sun-filled room of a nursing home. They could be looking straight at you and listening to you and talking to you. And still leave you searching.

The last time he'd seen his dad was in that day room. His father's body had looked floppy, almost flattened, like a pancake pressed into a seated position. This was the man who had taught him how to surf and jet-ski in the southern California breakers, who had installed windows and shelving in the jewelry store single-handedly. Now he seemed to have no muscles at all. His head was misshapen, the skin hanging off his cheekbones and jaw, his complexion marred by brown and black spots.

He'd taken his father's ropy hands in his. "Dad," he'd said softly, not wanting to draw the attention of the two men playing checkers in the corner or the woman in the wheelchair by the window. "Is there anyone else I need to contact?"

"Hey, pardner," his dad answered. "Two tickets, for my son and me, if you please."

Aidan felt his eyes sting. "No, Dad," he'd said. "I'm not selling tickets. I'm your son, Aidan. And there's a problem with the jewelry you took in for repairs."

"And we can get in early for batting practice?" his dad asked. "Oh, that would be fine."

"Dad, concentrate. Did you keep track? Is there a record?"

His father's watery eyes were unfocused. He blinked twice.

"Dad, we're in trouble. Me and Liam, your grandson. I need to make sure I've repaid everyone. How many were there? *Dad?*"

He could feel the presence of other people entering the room behind him. He didn't want to upset any of the other residents, and he definitely didn't want to attract the attention of the staff. He raised himself up and rubbed his jaw. How was this possible?

His dad was a man who never charged a dime more than he felt he was fairly entitled to, who wouldn't hire a bookkeeper because he knew he'd sleep better keeping track of the business himself. Had he done it because of the dementia? Was it fear about the opening of the new mall by the highway? Was it the stress of Emilia's illness? Had he thought he could get away with it? Or had he intended to somehow right everything before Aidan or anyone else found out?

Aidan had felt the urge to scream at him. But the truth was, he didn't blame him. He couldn't blame his dad. He'd seen the changes unfolding in his father's behavior during the months when Emilia was dying—the paranoid ranting on the phone, the unfounded accusations of stealing that he'd hurl, without warning, toward the UPS guy or the sanitation truck driver. But he ignored it. Emilia was so sick, and Liam was so scared, and there just hadn't been enough of him to go around. He abandoned his father at the very moment his father was losing a hold on reality. He had let this all happen. He was responsible.

"Two tickets, sir. Sure thing," he said to his father.

Then he looked down at his father's mottled scalp, with just a few strands of oily silver hair lying flat across it, and kissed the top of his head. "Bye, Dad," he said.

"Don't forget about the batting practice," his dad called after him. "That would be fine. Oh, I would enjoy that very much."

Aidan reached the corner across from Pearl's and leaned against one of the town's new lampposts. A few minutes later the screen door opened, and Liam emerged. He stopped when he saw Aidan waiting. Then he jogged across the street.

"What are you doing here?" he said, his tone an unlikely mixture of derision and appreciation.

"I picked up a couple of specials at the Grill for dinner," Aidan said.

"You didn't have to do that."

"We have to eat."

"I mean, you didn't have to go all the way up to the Grill."

"I knew you had a long day, and I thought you deserved a reward." He studied his son's downturned head. "And hey, I think I might have gotten you another website job. The dance store up the hill. You're going to have to start paying me a commission, bud. Although I don't want you to charge them. They're new and can use a break. I'll pay you for the work myself."

He waited for an answer. "What do you think? You interested?"

Liam kicked a pebble in front him, shaking his head. "It's a fucked-up way we live, Dad," he said. "I mean, it's a really fucked-up way."

Aidan nodded, trying not to think of Emilia, and how she'd never tolerate Liam speaking like that. "I know. I know."

"How am I supposed to handle this? I feel like my head is exploding. I'm out with the guys last night, I'm trying to hang out, and all I'm thinking about is what a stupid-ass liar I have to be."

"I know. But we've been here a while now. And pretty soon it's not going to feel like you're lying. You're just going to be living your life."

"But this whole California thing with the coach—"

"He only talked about California to introduce himself. From now on he's just going to talk to you about swimming. You're not a liar when it comes to swimming."

Liam scrunched up his nose and sniffed loudly, clearly trying hard to stop himself from crying. He pressed his lips together—the swelled upper lip and thin lower one he'd inherited from Emilia. Aidan felt his chest squeeze. His son was fifteen, but in some ways, he was such a little boy. Standing on a downtown sidewalk, desperately pretending that he was a tough guy, that he wasn't on the verge of all-consuming sobs.

"I know it doesn't seem like it at your age, but three years is a short time," he said. "And we'll get through it. I swear we will."

Liam pressed the heels of his hands into his eyes, then scrunched up his nose again and wiped it with the back of his hand.

"So… there's smothered onions and cheese," Aidan said. "And Maxine threw in a couple brownies for free. Hungry? Or did you fill up on Mrs. Pearl's chocolate muffins?"

Liam sniffed again and let out a small chuckle. "I'm *starving*."

"Great. Come on, bud. Let's go home."

He put his arm around his son's shoulder, and they walked together. The sunset was at their backs, and the growing darkness was just ahead.

CHAPTER TEN

That evening, Anna took the chicken from the oven while Evie brought plates to the table. "So Nicole says they're getting an air castle on Friday," Evie said, continuing the story of her day. "And Nicole says she'll help me find more of the tiny golden beads that I need to finish the bracelet I started."

"Nicole—she's Zac's counterpart for your group?" Anna said, carving the chicken. Evie nodded. "Sounds like you really like her."

"She's the best. Everyone thinks that." Evie went back to the cabinet for glasses. "And she said that tomorrow she'll braid my and Ariana's hair with the little braids going from the side to the back. But Ariana's is longer, so it might look better. But Nicole said mine will look good, too. Do you think mine will look good, too, Mom?"

"Yes, of course." Anna brought out the salad. In the living room, Zac was at the writing desk, streaming a baseball game on the desktop computer. "Zac, can you help?" she said.

He dragged himself into the kitchen and got the silverware.

Anna went back to the kitchen for the potatoes. She had decided on her walk to meet the kids after camp that she wasn't going to tell them the whole truth about the store. She thought it would confuse them and frighten them, just as it had done for her at first, and she didn't want to put them through that right now. Zac was old enough to understand what a huge amount of money was involved, and she was scared he'd worry about how they'd manage. Despite all the assurances she'd provide, she knew he would still be anxious, and she didn't want to give him yet another concern that would make it hard for him to sleep. And as for Evie, she craved certainty, and would no doubt have a lot of questions about why Greg had given Hope the money. Anna didn't want to make things up, and she didn't want to keep saying "I don't know."

Still, she wanted them to understand that the store was going to play a big role in their lives this summer, and to see that as a good thing. She wanted to do for them what Aidan had suggested she try to do for all the townspeople—to make them feel The Lilac Pointe was a place that could help them find themselves. Or… how had he put it? A place that could help them love their lives a little more. She still thought it a beautiful sentiment.

"So I went to visit Aunt Hope at her store today," she said. "And she needs our help. And we were talking about how it might be fun for us all to get involved making the store a very special place in town. I'm going to be there a lot, and it would be fun if you could be, too. There are a lot of things that go on in a store that you might enjoy doing after camp or on the weekends."

"Like what?" Zac asked, sounding as though he didn't believe there'd be anything fun to do there.

"Let's see… there's setting up displays and finding different sizes and colors of shoes and clothes for people… and there's going to be a website, and there's inventory spreadsheets. So there'll be lots of computer work… and you can even help choose what things to order. Aunt Hope wants families and kids to shop there, so she'll need you to help find clothes or other things that kids might want."

She looked back and forth between the two of them. "Can we give it a try? Make this a family project?"

Evie swung her feet beneath the table. "Is that what you want, Mom?" she asked.

Anna nodded.

"Okay," Evie said. "I'll help."

"Zac?" Anna asked. "Please?"

He shrugged. "Whatever. I go on the computer after camp anyway."

She let out a contented breath and raised her water glass. "Okay, then!" she said. "Here's to making The Lilac Pointe the best store Lake Summers has ever seen!"

Then she sat still for a moment and watched her kids eating—Evie holding her fork like a stake and sawing away at the meat on her drumstick, Zac pulling big mouthfuls of chicken breast off his fork, and causing a stripe of tomato sauce to form across his chin. They were hungry, her children—hungry after a busy day. There was something so right about her children doing the regular things of life. Just being hungry, tired kids. She thought about what Hope had said just before she left the store—that Greg would be proud of her. It was the perfect thing to say. It made her feel good for the way she handled the news today, how she had strategized a plan, presented it to Hope and her kids, and gotten everyone's buy-in. It felt like the first time she had done something productive in a long time, something that was more about the future than the past.

That night in bed, she began a list of ideas for the store—ways to do what Aidan had said, make people love their lives more. She wondered if they could offer a range of classes to appeal to different people. Hope was set to teach ballet, but what about ballroom? Yoga? Hip-hop? Salsa? They would have to find teachers, if Hope didn't feel she could teach those styles. And maybe they could host mixers, where singles could meet and dance. They could even have recitals. She imagined the studio filled with students—adults and kids—trying on costumes and practicing their steps.

The bell on her computer sounded. She clicked out of the document to look at the new email:

Hi Anna,

I talked to Dan from the Inquirer, and he wants to come see you on Aug. 12th to do the interview. Is that okay? BTW he said he talked to some officials in town who said Greg was kind of anxious last year. I said it was probably because he was working hard on Willow Center, but be prepared in case he asks you about it. Let me know when you have some ideas for the memorial.

Best,

Crystal

Anna closed the computer and put it down on her night table. It was surprising, what Crystal had written. She hadn't known that people were concerned about Greg. She thought about him now, all those evenings when he said goodnight to her, saying he wanted to go back downstairs and do a little more work. She would tell him not to stay up too late, and then she'd lie in bed, waiting for him to come back up, until she couldn't stay awake any longer. She would wake halfway when he climbed into bed, not even sure how late it was. Sometimes she'd hear him go back downstairs again. A bright beam would rhythmically illuminate the hallway—on, off, on, off—as he tested that old yellow flashlight in the downstairs closet.

Just then she heard footsteps in the hallway heading toward the bathroom, and she knew they were Zac's. She figured he was having a hard time falling asleep. She heard the bathroom door close, and she held her breath, waiting to hear him emerge again. But the minutes passed with no sound. She stayed still and strained to hear some kind of noise, even just the toilet flushing or the faucet running, but the prolonged silence was unnerving. So she climbed out of bed, switched on the hall light, and tiptoed down the hallway.

"Honey?" she said, knocking gently on the bathroom door. "Are you okay?"

"I'm fine," he told her from behind the door. "Go back to sleep."

"Are you sure?"

"I'm fine. Just go away."

She hesitated. "Okay, honey," she said. "If you need me, let me know—"

Suddenly the door opened. "The only thing I need is for you to tell Evie to learn to turn off the faucet!" he said. "Is she so stupid that she doesn't know how to turn the water off? Doesn't she know that people can slip?"

He walked past her toward his room, and she watched him, stunned. Was this what he'd been spending the last fifteen minutes doing—fuming about the faucet? She remembered the other night when he'd left so many towels on the floor by the sink. Was he really so worried about the water? But no, she thought—nobody could be this worked up about a drippy faucet. She followed him down the hall. "What's wrong?" she said. "Are you having trouble sleeping?"

"I'm having trouble with Evie being such a moron!"

"Honey, it's not her fault. The faucets are old, and they drip. Daddy always used to take care of it, so you never noticed it. I'll get a plumber this week, okay? Or do you want to go home? We don't have to stay here. It's fine if we go."

"This isn't about that. I like it here. I like my job. Okay? It was fine!"

"Then why are you so upset?"

"Because the faucet is dripping!" he said. "Mom, are you even listening? It makes noise, and it wastes water, and if it just keeps dripping it can overflow over the sink and someone can slip and get really badly hurt!"

He went into his room and slammed the door, and Anna stood outside in the hallway, her hand on his doorknob. She longed to hold him and hug him until he calmed down, but she knew that going in after him would infuriate him further. She pressed her hand on the door. "Okay. I'll tell Evie to be more careful," she called out softly. "And I'll call a plumber this week. Goodnight."

She heard the springs of his mattress compress and waited until the sound dissolved and she was reasonably sure he was settled in bed. Then she turned around and silently pressed the back of her head against the door. *Someone can slip and get really badly hurt.* His words reminded her of another time he'd sounded so fearful, out of the blue. It was two years ago when they went to Disney World for spring break. One evening when they were waiting to catch the shuttle back to the hotel, they came up to a small crowd gathered around a teenage boy sitting on the pavement, next to a bicycle with a wheel broken off. The boy's jeans were torn and his leg was cut up badly. The inside of his knee looked like raw hamburger meat.

Greg had taken charge of the situation, helping the boy to a bench and then jumping onto the bench to wave a police officer down. A little while later as the ambulance arrived, Zac had tugged her arm.

"Mom, I think I touched the blood," he told her, looking on the verge of tears. "I think it's gonna make me sick."

Anna had assured him that he hadn't touched any blood, that he hadn't been close to the boy's knee at all, and gradually Zac had calmed down. But his concern seemed so strange and intense that she brought it up with Greg the next morning.

Greg hadn't been worried at all, and Anna wondered if he'd feel the same way now: *Wet floors freak me out, too. He's right to want it dry.* But somehow Anna couldn't accept that. She knew that what was going on in Zac's head was much bigger than a damp bathroom floor.

She turned so her cheek was against the door, and the soft, rhythmic sound of Zac's breathing told her he was falling asleep. So she tiptoed down the hall and peeked into Evie's room.

Fortunately Evie was a deep sleeper and the noise in the hallway hadn't woken her up. Anna switched off the hallway light and went back to her bedroom.

In bed, she closed her eyes, and an image of the long track she'd described to Aidan started to form in her head. She could just barely see Greg, standing way back behind her. She imagined he was waving, trying to get her attention. She wished she knew what he might have been trying to tell her.

CHAPTER ELEVEN

When Hope showed up for breakfast the next day, Evie was prepared with pictures of hair accessories, necklaces, and wall hangings she had printed out from dance websites. Anna dished out the scrambled eggs, tickled at the way Evie had moved her chair closer to Hope's and was explaining why she thought girls her age would love the things she'd found. Hope's delight in Evie's ideas gave Anna confidence that she would appreciate the ideas she planned to discuss with Hope later at the shop. The only aspect of the breakfast that bothered Anna was the way Zac behaved—keeping his eyes fixed on his breakfast and then rushing off as soon as he'd finished eating. She told herself that she should have expected that—Zac was a teenage boy, and it was natural that he'd balk at the idea of spending extra time with his great-aunt and mom this summer. Plus, he had been so upset last night about the faucet, and she figured he'd probably had trouble sleeping. Maybe he would feel better once she got the plumbing straightened away.

After breakfast, Hope headed to the store, and Anna brought Evie to the lake. Evie checked inside her backpack, presumably for those sunglasses, but then went willingly down the hill. Anna waved and took off for the store, her laptop with the list of ideas she'd come up with tucked away inside her tote bag. She suspected that Hope would resist some of her ideas, such as holding singles mixers in the studio. She knew that when it came to anything involving dance, Hope was a purist, and no doubt thought that beautiful studio of hers should be used only for formal dance training. Anna had never seen herself as a ringleader, someone with the skill to bring other people around to her way of thinking. And this was her aunt—someone who was supposed to know more than she did, who was supposed to give directions. But she had to step up. She needed the store to be on a solid footing by the end of August, and it wasn't going to turn out that way if business stayed on its current course.

When she got to the store, she found her aunt once again kneeling amid a sea of strewn pointe shoes. Two girls with long ponytails and Jayson-logo leggings were sitting on the ottomans, comparing toe boxes and soles.

"So, Hope, do you think Gaynors would be too soft?" one of the girls said. "Melanie said you could look at my feet and tell me if you think they'd be too soft."

The girl stood up and pressed high on her bare toes, and Anna watched her aunt circle around her, studying her feet from every angle. "You've got a pretty strong relevé, you could handle a hard shoe," she said. "But the Gaynors are in a class by themselves—it's not that they're soft, it's that they feel broken in when you first put them on. Some dancers like that, some don't. So why don't you give them a try, and if you don't like the feel, I have a couple of other ideas for a high arch like yours. They're still in the basement, let me go get them."

She went across the room and started down for the basement. Anna followed her, shutting the door behind them and grabbing her elbow.

"Wait," she said. "I don't mean to get in your way, but before you spend any more time with these girls, we have to establish a rule. Either they buy the shoes from us, or they pay for the fitting. We'll tell them as soon as we go back up."

"What?" Hope said. "No, no, we're not going to do that. I know these girls. If we say that, they'll just leave."

"They weren't buying anything anyway."

"Maybe they would."

"They never do. You told me that yourself."

"But they're students. They don't have money. You remember what that was like."

"They're college kids studying dance, and shoes are like textbooks—they need them for their classes," Anna said. "I'm not saying to rip them off. Price the shoes as low as you can, and we can give a free sample dance class or a pair of tights as a reward. But stop giving your expertise away."

Hope thought for a moment and then shook her head. "I don't think so. It feels too manipulative. Look, I think it's great that you want to try something new, but we're not retail experts, at least not yet, and I'm scared it could backfire…"

"But it is an expert's idea," Anna said. "I went to Village Hall yesterday. I spoke to that consultant—"

"You talked to that guy about our store? I told you, I don't have a good feeling about him."

"He's nicer than you think."

"I doubt it. If he's so nice, then why is he always alone at the Grill? He's got the wedding band, so where's the wife? Anna, I'm your aunt, and I'm telling you to stay away from him. I've been around guys like that. They act like their marriage is ending, but then they parade the wife out when they want to get rid of someone—"

"His wife isn't around because she died," Anna said. "And if he's alone, it's because he misses her. And he probably wears his wedding ring because he isn't looking to date and doesn't want to give people the impression that he's available." She lifted her left hand. "See? I wear mine, too."

Hope sighed and rubbed the inside corner of her eye. "Okay, so I'm a jerk. I guess I've been around so many bad men in my life, I don't even recognize a good one anymore."

"It doesn't matter. But we need to settle this."

Hope glanced to the side, as though searching for an escape. "Look, I care about these girls," she said. "I feel motherly toward them. They're just starting out, and they need me."

"I understand that you care about them," Anna says. "But if the store fails, you won't be here for them at all, and then they'll really be lost. So how about we try the fitting fee? And if it's a disaster, we'll get rid of it, and we'll find a way to track down the girls and refund any money we took. Is that okay?"

Hope pressed her lips together, then shrugged and continued downstairs.

Anna went back up, smoothing the ends of her hair along her neck. She hadn't thought before about which one of them would tell the girls about the fee—but it was her idea, so it was her responsibility to do it. She walked to the ottomans and began gathering up the rejected shoes. "Hi, I'm Anna, I'm one of the owners of the store," she said. "And you are…?"

"I'm Diana, and this Joelle," the first girl said. She looked a little reluctant to introduce herself, and Anna suspected it was because she felt ashamed that she had no intention of making a purchase. Anna smiled to herself. These weren't bad girls, she could tell, but they needed to set some boundaries.

"You both go to Jayson, right?" Anna said. "I was a dance student, too, a long time ago. I used to be so scared shopping for pointe shoes. If they don't fit perfectly, you can really get hurt. You both are so lucky to have Hope here to fit you."

Diana nodded. "That's why we're here. Our other friend, Melanie, told us about her."

"It's because she used to be a soloist," Anna said. "Did you know that? She danced with the Hamburg Ballet Theatre. She danced all over Europe."

The girls looked impressed. "Whoa," Joelle said. "Melanie never told us that."

"She probably doesn't know. Hope's very modest," Anna said. "But she really cares about dancers. I know that for a fact, because she's my aunt. And she's the nicest person in the world."

The girls exchanged guilty glances.

"Hope will be right up, she's just finding some styles she thinks you'll like. She works so hard. Which is why she was upset the other day. Do you know that there were dancers here who asked Hope to fit them and then bought the shoes online? It's so sad, because we know how much dancers like you need a great store like this, but we won't be able to stay in business if people take advantage of Hope. Can you see what a problem that would be?"

The girls looked down at their laps and slowly nodded.

"So I feel kind of bad telling you this, but we've had to establish a fitting fee," Anna said. "To guard against people like that. The idea is that it costs a hundred dollars for Hope to fit you for shoes. But the good news is, you can apply the fee to the cost of the shoe. So for customers like you, it doesn't matter at all, since you're planning to buy shoes here anyway, right?"

Anna watched the girls look around, as though trying to come up with a strategy for this unexpected turn of events. Out of the corner of her eye, she saw Hope come back up.

"Well… but I'm not sure I'm buying shoes today," the first girl said. "I just wanted to try them. And, like, go home and think about it."

"That's fine," Anna said. "You can pay the fitting fee now, and we'll give you a credit towards shoes when you come back." She paused and smiled at the girls. "I know this is a lot to process. So why don't you take a little walk down the hall and think about it? You can look at our beautiful studio while you're there. Hope's summer session starts next week."

She watched the girls head down the hall, feeling as if she were playing chess, waiting for a response to her opening move. She knew she had the upper hand, and her parenting instincts told her she was getting through to the two dancers. But looking at Hope, who was standing by the armoire, she started to second-guess herself. Maybe the girls weren't as moved by the conversation as she thought they were. Maybe they weren't going to budge. She would feel terrible if she'd chased away the dancers Hope cared so deeply about. What if, by the time she and Hope decided to cancel the fitting fee, the girls had already found a different place to shop?

But then the girls came back. "Okay," Diana said. "We're sorry about what happened to Hope. We both want her to do the fitting."

Fifteen minutes later, Hope rang up two pairs of shoes. When the girls left, Anna let out a sigh of relief. And then, since the fitting fee had worked, she went on to describe the other ideas she'd had—the grand opening promotions, the website, the broader range of classes, and SummerFest.

Hope sat down on one of the ottomans. "You did a lot of thinking last night," she said. "And I guess you had quite a talk with Aidan."

"I'm not trying to take over," Anna said. "But I do want to be your partner. I fell in love with the store when I first saw it…" She paused for a moment to gather her thoughts. "But now I'm falling in love… with the whole idea of working with you to create something spectacular."

Hope pulled herself up and walked over to Anna. "Then I'm excited, too," she said. "Because for the first time since last summer, I think I see you coming back to life."

Anna gave Hope a hug, and a few moments later, the two were hunched over the computer, working to design a promotional flier. They created a border with images from famous ballets, like *The Sleeping Beauty*, *The Nutcracker*, *Swan Lake*; stills from dance movies, like *Footloose*, *An American in Paris*, *Saturday Night Fever*, and *Dirty Dancing*; and photos of famous dancers, like

Fred Astaire, Ginger Rogers, Gene Kelly, Mikhail Baryshnikov, Michael Jackson, and Misty Copeland.

Then they shared memories of promotions they used to love, recalling the offers that spoke to their identities as dancers. They settled on three that would run through July: get a free dance tutorial when you spend $100 or more (they would let the girls from today use this retroactively); get two free classes when you buy a twenty-class series; and get 10 percent off when you spend $150. Anna threw her arms around her aunt's neck and kissed her cheek. Even now, it felt so good to have her aunt's approval—almost as good as when Hope would come back to New York City for a visit, and she'd demonstrate how she'd mastered a double pirouette or a grand jeté, and Hope would say she was good enough to dance at Lincoln Center. Hope's cheek was a little softer and her spine a little less straight than it had been back then, but she was still the best hugger Anna knew.

Anna put the document onto a thumb drive and left to make copies. Her first thought was to go to the Staples on Route 35. But she changed her mind and went to the small print shop a few doors down instead. Knowing what she knew now about how hard retailing was, she felt compelled to support other local merchants. She introduced herself to the owner of the print shop and asked for 250 color copies of the promotional flier. He was glad for the business, and threw in fifteen extra copies, then agreed to post one on his bulletin board.

She left the shop and went door-to-door, meeting the other merchants and asking if they'd carry or post her flier. It was strange and intimidating at first; whenever she'd made campaign stops, the crowds knew who she was and were happy to see her. And when she spoke, Crystal always gave her prepared speeches. But even though her task was harder now, she enjoyed it more. The Lake Summers retailers—the father-daughter owners of the sports store, the manager of the formalwear place, Mrs. Pearl of

Pearl's Café, and so on—were remarkably nice. There was a vibe in the downtown area that she'd never noticed when she was just a summer resident. Now she was part of the town's commerce, and she was starting to feel a real sense of belonging. The pizza place owner and the manager of the Ice Creamery praised the dance shop's facade and patio, and she promised to email the name of Hope's contractor. At the real estate office, she mentioned that she planned to put her house on the market before she left town in August. The manager sounded smart and savvy, so she took the woman's business card and said she'd be in touch.

Her final stop was Village Hall, where she left a stack of fliers, as Aidan suggested. She glanced over at the seating nook and behind the wooden reception desk as she moved through the lobby, thinking she might run into him. She was proud of what she had accomplished today, and wanted to share it with someone she thought would appreciate it. When he didn't appear, she went up to the receptionist and asked for him so she could turn in her SummerFest application.

"He's in a meeting," she said. "But I can take your form and give it to him as soon as he's out."

Anna held onto the sheet for a moment, then took a pen from the cup and wrote a quick note across the top: *If your son is available, we'd like to hire him to build us a website.* She handed the form to the woman and thanked her for her help.

She was surprised at how sorry she was that Aidan wasn't around to say hello to.

*

"So I tell them, 'This one's for Josiah!' and they all freeze like I'm the king or something, and then I lob the ball over the net, and Josiah swings and of course he misses it, like they always do, then I say, 'Go!' and they all go chasing the ball and they're banging into each other and falling all over the place and laughing like crazy!"

It was later that week, and Anna was walking Zac and Evie to the lake for camp, reveling in Zac's story. She was glad that things were looking up with her kids, as they both seemed to be enjoying camp. Zac had won the tennis round robin the day before, and according to Evie, the counselors had hoisted him on their shoulders. "You should have seen it, Mom!" Evie told her. "They carried him all the way back to the lake, and everyone was following and shouting his name!" And he also seemed well suited to watching the six-year-old boys in his group. He found their antics hilarious.

She gave Zac some money for ice cream later, and reminded him that she'd meet him and Evie at the Ice Creamery around five o'clock. Then she kissed his cheek and watched him jog down the sandy slope. Turning her attention to Evie, she leaned down and wrapped her in a hug.

"Don't be fooled, Mom," Evie said. "The reason he's so happy isn't because he likes his group. It's because of Nicole, from *my* group. He has a big crush on her. And everyone is saying she likes him, too!"

"Oh?" Anna said. "The one who braided your hair?"

"She talks about him all the time. I think maybe they're gonna fall in love," she added as she took off down the hill.

Anna watched her. So that was it, she thought. Zac had a crush. She smiled as she walked back toward town, excited by this added piece of good news. But was Zac ready for all of that? Was she?

Back at the store, she turned her attention to business. Hope was hanging up a poster-size write-up of the fitting fee policy, and she stepped back against the opposite wall to let Hope know if it was straight. That's when the door chime sounded. A teenage boy was standing at the entrance.

"Is one of you Mrs. Harris? I'm Liam Lawrence. My dad said you need a website?"

"Liam… hi," Anna said, putting down the pushpins in her hand and going over to greet him. He was fair-skinned and long-limbed—she supposed he took after his mother in that way. His hair was short and a very light blond, which made him look as though he belonged on the coast somewhere and not in the middle of New York State. He was dressed nicely, in a button-down shirt over tan shorts. He held out his hand, first to her and then to Hope, which surprised her. She didn't know fifteen-year-olds thought to do that.

"My dad said you probably want something simple to start with, so you can update it easily," he said. "I can get that done in a couple of hours."

"And how much would that cost?" Hope asked.

"My dad said to do it for free."

"What? No, we can't accept that," Anna said. "We have to pay you."

He closed his eyes and shrugged, with an ease that Anna thought must also come from his mother. Aidan moved and spoke with far more intensity. "That's what my dad said. He wants to help. Don't worry, he'll make it up to me. Where's the computer?"

Anna led him to the laptop in the back office. She wasn't going to let him work for free. They'd definitely pay something. But she thought it sweet that Aidan had done that.

Liam sat down and began typing, then looked at the screen, one palm perched on his thigh and the fingers of the other rubbing the side of his mouth. "The first thing is a domain name," he said. "I checked on my way here, and TheLilacPointe.com isn't available, but we can do something close, like TheLilacPointeStore.com."

"Is that bad?"

"It's not the best, but it's okay. Now there are different hosting sites, but they're pretty much the same, so it doesn't so much matter which we pick. They have lots of deals if you register the domain for more than a year, but there's pros and cons to that…"

Anna watched him work, taking in his explanations and answering his queries: yes, they wanted the store hours on the homepage; no, they didn't want a blog, at least not yet; yes, they wanted to offer an incentive for signing up for emails; no, they weren't ready for online shopping. The more she listened, the more impressed she was. He reminded her of his father—patient and knowledgeable and even-keeled. She felt in good hands as she listened to him present choices and suggestions. She thought that Aidan must be a great dad.

"So I'll set up the templates, and then I'll take some photos and insert them," Liam said.

She left him to his task, and he came out from time to time to snap photos on his phone. Hope brought him pizza for lunch, and he ate a couple of slices as he typed. True to his word, in a couple of hours he emerged to tell them he was done.

They followed him into the office to take a look at the website—and it was far more than basic. It was spectacular. The homepage had an image of the storefront that Anna had had on her hard drive, the porch dappled from the sun and the blue sky lining the background. The hours and location were listed in a coral font that harmonized perfectly with the violet on the storefront's sign. Another page showed the sales floor, with a photo Liam had taken of the shoe armoire that did justice to its extensive assortment. An exquisite image of the dance studio, which Liam had also snapped, decorated a third page, the light from the skylight making the floor gleam.

"It's gorgeous," Anna said, and Hope nodded.

Liam shrugged, as if it had barely been any work at all. "There's just one other thing," he said. "There should be a shot of the two of you on the 'About' page."

Hope suggested they go outside and stand on the top step, framing the front door. Anna held back at first, wondering if she should be in the photo, since she wouldn't be around past the summer. But then she decided to do it. She didn't want to stress her aunt out by reminding her of that late-August deadline. And what was more, she was feeling a strong sense of ownership. She wanted to be included.

She gave Liam her phone and he took a few shots.

"Now, how about a picture with you, Liam?" Hope asked. "I'll ask one of the smoothie guys next door to take it."

Liam shook his head.

"But you're our web designer," Hope said. "Your photo belongs on the website."

Liam handed the phone back to Anna. "No, that's okay. I'm good. I'll stop by tomorrow to make sure everything's working. Thanks for the pizza."

They watched him leave and then went back inside. "I thought teenagers were all about putting their pictures online," Hope said.

Anna shrugged. "Maybe he doesn't want to be associated with a store that's so pink. He is a teenage boy, after all."

Later that afternoon, Anna went to meet Zac and Evie. At the Ice Creamery, she looked through the window and spotted her kids, seated at a round table with a girl that Anna suspected was Nicole. She had long, dark brown hair, her slender, tanned arms emerging from a sleeveless tee shirt, and she looked at Zac with huge, adoring eyes. Anna started to walk into the store, but then stopped. She was a little early, and they weren't expecting her. She didn't want to embarrass Zac by showing up unexpectedly. She figured she'd wait another ten minutes or so.

Sitting down on a nearby bench, she imagined what it would be like if Greg were right there next to her. *Look through the window—she's adorable, isn't she?* she heard herself saying. *And Evie says they're falling in love. He looks so happy. But do you think he's old enough for a girlfriend? Should we ask him about her?* She knew Greg would tell her to ease off and wait. And she'd protest a bit, worried that Zac might have questions about what he was feeling, before agreeing that Greg was right. Oh, how she missed telling Greg about the kids, or her day! She'd always loved feeling his warm body alongside hers in bed at night as they shared their thoughts in the dark. The pressure to be with him felt overwhelming, like an itch she couldn't reach to scratch.

The only thing to do was to keep moving forward, she thought as she waited alone on the bench. But she couldn't stop wondering if that desperate itch would ever, *ever*, go away.

CHAPTER TWELVE

It was a few days after Liam designed the website, and Hope was admiring how beautiful the store's pictures looked, when the door chime rang and a deep voice sounded from the entranceway.

"Hi, I'm Keon Carter. Would you happen to be Ms. Burns?"

Hope startled. It was unusual to hear a deep, booming voice in the store. Or to see someone who looked like he did: extremely tall, extremely bald, and extremely broad-chested. By the lines along his forehead and framing his mouth, she'd have guessed he was about her age, late fifties or so, but he had the build of a man much younger. The outline of his chest muscles could be seen pressing against the front of his royal-blue polo shirt. She figured he must have been an athlete at one point. A tattoo with some kind of inscription peeked out from the underside of his taut forearm.

"I'm Hope Burns," she said. His name, Keon Carter, sounded familiar, and she wondered if he was a vendor or a contractor, if maybe she hadn't paid some bill on time, and she owed him money. She looked at his large, outstretched hand and tentatively met it with hers. "Can I help you with something?"

"Yes, you can let me apologize," he said. "We spoke on the phone the other day, and I was extremely rude. I thought you were someone else—not that that's an excuse." He pointed to the logo emblazoned on the left side of his shirt. "I'm Dean of Student Life at Jayson College."

"Oh… Dean Carter," Hope said. Relieved that this wasn't about anything she'd messed up, she let the name sink in. "Yeah, you were pretty rude. You basically hung up on me." Her tone was bold but also playful. It seemed the perfect response to his friendliness.

"It was a long day, and I was tired, and I mistook you for a telemarketer," he said. "But then we had a meeting with our dance majors, and your name came up. And it rang a bell, so I checked my recent calls… and anyway, I'm here to say I'm sorry."

She smiled, flattered that he had made the trip over for this reason. "That's very nice of you."

"I behaved badly, and I wanted to make amends. And to see the place, if you wouldn't mind. Our students speak very highly of the store, and of you. They say you know more about pointe shoes than anyone on the planet."

She paused, savoring his words like an unexpected treat, a festively wrapped gift from someone you didn't think knew it was your birthday. When she'd seen the girls run out after noting down those style numbers, she'd been sure they took her for a fool.

"I can show you around if you'd like," she said.

She led him across the sales floor, stopping to make a quick introduction to Anna, who had just carried up a fresh box of leotards from the basement. Then she brought him down the hall to the studio. He stopped at the threshold, and she watched, charmed, as he bent over to untie and take off his sneakers. Even though he wasn't a dancer, he clearly had an appreciation for her world. She slipped off her sandals, and as they both walked in, she explained all the design elements—the construction of the subfloor, the quality of the mirrors, the color and placement of the lighting. He nodded as she spoke, and his clear interest gave her the confidence to go into detail.

"How did you get so knowledgeable about all this?" he said when she finished. "Do you have a construction background?"

"No, not at all," she said, amused that he would think that. "But I always dreamed of owning my own dance studio. I've danced in so many different studios and on so many stages, and I was always trying to figure out what made one so magical and another so uninspiring. I wanted to make this place the best in the world. The kind of place I could devote myself to for the rest of my life."

"I'm impressed," he said. "So, what's your story, Hope... may I call you Hope? I assume you're a dancer?"

"Of course, about Hope, and I used to be a dancer," she said.

"What company did you dance with?"

"It was in Europe. But that was a very long time ago."

"Miss it?"

"I did, for a time. But I think I was ready to leave. I was young when I started, and I got a little in over my head. It's not an easy life."

"I'll bet," he said. "Especially in a foreign country."

"I taught and did some choreography after I stopped dancing, and I realized I liked that more. I know that's hard to believe. People always think that everyone's first choice is to be on stage, right?"

He chuckled. "Don't look at me. I'm a school administrator. I'm like you—I like being behind the scenes. That's where you have a pretty big impact."

She walked further into the room, enjoying the soft snap of her bare feet as they pulled up off the wood floor with each step. She rubbed the pads of her fingers along the barre and looked back over her shoulder at him. "I think so, too," she said. "I love bringing all the pieces together—the dancers, the steps, costumes, lighting. Making the dance more beautiful by elevating the dancers, making the dancers more beautiful by enhancing the dance."

"So you're an idea person," he said.

She liked the sound of that. She remembered the last time she visited David and Anna, when she taught Anna the Lilac Variation so she'd have a dance ready when she began auditioning for roles. She'd found tapes of the solo, performed not just by her, but by a range of ballerinas from different dance companies and different decades. She'd studied the tiny differences among them, trying to find subtle ways to show off Anna's strong feet and high arches, her long back and neck.

"I guess I am," she said. "And the thing I most loved about choreographing was that there was this freedom to experiment. Oh, I suppose as a dancer I was free to express myself, too, but only to a certain extent. Mostly I was executing the choreographer's vision—at least, that's how I saw it. But a choreographer can change things over and over, even before she shows it to anyone." She looked at herself in the mirror. "Dance was a lot more forgiving than real life, in that way."

She saw his reflection take a few steps in her direction. "You sound like it's in the past," he said. "Aren't you teaching here?"

"Well… I will be," she said, turning to face him, her back against the barre. "The store is still getting off the ground. But my hope is to fill up my classes and maybe even launch some careers. Maybe some of your students, even."

She looked past Keon, and her eyes rested for a moment on the mirrored wall at the back of the studio, and she saw the multiple reflections formed by the surrounding mirrors. There she and Keon stood, their bodies revealed from different angles. Their adjacent bodies and their limbs looked like a work of art.

"I'm an idea person, too," he said. "And I feel a big one coming. And like you said, if it's a dud, we'll just kick it aside. But I think it might turn out pretty good. Is there a place we can sit and talk?"

They left the studio, and she slipped her sandals back on and watched as he retied his sneakers. Then she led him back down the hallway and into the office. She'd thought she was so smart last winter, shopping at tag sales for her office furnishings, but now she regretted it. She hadn't expected to have people sit down back here, and she was embarrassed. The chairs, which had clearly once been part of a kitchen set, had cracked wooden frames and frayed wicker seats. The metal desk had to be thirty years old. She sat down behind it, and as Keon took the opposite chair, she hoped it was strong enough to hold him. She wished she could offer Keon something to drink, but she didn't have a coffee maker and hadn't gotten around to stocking the little fridge with water bottles.

He didn't seem to mind about the chair or the lack of a beverage. He leaned forward, his elbows on his knees. "So, the meeting with our dance majors, where your name came up, was about our summer session," he said. "It was supposed to start next week. A lot of our students have double majors, so taking summer classes is essential for graduating on time. But the air conditioning in the theater arts building gave out for good, and it's going to take a few weeks to replace the system. So we have no studios for dance classes this summer.

"But now I'm thinking—like I said, I'm an idea guy, too—I'm thinking that we can rent your studio a few times a week to hold our summer classes. I don't know what we can pay, but I'm sure we can do something fair. It's a lot better than trying to place our students at this late date at other colleges in the area. And maybe you could even teach a class or two."

"Me?" she said. It sounded like a dream, working with college students again. But then she remembered all those years she'd fudged her credentials so she could land teaching jobs, and how ashamed she'd felt each time someone from administration discovered that she didn't have a college degree and called to say they were letting her go. She never wanted to go through that again. "I don't know if I'd have the time…"

"Obviously you'd need to meet with Dara Steen—she's the chair of the department," he continued. "Look, it's just an idea now, and I'm sure there are lots of problems that would need solving. But on first blush… is it worth pursuing?"

Hope sat back in her chair. She didn't even care anymore about how rickety it was. For months she'd been worried about telling

Anna about the store, and facing the fact that she'd taken money Anna needed for herself and her kids. She had spent the whole of last year feeling guilty and worried. But now she was sitting here in this place she'd designed from scratch, fielding a request to hold college-level courses in her studio—and to teach one or more of them. And if Jayson students were here all the time, they might buy more dance gear, since it was convenient. And their presence could spur others to sign up for classes. Hope realized that she couldn't say no to any of this. She needed to do whatever she could to make the store a success—not just for herself, but for Anna and her kids as well.

"I'm going to have to discuss this with Anna," she said. "But I would love to give you a tentative yes."

He stood and reached out his hand to shake hers. "Hey, Hope, that's terrific," he said. "I'll go back and talk with the rest of the administration and with Dara. And we'll reconnect tomorrow."

They walked out of the office to find the sales floor humming. Anna was helping some women who were admiring the sweaters and pullovers, and several other customers were sorting through the shelves of leggings and looking at the picture frames and jewelry. Clearly the promotional flier Anna had distributed was starting to work. Stan, in his Smoothie Dudes apron, was moving among the customers, holding out a platter with samples of Trey's finalized July Fourth smoothie. The place had a kind of Mardi Gras feel. Hope took two little cups off the platter and handed one to Keon, then raised the other one to her mouth to take a sip. It was crisp and fruity, with just the perfect balance of sweetness and tang.

"I wish I could stay, but I should be getting back to the office," Keon said.

"And I should be helping with the customers." She took his empty cup and threw it away with her own, and then walked him out the door and onto the patio.

"Thanks for your time," he said. "I can see what my students have been raving about."

"I should mention that they spoke well of you, too," she said.

"Oh? What did they say?"

"That you believe in taking personal responsibility."

"And that's it? Nothing bad?"

"They also said you talk a lot."

He laughed and rolled his eyes. "They're right. I do."

"But that wasn't such a big part of it. Mostly they were saying you wanted them to do the right thing."

"I try. Not always successfully, but I try."

"You know, that's the reason I called you the other day," she said, and went on to tell him about the pointe shoes and the fitting fee.

"A good, practical solution," he said. "Easy, and does the trick. But if you thought they were disrespecting you, you could have spoken up. You could have told them how you felt."

"It wasn't my place. I'm just a store owner."

"You're more than that. You're someone they admire. And the truth is, by speaking up, you'd be teaching them a lesson."

He shook his head. "Or maybe not. Hey, I don't mean to make you responsible for Jayson's students. That's *my* job. I come from a long line of people who spend their time looking out for other people. It's in my DNA."

The screen door opened and Stan emerged, his platter under his arm, a few tiny beads of sweat above his bushy mustache. "Whew, busy place! Well, Hope? Did we do it?"

"It was delicious," she told him. "You'll sell a million."

Keon nodded his agreement and then introduced himself. Stan shook his hand and went back to talking about the new smoothie.

"Finally! We were getting close," he said. "July Fourth is next week already. We're going to give out coupons before the fireworks and then stay open late for people to stop by after. You're going, right?"

Hope raised her shoulders. "Maybe. Not sure yet."

"What? You have to go. I hear that Aidan got the town to fork up some extra bucks. It's going to be the biggest show we've ever had." He continued down the steps, then looked back over his shoulder. "And guess what? Trey's next invention is going to be a lilac-themed smoothie in honor of your store!"

Hope waved, then turned to Keon and groaned. "That's a scary thought. It usually takes them a few tries to get it right. I better make sure we have Tums around."

Keon laughed. "But what's this about you not going to the fireworks? I hear Lake Summers puts on a great show."

"It's beautiful. I used to go with Anna and her family. But I don't know if she's going this year. And I wouldn't want to go alone."

He pursed his lips and nodded as she spoke. "I've got no plans yet for the Fourth," he said. "What if we went together? Or if you do end up going with Anna, would it be okay if I tagged along? I've always wanted to see the fireworks here."

Hope smiled, enjoying how easygoing he was. She had the feeling that although he wanted her to go, he'd be fine if she said no. He wouldn't feel rejected or foolish. He'd just move on.

But she didn't want to say no. "Sure," she said. "That would be fine."

A moment later he went to his car, and she walked back into the store. Anna finished up with a customer and then grabbed her bag to go get Evie. Hope took over at the counter, thinking that after closing, she'd go into the studio and begin to choose music and plan a possible pointe lesson for the Jayson dancers.

For the first time since her family had arrived back in town, she truly believed in herself.

CHAPTER THIRTEEN

"A sycamore or red maple," Anna said into the phone to Crystal as she looked out onto the backyard from the porch swing, comparing what she saw to the thumbnails on the sheet Crystal sent. "Those are the ones that look most like what's here. Greg loved this yard."

It was nearly three weeks after she'd found out about the store, and things were starting to look hopeful. The Jayson summer program had begun, so students—both girls and guys—were coming in and out of the place all day. Plus, the fitting fee had done its job, and dancers were actually buying their pointe shoes at the store after receiving Hope's assistance. Anna had convinced Hope to offer a wider range of classes, and thanks to Keon's recommendations of local teachers, they were able to add yoga, hip-hop, and ballroom to their mix. At the same time, store traffic was picking up, as people got their hands on the promotional flier and increasingly stopped by to take a look. She and Hope had even arranged to bring Melanie on as a part-time intern, getting the school to agree to reduce her summer tuition in exchange for her help on the sales floor.

With Melanie coming in, Anna asked Hope to step out one morning and help her choose some new clothes. She'd started to grow tired of the blouses and capris she always wore—they'd been perfect when she spoke at campaign events or went to Greg's office to work on volunteer projects, but they seemed out of place with the casual vibe of the dance store. She wanted some more playful and prettier options, like the dresses in the window of The Look, Lake Summers' most popular boutique. Hope had great taste, and always wore jersey or gauzy dresses with gathered waists or drapey silhouettes that showed off her dancer's body. Hope said she'd love to come, and in the end they settled on three dresses—a silver-blue racerback style, a mini-floral print with an A-line silhouette, and a pale yellow sundress with a camisole bodice and handkerchief hem, which seemed maybe a bit too dressy for work, but was too pretty to pass up.

Over coffee at Pearl's following their shopping trip, Anna and Hope brainstormed some ideas for their booth at SummerFest, with Hope offering to choreograph some mini-dances for the Jayson students. "I'd love to give them some stage experience and show off their strengths," she said. "Diana has beautiful feet—and Melanie has such presence. If I create a contemporary piece for her, her personality will really shine. Something fun... kind of light..."

Anna looked over her coffee cup at her aunt, who had started scribbling notes on a napkin. She'd never heard Hope express sadness about not having children of her own, but she'd always known Hope was a nurturer. "You really care about these kids, don't you?" she said.

Hope looked up from her scribbles. "Oh, they're a little trying at times, and they definitely have sass," she said. "But they're so young, and they have their whole lives ahead of them. I want so much to help them discover their dreams, and maybe see some of them come true."

They finished their coffee, and Hope went back to the store, while Anna went home to take care of a few chores before returning later with the kids to do the late shift. Now she looked at the woods that Greg used to love, as Crystal tapped at her computer on the other end of the phone.

"Sycamore or maple," Crystal repeated. "And the quotation?"

Anna thought about the small Sleeping Beauty doll Greg had given her the day they met. "All I can think of is that thing he always used to say, how you can't change everything but you can do what you can do. Not so appropriate for an inscription, I guess."

"He did say that a lot," Crystal said. "But I think it was his voice that made it sound inspiring. Don't worry, you can think a little more about it. We just want to be able to talk about the memorial at the August city council meeting. Which reminds me… is August twelfth okay for Dan Groner to come up there and do the interview for the *Inquirer?*"

Anna hesitated. "Are you sure I should do this? You know I'm not comfortable by myself with the press—"

"The council is voting on Willow Center in late August, and a big article on Greg and all he stood for could be very helpful. We've heard that two of the seven council members are withdrawing their support. We can't lose any more."

"They're withdrawing? Why?"

"Without Greg, the opposition has more influence. So we need Dan's article."

"But what about the email you sent me, about how some officials told him that Greg looked anxious last fall? I don't know what I'll say if he asks me about that."

"Say he was concerned about the future of Willow Center. That's the truth, isn't it?"

"Yes, of course it is."

"I don't think it's a big deal," she said, sounding like she was losing patience. "Everyone knew that Greg was working hard. I didn't mean to freak you out. I just wanted to prepare you. It'll make things worse if you change your mind now. And you can be tough, too. If you don't like a question, don't answer it. Okay? Can I tell him it's a go?"

Anna sighed and said it was fine. She'd only met Dan Groner once before, on that day last September when he'd accompanied her, Greg, and Crystal to visit a prototype for Willow Center in Connecticut. Greg had been his usual, friendly self as he'd toured the facility, meeting counselors who were there to lead support groups or give one-on-one advice about jobs and housing. But on the way back, Dan had been aggressive, plying Greg with questions about costs and staffing—and while Greg was normally good at speaking off the cuff, that day he'd been strangely uncertain, answering often with "I don't know offhand," or "I'll get back to you." Anna had been happy to drop Dan off at his office.

Back home, Greg had collapsed onto the sofa. "So what do you think if we bagged all this and moved up to Lake Summers for good?" he'd said. "A nice, quiet life. I could be a landscaper or something. What do you think?"

"Hah," she said as she went to hang up his coat. "You wouldn't last a week before you'd be looking for some huge new project to get involved in."

"And wouldn't that be okay?"

"No, it wouldn't be okay," she said with a laugh, and left to get Evie from school.

And wouldn't that be okay? That's what he'd said, right? Or had he said, *Wouldn't* it *be okay?* She'd thought he was teasing, asking if it would be okay if he hated their quiet life and pined for new projects, and she'd meant to tease back: *No, if you're going to pine for new projects, you may as well keep things as they are.* But now she heard the question differently. Had he been asking if a quiet life would be okay? And had she dismissed him? She never would have intentionally said no to that. She would have loved a quiet life if that were what *he* truly wanted. The conversation felt so distant, like the sight of Greg on the imaginary track. She couldn't remember now. She had no idea which question he'd asked.

She ended the call with Crystal and went upstairs to get the kids' laundry, and then went down to the basement to start a wash. But when she turned on the machine, no water flowed into the tub. That was odd—she'd done a wash just the other day, and had had no problem at all. She reached up to the hot and cold water valves behind the machine, and noticed that they'd been turned off. She didn't think she'd done that—she never turned the valves off in between washes. And yet nobody else had any reason to be down here besides her. Had she done it without thinking? It didn't make sense, and yet there was no other explanation. She looked behind the machine again, where a few tiny droplets of water were running along the length of the cold water hose. Evidently Greg had never gotten around last summer to replacing the water hoses, as he had promised to do. She made a mental note to stop by the hardware store and see if they carried a replacement.

She went upstairs and into her bathroom to grab the rest of the laundry. On her way back out, her eyes landed on the toothbrush holder, which only held her toothbrush. That was strange, too; she thought Greg's orange one had been there all along. He would always leave his toothbrush there at the end of the summer, and she'd always throw it out when they arrived back in town. But she didn't remember throwing it out this time. Had she tossed it without paying attention? Or was it never there to begin with this summer?

She walked into her bedroom and sat down on the bed, feeling unsettled by the missing toothbrush and turned-off water valves. It had never been so hard to get through her daily chores before. She wondered if maybe she was spending way too much time in her own head; if maybe she was just very lonely. Yesterday on the way home from camp, Evie had shown her an invitation she'd gotten to a Fourth of July party at Sophie's, a new camp friend.

"Are you happy, Mom?" she'd said. "Are you happy that I'm gonna be with my friends and Zac's gonna be with his on July Fourth?"

"Yes, of course," she'd said.

"Even though we won't be with you?"

"I'm fine, honey. You don't need to worry about me."

"You're fine? Being all alone, you're fine?"

"Yes, I'm fine, I'm fine," she said. "Okay, Evie? I'm fine."

"Okay, Mom," Evie said. "But if you're fine, why are you yelling at me?"

*

July Fourth arrived, and store traffic slowed as five o'clock approached. Knowing that Hope had plans to see the fireworks with Keon, Anna offered to close up on her own, so Hope would have a little time to freshen up if she wanted.

"Why don't we close up now?" Hope said. "Nobody's shopping, everyone's heading down to the lake. How about we go to the Grill for an early dinner? I'll still have time to shower and change before Keon comes by."

Anna agreed—she didn't have any other plans, and it was nice not to have to eat dinner alone. They got a table on the deck and Anna was amazed at how quickly their order arrived—although then again, the place was almost as empty as their store had been. Nearly everyone in town packed a picnic to eat at the lake on July Fourth. Last year, she and Greg had done exactly that.

"For the last time, will you please come with us?" Hope said, as they both dug into their salads. "Your kids both have plans, why not come?"

Anna tilted her head. "You don't want me there with you two."

"You think this is a date? Believe me, I am way too old for that. He just wanted to see how they do fireworks here. He didn't ask me to go—he asked if it would be okay if he tagged along with you and me. *He's* the one who'd be tagging along."

"I'm tired. I want to go home. And I don't like fireworks that much, anyway."

"Okay, if you're sure I can't get you to change your mind." She finished eating and wiped her mouth with her napkin. "Would you mind if I took off, then?"

"Go," Anna said. "Have fun."

"My treat," Hope said, and threw some bills on the table, then hurried toward the metal staircase before Anna could protest. She gestured to Maxine for the check. The truth was, she couldn't bear to go to the lake without Greg. They had spent so many wonderful July Fourth evenings there together, mostly sprawled out on a blanket with the kids, taking in the glorious show. And last summer—the first time that Evie had run off to watch with her friends, like Zac always did—had in some ways been the most wonderful. She had lain down next to Greg with her head on his chest, pleasantly buzzed from the wine they had shared, missing cuddling Evie on her lap but also feeling proud of her growing children.

"Don't you just love our life?" she'd said. "Don't you just love our kids?"

Greg had lifted his head to kiss the top of hers. "We done good," he'd said.

Anna paid Maxine and then got up from the table. On her way toward the staircase, she noticed a lone figure at the bar.

It was Aidan.

She stopped, not sure what to do. She wanted to say hello. She wouldn't mind talking with him again. But as she watched him twirl his drink, clearly engrossed in his thoughts, she wondered if maybe he was also remembering past July Fourth evenings. She thought he probably didn't want to be interrupted, but suddenly he was looking back at her.

"Hi," she said. "I was just having dinner with my aunt"—she pointed toward the staircase, as though he could still catch a glimpse of her, even though she had left fifteen minutes ago—"she had to leave… we had an early dinner."

"Oh," he answered. She didn't know why she'd felt compelled to share all that. She thought it was probably because she felt self-conscious about being alone on the holiday, and to be caught looking at him from the staircase.

But he didn't look unhappy that she'd come over. "Does that mean you have to leave, too?" he asked. "Or can I buy you a drink?"

He gestured toward the stool next to him, and she nodded and slid onto it, thinking that she was glad for the invitation. It was hard to be alone and melancholy on a night when others were celebrating. She'd felt compelled to say she was fine over dinner, so she wouldn't ruin her aunt's evening, but the nice thing now was that she didn't need to pretend around Aidan. She had felt so unburdened the other day at Village Hall, talking with Aidan about losing Greg, and seeing so much of him in her children, and worrying about how they were handling their grief. It was the first time she'd ever spoken about those feelings.

He motioned to the bartender, and she ordered a glass of wine. "So, how's it been going with the store?" he asked.

"So-so," she said. "The promotions are definitely bringing people into the store. But I'm waiting to see a sustained bump in our sales. I'm worried that people are still mostly browsing."

"There's always something to worry about in retail," he told her. "But I think you should feel good. You've done a lot in a very short time. Liam's been giving me updates."

"Thanks for sending him over to do the website. He's a great kid."

"Glad it worked out," Aidan said. "He enjoyed it."

"He stopped by a few times to see how the website is working. And he helps out, too, when we need to lug big boxes. But you have to let us pay him. He won't take any money because you told him not to."

"You mean he actually listened to me for a change?" Aidan's eyes smiled. "Sure, I'll tell him it's okay."

The bartender returned, and she took a sip of her wine. Aidan was easy to speak to. Greg had been like that, too. Still, with Greg there'd always been that theatricality, a look in his eye or an expression on his face that said he'd nailed it. Aidan's demeanor was different.

"So, what are your plans for this evening?" he asked.

She shrugged, no longer self-conscious. If anyone would understand her feelings about tonight, it was him. "Seeing as how my kids have both dumped me for their camp friends"—she paused and he laughed—"I think I'm going to go home and take a nap until they get back. And you?"

"I'll probably go to the fireworks with Liam after he gets off from Pearl's. Or if he dumps *me*—which is a clear possibility—I'll watch from our porch. Turns out we've got a good view."

"I can see them from Zac's bedroom window," she said. "They're pretty. Worth a look."

"I ordered a couple of sandwiches to go," he continued. "Although I don't expect to be hungry. I spent the day helping Lonny Brines adjust his new hot dog grill. And we strung some lights along his new deck. He wanted to be ready for people stopping by later, needing a snack after the big show…"

She listened to him describe working with Lonny, impressed at how pleased he sounded to crawl on the floor and climb up on ladders, inserting screws and tightening bolts, and twisting light bulbs when they didn't work. She remembered that among Greg's staff, a common complaint about consultants was that they never wanted to get their hands dirty. They never "owned" the project. But Aidan was different. He hadn't just been Lonny's consultant today. He'd been Lonny's friend and partner.

"Forty different types of hot dogs on his menu," he said. "And I must have sampled at least a third. Have you been there yet?"

The question snapped her back to the present. "The hot dog place? No. I'm not a hot dog eater."

"You don't like hot dogs?"

"I've never had one."

She wondered if he'd find this strange, but he seemed a little charmed by it. "You've never had a hot dog? Really?"

"My father worked at a fancy restaurant when I was young, and he formed some pretty strong opinions about food. He had strict rules about what to put into our bodies."

"But what about as an adult? Never even a taste?"

The memory of a county fair from years ago sprang to her mind. "My wife doesn't allow me to eat hot dogs," Greg had said to the white-haired ladies behind the food table, pretending to walk away but then sneakily seizing one, as the women laughed and Anna feigned disapproval. Greg loved to cultivate the idea that he was a slightly naughty husband, and she was his disciplined wife. She'd thought it was fun to go along with it. Even though those hot dogs had smelled awfully good.

She shook her head. "I grew up in New York City, and I'll never forget how my dad would describe them when we passed the food trucks outside Central Park: 'Ugly red chunks of spongy rubber waste—'"

"Well, when you say it like that, I wouldn't eat them either," he said. "But Lonny's dogs are different. He grills them just right, so there's a burst of juiciness when your teeth pierce the skin"—he pressed his thumb and fingers together and then sprang them apart to illustrate the burst—"and then your mouth is overcome with flavors, complemented by the crunch of a perfectly grilled bun—"

"I think maybe Lonny brainwashed you this afternoon…"

"No, it's all true," he said. "Look, let me get this straight. It's not like you're allergic to hot dogs or anything, is it? It's just a choice?"

She nodded.

"Then how about we meet at Lonny's and you try one? Just a bite. And if it's bad, dinner's on me. What's the best place in town? Maybe that Italian place across the lake, Sogni di Lago? If you hate the hot dog, I owe you a dinner there."

She nodded, thinking how comfortable she felt right now, and how much she'd enjoy seeing him again. "Okay," she said. "It's a deal."

"How's next Monday? What time's good?"

"I'll want to give the kids dinner first. So, seven?"

"I'll meet you at Lonny's. And I promise, you're going to love it."

"I don't know. I think I have a fancy dinner in my future…"

Maxine came by and dropped a bag on the bar. "Here you go, Aidan," she said. "Say hello to your boy."

"Thanks," Aidan said. "Happy Fourth."

The waitress walked off, and Anna felt the air change, as though the takeout food had transported them back to reality. They were no longer carefree friends bantering about hot dogs, but grieving single parents trying to get through the holiday. Aidan looked down, and it seemed something weighty was on his mind again. She decided to leave before the conversation turned back to fireworks.

"I should get going," she said. "See you Monday."

"You bet," he said. "See you Monday."

When she reached the metal staircase, she looked back over her shoulder. Aidan was leaning on his elbows and rubbing his forehead. He took his wallet out of his pocket and put some bills on the bar, then went back to twirling his glass. He had told her that afternoon at Village Hall that losing a spouse gets easier after the first year. But watching him now, she didn't believe that he'd meant it. He slowly brought his glass to his lips, and she kept her eyes on him a moment longer. There was so much she wanted to know about him. Like where he came from and what had brought him to this little town. Like whether he and Liam had family elsewhere, and why they would choose to live here if they could be closer to relatives. Wouldn't Liam have felt better being surrounded by people who knew and loved his mom? Wouldn't Aidan have preferred that, too? After all, the only reason Anna came back to Lake Summers was because Hope was here, and she knew Hope would take care of them in a way no one else could. She remembered that Aidan had mentioned owning a jewelry store with his father, and she wondered whether his father was still alive, and what had happened to the store.

At home, she changed out of her work clothes and into an old white tee shirt and a pair of pajama pants. She watched TV for a little while, and when it grew dark outside, she went upstairs to Zac's bedroom. Kneeling on his bed, she looked out the window. She and Greg had sometimes watched the show from here, back when the kids were tiny and the loud booms and crackling sky would scare them. She'd put the kids to sleep early, after Greg had exhausted them with a raucous tickle session, and then the two of them would sit on the edge of Zac's bed in the darkened room. Greg would usually grow uninterested once the sky came alive, disappointed to be so far from the action and the crowds. But Anna never cared that they weren't by the lake. She was with her family, and the view through the window was still brilliant and beautiful.

Sitting by the window now, she wondered if Aidan was on his porch, also waiting for the show to start. There was something comforting about the idea that she and he were both watching the same black sky. The first few rockets launched, and a series of white sparklers rained down. Then came a huge blast that sent fiery red lines bursting in broad, eye-popping arcs.

And for just a moment, the red lines made her think of hot dogs. Hot dogs that burst with juiciness when your teeth pierced the skin. Filling you with anticipation of all the deliciousness to come.

CHAPTER FOURTEEN

On Saturday, Anna took the kids to the store to help out. She put Evie in charge of sorting the new leotards by color, and let Zac add updated sales figures into a spreadsheet, and promised that if they got a lot done, she'd arrange with Hope to leave early so she could take them for lunch at the Grill and then kayaking on the lake. It should have been a fun morning. But they were tired from the July Fourth festivities, or maybe the high humidity from the past week was getting to them—whatever the reason, things didn't work out so smoothly. Evie started in on Zac, saying that Nicole was talking about him at camp, and Zac grew red in the face and demanded that she tell him what she said, and Evie kept saying it was a *secret*, delighted with the power she held over him. Anna threatened Evie with no kayaking unless she behaved—a threat she desperately didn't want to carry out—and that's when Hope invited Evie to take a walk to see how Stan and Trey were coming along with the new lilac-inspired smoothie they'd promised to invent.

Alone in the shop with Zac, Anna helped a few customers find tops and leggings, all the while keeping her eye on her son as he sucked his bottom lip and typed numbers on the spreadsheet. His initial optimism about camp was waning, and lately he seemed unsettled again. She worried that he was having trouble processing his feelings for Nicole. She ached for him, knowing how hard it must be to like a girl for the first time in his life, and not have Greg around—maybe not even to talk to, maybe just to watch and identify with. At night she would try to talk to him about camp before he went to sleep, but he only either complained about Evie or told her he was fine and she should leave him alone. She thought maybe it was hard for him to talk to her at night, when he was tired and likely feeling lonely, remembering how it used to be with Greg around in the evenings to watch the Yankees with. She wondered if maybe he'd open up a little to her now, when it was daytime and they were out of the house.

She rang up the purchase, and as the women left, she leaned her elbows on the jewelry counter where Zac was working. "How's it going, honey?" she asked.

He stared at the computer. "Fine."

"I wouldn't worry about what Evie is saying. I think she's just trying to get your goat."

He shrugged. "Whatever."

She paused, then decided to plunge ahead. "Is there anything you want to talk about? I mean, maybe about Nicole, or anything you're feeling?"

He shook his head.

"I'm just wondering if you have any questions about… girls," she said. "I know I'm not Daddy, but I was once a girl like Nicole, and I'm your mom. You can talk to me about anything."

"I'm fine," he told her.

"Are you… missing Daddy a lot?" she asked.

He dropped his head forward, and she knew she was getting on his nerves. "No. Can you just let me get this done?"

"Okay," she said, mostly to herself, and started to walk away.

"You know what the best thing was about Dad?" he suddenly said. She held her breath, thinking any sudden sound or movement could scare him off from continuing. She didn't know what had triggered him to ask this question, but she so badly wanted to know the rest of his thought, to know what was churning up inside of him. She had never felt so distant from him as she'd felt this summer.

"What, honey?" she asked, almost in a whisper.

"It was always easy with him," he said.

She nodded, because she knew exactly what he meant. "He made it seem that way, didn't he?" she said. "That's why people loved him."

"Like even with the train accident," he said, and she knew he was thinking about the night he was born, the story she had told him over and over when he was little. "He just went in there and saved people. Like it was nothing."

"I think it was harder than he let on," she said. "But *you* were on your way. He knew that after all the bad was over, he'd go to the hospital to meet you. I think that's what always kept him going. Knowing we'd be there for him."

She looked up and saw Hope and Evie coming back, Evie holding a tray with four bright green smoothies. Zac was staring at the computer again, showing no emotion. She could only imagine how hard he was working to keep everything bottled up so securely inside, and wondered if she had made him feel worse, instead of better, by talking with him about Greg. She sighed and wiped her eyes, and then went to open the door.

*

Dusk was falling, and the air had a misty, purplish glow as she walked by the green and came upon Lonny's on Monday night. The twinkling lights threaded through the trees were festive and inviting, so she wasn't surprised that the place was crowded. She walked up the stairs to the deck, and near the railing she spotted Aidan, sitting at a small table, a platter of food in front of him. He stood and pulled out a chair for her. In his tapered gray shirt tucked into light tan pants, he looked nice, and more dressed up than usual.

"Hey," he said. "I was scared maybe you'd back out."

"I'm no quitter," she joked as she sat down opposite him. The truth was, she had thought about cancelling at the last minute, because she felt guilty leaving the kids. But they were both wiped out after a long, hot day at camp and looked perfectly content to relax on the sofa, watching TV and munching on the pizza she'd ordered in. They murmured their consent when she said she was going out for a quick bite, and didn't seem to notice or care about the pale yellow sundress with the camisole bodice that she'd bought with Hope and chosen to wear tonight.

Now she studied the platter. It had five wide cardboard cradles on it, each holding a blob of toppings so massive, she could only make out hints of the hot dog underneath.

"Wow, that's a lot of food," she said.

"I wanted you to have choices," Aidan said. He pointed to the first cradle. "Here we have the Caribbean style—topped with a little lime juice and some mango, pineapple—you know, a healthy alternative to start you off."

"Oh yes. Very healthy."

"Next is the classic—brown mustard, some onions, relish, and sauerkraut. Then the Latin variety—jalapeños, guacamole, some salsa, and a little Jack cheese. The chili dog—tomatoes, beans, cheddar, and some sweet pickles. And finally, it's the meat lover's special—ground beef, bacon, pulled pork, shredded barbecued chicken." He handed her a tall paper cup with a straw in it. "And to wash it all down, unsweetened iced tea, which my son says is your go-to beverage."

She smiled. Liam must have heard her ask for an unsweetened iced tea from time to time when Hope was taking drink or snack orders. She was flattered that Aidan had talked to Liam about what she liked to drink.

Reaching toward the Caribbean hot dog first, she hesitated, unsure of how to get her hands around the whole thing. Aidan picked it up for her, and she took it and examined it, looking for an entry point. Finally, she just dove into the mess. It was surprising how tasty it was—tangy, sweet and juicy—and how the ingredients blended and melted in her mouth. These were not the thick, rubbery logs her father had warned her about.

"Well?" he asked.

She held up an index finger until she had finished chewing and swallowing. "Life-changing," she said.

"No, no," he told her. "No sarcasm. Tell it to me straight."

"It's delicious. Really, you were right."

She gave it back to him, and he took a big bite, nodding his agreement with her assessment. It surprised her, and kind of tickled her as well, that he felt casual enough with her to eat the same hot dog.

Twenty minutes later she had tried them all, including the meat lover's one. And while she wasn't a big meat eater, she had to admit that it, too, was tasty and satisfying. As a dancer and then a politician's wife with a reputation as the family stickler, she had never really eaten with abandon before. And although she couldn't imagine eating this way regularly, it was fun to do it for a change.

Leaning back, she surveyed the platter and put her hand on her stomach. "Oh, boy. So much left over. But I am stuffed."

"Trust me, you have to move after eating these babies," he said. "Otherwise you'll fall fast asleep in your chair. How about a walk? Or do you have to get back to your kids?" he added.

"No, they're okay, probably fast asleep in front of the TV right now," she said. "A walk sounds nice."

He handed her their drinks and was going to toss out their trash when a photographer called over and asked Aidan to pose with Lonny for the *Lake Summers Press*.

"No, that's okay," Aidan said. "It's Lonny's deck, not mine. Better just him alone. I'm good."

The photographer shrugged, and Anna waited as Aidan continued to the trash basket. Liam had said the same thing at the store that day he designed the website. It was interesting that neither father nor son wanted to have his photo taken.

They walked down the stairs of the patio and began strolling along Main Street. Anna sipped her iced tea from time to time, enjoying the glimmer of the streetlamps, the close night air, and the feeling of being next to Aidan. On the green, she could see the shadows of young children as they licked ice cream cones, climbed on the gazebo, or ran across the makeshift stage still set up from that week's jazz concert. She knew that their moms were probably conflicted, regretting keeping them up so late—there would be crankiness tomorrow!—but choosing to stay a little longer because it was just so much fun. She envied the moms their ease, their confident expectation that their biggest problem tomorrow would be an overtired toddler. Those had been wonderful years for her, when she was in their shoes.

"What is it?" Aidan said. "You're smiling."

She shook her head. "Just watching the families," she said.

They walked a bit more. "So how did you end up in Lake Summers?" he asked quietly. It was as if he recognized she was feeling wistful and nostalgic, and he wanted to give her the chance to talk about it. She decided to take him up on it. Maybe it was the charm of the town or the pleasant feeling of comfort food in her belly or the company of a nice person, but she felt like opening up.

"My husband and I met here," she said. "At the Lake Summers Resort. We worked for the same marketing company. They brought all the new MBAs here for a company retreat. Greg was one of the MBAs, and I was in charge of planning the event." She paused, remembering how young and delightful Greg had been. How she'd been reeling from losing her father and her dancing career. How, somehow, in ten minutes, he'd seemed to set everything right.

"But neither of us stayed with the company very long," she added. "He went into politics, and I went into... helping him, I guess."

"No kidding. Politics?"

"He was a state senator before he died. We bought the house here a year after we got married."

She looked up at Aidan. "And you? How did you end up here?"

"It was after I lost my wife," he said. "We were living… in Rochester, Liam and me. And I needed to make a change. Wanted to make a change."

"Did it help?" she asked, thinking of her own plans to sell Lilac House. "Leaving, I mean?"

"Honestly? Not really. Just a different kind of hard."

They continued ahead in silence for a few moments, with the sound of the children behind them. She finished her iced tea, and he took her cup and threw it out with his own in a curbside trashcan. Eventually they wound up at her shop. Wordlessly they walked up the steps and onto the porch. Anna sat down on the sofa.

"Can I ask you another question?" he said.

She didn't know what he might want to ask, but he looked a little playful, and she was curious. "Sure," she said.

"I know I'm not the most sophisticated guy on the planet, so I'm sorry if the answer should be obvious," he said. "But what, exactly, is a lilac pointe?"

She laughed. "No, it's not obvious. Pointe refers to pointe shoes, the kind of shoe that ballerinas wear. And lilac—that has to do with a dance, this ballet solo. It's from *The Sleeping Beauty*. I don't know how much you know about fairy tales, but there's this lilac fairy… oh, you don't want to hear this."

"No, I do," he said, sitting opposite her on the rocker.

She studied him, remembering how Greg would coach her before campaign dinners and meet-and-greets. "They ask you about you, but they really want to talk about themselves," he'd say. "So please, don't start talking about ballet, even if they act like they want to hear it. They're just being polite. Believe me, it gets boring!" She'd roll her eyes and slap his arm, but he was so boyish and good-natured when he teased her like that, she never could get mad. And deep inside, she suspected he was right. Nobody they met was actually there for an intense talk about ballet.

But Aidan wasn't one of Greg's donors or supporters. And he looked like he genuinely wanted to hear her.

"Okay, if you're sure," she said, not certain how to begin. It had been a long time since she'd covered this ground. "The story starts with the birth of a princess. And some good fairies give her nice presents, like beauty and courage. But a wicked fairy plants a curse, saying the princess will die when she turns sixteen. Then it's the lilac fairy's turn, and while she can't erase the curse, she changes it, so that instead of dying, the princess falls asleep for a hundred years and is awoken by a prince's kiss. So the lilac fairy basically saves the day."

"And that's why the dance is important?"

"It's important because it's beautiful," she said. "It's big and grand, and it has these"—she grasped for the right words—"these repeating phrases of glorious steps that the ballerina gets to do again and again. Lots of chances to get it perfect."

"And was that you? The ballerina in the dance?"

She held his gaze for a moment, wishing she could say yes. "It was supposed to be. I was supposed to dance it in my first performance in New York. But right before the dress rehearsal, my father went back into the hospital. I was so upset. I never should have gone on. I fell, and basically destroyed my ankle."

"I'm sorry," Aidan said. "What happened with your dad?"

"He died that night. He'd been sick for a while." She looked down, clasping her hands together against her chest. It rattled her, revealing this long-ago episode. She never talked about this period of her life. It was so painful to remember, how she'd gone from having so much to having nothing. She'd tried to track down Hope, but couldn't reach her anywhere. And then there were the money problems. Her father's savings had been eaten up by medical bills, and with her ankle ruined, there was no longer any chance of her receiving an invitation to join a dance company. She was just one month away from being evicted from the apartment she'd shared with her father when she got the job offer with Roe & Durst. She'd known that she wasn't qualified. She'd known that her lecherous boss wasn't hiring her for her event planning experience. But she had to take it. She needed the job.

She wiped her cheeks. "I don't normally get like this. The truth is, if I hadn't broken my ankle, I wouldn't have met Greg, or had my kids, or anything. So it was all for the best."

She felt him watch her, and she thought he was staying quiet because he believed she needed him to. "Lots of chances to get it perfect, huh?" he finally said. "No wonder you loved that dance. Who wouldn't?"

"Would you like to see it?" she asked. She didn't know what had given her the nerve to ask that. She thought maybe it was like the hot dogs. They were developing that kind of friendship. Where they invited each other into their worlds. Where they were grateful to accept the invitations.

"It's on YouTube," she said. "The Hamburg Ballet Theatre does my favorite version."

She reached into her bag for her key and unlocked the door. The silvery chime whispered as they stepped quietly inside. She put on one set of lights. The sales floor glowed golden. There was something deliciously tantalizing about her inviting him in like this. About having the power to enter this space at night. It was like knowing a secret.

She led him to the office, apologizing for the time it would take to get the desktop computer going. "I planned to use Greg's iPad this summer, but I can't find it anywhere. I thought he kept it in his desk."

He told her it was no problem, he wasn't in a rush, and he brought the chair around from the other side of the desk. She typed into the search box, and when the YouTube video started, she maximized the image so it filled the screen. The orchestra began, the semicircle of purple- and red-costumed dancers filled the stage, and then the gorgeous prima ballerina—dressed in lilac and gold, her perfectly done hair pulled back into a jewel-encrusted bun—appeared in the corner. She performed the sequence, a high battement to the side, a bow with the leg forward, a crossover step and an arabesque, and repeated it three times. Each time bigger and better than the time before. She filled the music with grace and confidence, life and movement. She was the most beautiful prima ballerina in the world.

"That's my aunt," Anna said.

"Hope? Wow, look at that. She's stunning," Aidan said.

"Isn't it amazing, how easy she makes it look?" Anna was almost whispering. "That's the magic. And she was so good at it. The harder it is, the more effortless she makes it seem. People think ballet is so artsy and flowery, but…" She tensed her fingers, looking again for the words. "That's an illusion. It's about lines and angles. Precision. It's strength and control. And my aunt had it all. I love that."

The young Hope progressed to the next sequence of steps, a pirouette combination, repeating it four times as she moved backward along the same imaginary diagonal line on which she'd come forward. "She looks so joyful, doesn't she?" Anna said. "Like the steps are a gift she's giving the world. See? It gets more and more perfect as the music goes on."

The video ended, and she put her elbows on the desk and looked at him. "I get goosebumps whenever I see it," she said.

He nodded. "But I didn't see… look, I'm totally in the dark, I don't know anything…"

"You didn't see what?"

"I didn't see her doing the steps more perfectly. They looked perfect from the beginning. I just saw her doing them… differently."

"*Differently?*" She'd talked about the solo hundreds of times, maybe thousands. She'd never heard anyone say this before.

He pressed a hand to the middle of his chest. "Okay, I'm a guy who doesn't know what he's talking about. But… here, can I show you what I see?"

She nodded, intrigued, and he reached over to the computer to replay the video, his sleeve lightly grazing her wrist.

"Okay, so the first time, it's beautiful," he said. "And now she repeats it and… okay, her chin's a little higher, but is that better? It doesn't look better to me, just a different way of doing it. And now… her body is a little more turned to the side I guess, but the first time was just as good."

Anna rested her chin on her hand and watched the dance one more time, not sure if he had said something naive or pointed out something very profound.

"I don't know… to me, she's doing it better," she said. "The steps look better, prettier, each time. At least, I think they do. Because that's the whole point of ballet. You learn to start out small, so you have room to build."

She shook her head. "I always thought that's what made ballet better than real life," she said. "You get second chances to do it better."

They were both quiet for a moment. Then Aidan spoke.

"That sounds better to me, too," he said.

A little while later she locked up the store, and as they started for her house, the conversation turned to business. She told him that one of the local churches had booked a salsa night for singles, and the Seniors Club was planning a night of swing dancing. He told her he would give The Lilac Pointe a central spot on the hill for SummerFest, so they could run a series of sample dance classes.

"Are you this good to everyone?" she asked. "Or just to people who have no idea what they're doing and have no business owning a store?"

He laughed and shook his head. "It's my job, helping store owners and making the town stronger. I don't play favorites. But don't sell yourselves short. You and Hope are doing something very interesting. Creative. It reminds me of when I had a store. How much fun it was for my family."

He looked at the pavement. "And just now, listening to you and watching that dance—it got me out of my own head for a while. I needed that."

She felt her cheeks warm. She had enjoyed Aidan's company tonight, just as she had the other times she'd talked with him. But she hadn't given much thought to how he was feeling. It was nice to know that he enjoyed her company, too. And now that she knew that, she was moved to hear more about him. He had invited her to tell him about herself tonight, and it had felt good to do it. She wanted him to have the same chance.

"Tell me about your store," she said.

"My jewelry store? It was a neighborhood place. My mom would set up fresh coffee and people would come in and stay for a cup, look at the newspaper my dad kept on the counter, and argue about politics. People liked my dad. He made everyone important. On 9/11 everyone stopped by, just to check in on everyone else. My dad set up a TV on the counter."

Anna looked at his profile in the darkness. No wonder he grew up loving retailing.

"And people bought stuff, of course—not enough to make us rich, but enough," he said. "When I turned eighteen, my dad made me his partner. I was so proud of that place. A pretty store not too far from the beach. When it was quiet out, you could hear the waves."

"Waves?" she said. "Somehow I thought you said you were from Rochester."

"What? No, I am." He dug his hands deeper into his pockets. "Lake, I meant near the lake. You could hear the lake water, the lapping. Anyway, my mom's been gone for a long time, and my dad has dementia. The last time I saw him, he didn't know who I was. He started failing just when my wife was dying. What a horrible time."

"I'm sure," she said. Then, wanting to say something positive, she added, "It sounds like your dad was a great father."

They reached the start of her front walk. "We should probably say goodbye here," she said, looking at her watch. It was almost ten. "My kids will be asleep. I don't want to wake them."

He nodded. "I should be on my way, anyway," he said. "I told Liam I'd be home when he got back from swim practice."

"Thanks for introducing me to hot dogs," she said.

"Thanks for agreeing to come. You were pretty adventurous."

She stood still, letting the word linger. *Adventurous.* It wasn't a word she typically associated with herself.

"Well, goodnight then," he said, and as she watched him walk away, she couldn't help feeling let down that they hadn't arranged to see each other again. But she figured it was just as well. They both were busy. They both had kids to take care of. And she was leaving at the end of the summer, anyway. Still, he was someone she could talk to. She would have liked to see their friendship grow.

She was starting up the walk when she heard him jogging behind her.

"Anna?" he said quietly.

She turned, surprised.

"I know I won the bet and all, and I don't owe you a dinner," he said. "And I know you've got kids, and I've got a son, and there are probably a million reasons I shouldn't do this. But can I take you to dinner at Sogni anyway?"

She started to speak, intending to say no, because of all the things she'd listed in her head. And yet something felt right.

"I would love to," she said.

CHAPTER FIFTEEN

"So the kids at the New Manorsville Kids Club, they basically have nothing. I mean, *nothing.*"

Keon looked at her, his eyes squinting in the sun, his elbows on the round bistro table. "And it's crazy, Hope—it's crazy when you think they're in New Manorsville, less than two miles from all this wealth." He stretched his arms wide.

Hope leaned forward, matching her elbows with his. They were sitting on the patio of Smoothie Dudes, each with an untouched cup of pink, frothy liquid. It was a week after July Fourth, and Keon had stopped by the store that morning on his way to work and asked if she could break away for a few minutes. They'd decided to go next door, since she didn't have much time before her next class. Trey had come right over with his latest trial of the lilac-themed recipe, but Hope hadn't even taken a sip. The smell was overpowering, like a cheap, plug-in air freshener. She'd pressed Keon's hand down before he lifted his cup, and whispered that if he was thirsty, there were now water bottles in her office.

"Jayson is big on community service," Keon continued. "We encourage our students to help the kids at the Kids Club with homework during the year. So, I'm thinking—why wait until fall this year? Why not start now?"

Keon was one of the most amazing people she'd ever met. He was so effusively enthusiastic, and such a cheerleader for Jayson, almost to the point of being a cliché: the cheerful and ultra-involved academic administrator you'd find on some high-school-based TV show. He always wore shirts with a Jayson logo, and carried a Jayson backpack, and when he saw his students in the store, he always addressed them by their last name: "How are you doing today, Ms. Reynolds?" "How is your morning going, Mr. Tate?" When someone asked him how he was feeling, he never said fine or okay, but "Super," or "Could not be better!" And he never said "Bye," or "Thanks," to people; it was always, "Have a wonderful afternoon," or "Make it a good one, now."

Who would have ever imagined that she'd enjoy being with someone like that? Not her, that was for sure. But his candor, and his enjoyment of life, and his total lack of even a shred of irony—it was so refreshing. They had had a perfect night on July Fourth. The humidity had lifted earlier that day, and the gentle sound of the lake lapping against the rocks had been hypnotic, as they'd waited in the dark for the fireworks to begin. He'd brought a blanket to spread over the sandy bank, which was wonderful since it hadn't occurred to her to bring one. And he'd put his Jayson windbreaker over her shoulders, which had also been wonderful, since she'd worn her favorite camisole top but hadn't given a thought to the predicted drop in temperature that night. He was a planner, but it came naturally to him, so he wasn't self-righteous or prideful. She didn't feel stupid or embarrassed for leaving her apartment so unprepared. She felt like she was okay the way she was.

"So, my idea is… Hope, are you listening?" he asked.

"I am, I am," she assured him, not wanting to admit that she'd been reliving July Fourth. "I'm sorry, it's just that I'm teaching in a few minutes. I should head back."

She grabbed the smoothie cups so Trey wouldn't see that they were still full, and threw them into a trashcan.

"A little too intense, maybe mellow it down a little?" she called over. He waved and went back into his shop.

"So your idea is…" she said.

"My idea is, we bring the kids from the Kids Club here, say, twice a week. Maybe you do a short pro bono ballet class. Maybe Maz—the hip-hop teacher, he's started teaching here, right? Maybe he does a pro bono class, too. Then we get the Jayson students to donate their time as teaching assistants, which involves them in community service while also giving them some real teaching experience."

They reached the front door. "What do you think?" he said.

"I think you're exhausting," she teased. "You're like Anna's little girl, Evie. You never slow down. But she's ten!"

"Hey, don't change the subject. Do you like the idea or not? If it's a go, I can get this thing moving pretty fast. Jayson has an endowment for community service—it's not big but I bet I can get some money to pay for a bus to bring the kids over."

"I think it's an amazing idea," she said. "Now get out of my way, I have to get to work."

She went into the store, sure that Anna would go for the idea, too, once they had a chance to talk about it. Anna loved helping people, which was one of the reasons why she'd been such an asset to Greg's career. And she'd been in an especially upbeat mood lately. Ever since her hot dog date with Aidan two nights ago.

With a wave to Anna on the sales floor, she headed down the hall and into the studio to begin the pointe class, one of two classes she'd been hired by Jayson to teach. It was her third pointe session with the girls, and she initiated the warm-up hopeful as always. But as with the previous two sessions, she found herself disappointed as the class went on. The girls were talented, there was no doubt about that. But there was something disturbing in their attitude—a swagger, and arrogance. It showed up when they failed to finish a combination, claiming they couldn't remember how it ended, or they were too tired. Or when they dropped down after a single or double pirouette, acting like it wasn't worth the effort to go for a triple.

"That's it for today—good class, but I need you all to put more into it," she said when the hour was up. "Let's work a little harder next time—and dancers? Excuse me?"

There were a few groans as the students, who were nearly all out the door, filed back into the studio and formed a semicircle. Hope saw Melanie roll her eyes at Kristin, as they all placed the toe of one foot behind the heel of the other, then dropped their chins, opened their arms, and sank into their final curtsy.

"Thank you, Hope," they said in singsong unison.

"You're welcome," Hope said, and lowered her head in return.

They giggled their way out of the studio, and Hope followed behind. That bothered her most of all, their mocking of "reverence," the traditional practice of thanking the teacher at the end of ballet class. She suspected their scorn masked some fear—of losing status and looking uncool in front of their friends. She knew this wasn't new or unique—no doubt there'd always been dancers who behaved this way. But those dancers never got anywhere. She remembered how Anna had been when she trained—earnest and open and vulnerable. You had to be that way if you wanted to succeed as a dancer. Hope worried that this attitude would hold the girls back—in dance and maybe in life as well.

"And I don't know what to do about it," she told Keon the next evening, as they had dinner in her kitchen. Actually, it was a stretch to call it a kitchen. There was just a table in front of a sink and a row of appliances: a small refrigerator, an oven, a tiny dishwasher that didn't work, and a small stacked washer-dryer. And it was a stretch to call her place an apartment—it was basically one room, with an oversized closet where she kept her bed, and a tiny bathroom in one corner. It was the kind of place a young person just starting out should live in, Hope thought as she went to open the door for him; not a place for a woman old enough to have a grown niece with children of her own.

But Keon hadn't looked surprised or appalled or anything when he entered, after he'd climbed the stairs of the building. He'd looked happy to see her, and glad to offer up the Chinese food he'd brought, along with the box of brownies he'd picked up at Pearl's.

"There's a lot you can do about it," he said. "You can talk to me, or to their other teachers, or even to Dara, the department head. Just because you're not a full-time faculty member, that doesn't give them the right to disrespect you."

"But I want them to like me. I don't want them to leave."

Keon rubbed his forehead. "Where would they go? Hope, this is absurd. This isn't about liking or not liking, leaving or not leaving. What's that thing you said—that ritual, the bowing to the teacher at the end of class? That's about respect. For you. If they're not taking that seriously…"

He poured himself more of the lemonade she'd made after work. He never touched alcohol, he'd told her, because he wanted to be able to tell his students honestly that you didn't need alcohol to have a good time.

"Tell me, did you ever talk to them about the shoe fittings, and how you knew they were taking advantage of you?"

She shook her head. "Not directly. I didn't want to embarrass them. I didn't want to confront them." She rolled her eyes at how childish she sounded.

"Okay, but you're their teacher now," he told her. "*You* have some responsibility here. You're not doing your job if you don't address their bad behavior and make them accountable." He waited and watched her as she let his words sink in. Then he got up and started clearing the table.

She followed him to the sink. "How are you so smart about all this?" she asked.

"I can't take credit," he said, and explained that he'd learned from the best—his parents were schoolteachers, his aunt was a minister, his uncle was a social worker, his sister ran an after-school program in the Bronx, and his cousin was a nurse.

"I grew up not too far from the Kids Club I told you about," he said. "We lived in a two-bedroom apartment when I was little, and I slept in the living room until my parents saved enough to buy a small house. But they taught us about love and they taught us about faith, and they took us to church every Sunday, and they encouraged us to work hard. And in the end, we turned out pretty well." He pointed to the tattoo on his forearm, a thin, blurry string of numbers and symbols. "I got this fifteen years ago, when my parents couldn't handle the stairs anymore and decided to move," he said. "It's faded so you can't see it so well, but it's the coordinates for that house. It was the happiest place on earth, no matter what the Disney folks would have you believe."

She'd wondered what the story was behind that tattoo, but had been too self-conscious to ask. Now she thought about how lucky he was, to have such good memories of his childhood. She thought about her own childhood, how she never knew her father, how her mother had flitted from man to man and seemed to consider her late-in-life daughter a burden. She knew how relieved her mother was when she finally left home and went to live with David and Anna. She wondered now if her life would have been different, and whether she'd have stayed alone and estranged from her brother and then from Anna for so long, if she'd had a mother who truly wanted her.

They finished the dishes, and he sat down on the sofa to continue his story. "I went to the state university at Albany and stayed on for a Master's in education," he said. "But I didn't want to be a teacher. I'd seen how frustrated my parents were. They never had enough funding or support, or freedom to do the kinds of creative projects they wanted with the kids. I decided to go into administration. I wanted to fix the system from the inside."

She put the leftovers in the refrigerator, and he scooted over on the sofa to make room for her. "I stayed in the public schools for a while, but I always liked the idea of working with older students. So I moved to Jayson. I've been there… let's see, I'm sixty-two now—more than twenty years."

She sat down where he'd gestured. "So you're sixty-two and you've never been married? How is that possible? You're such a good guy."

"Well, I've had relationships. I even lived with someone for a few years. But I could never pull the trigger. I don't know, maybe I spent too much time thinking there was someone better out there. Maybe I idolized my parents' marriage too much. Anyway, I got busy with work and was helping my parents as they got older—and here I am. Life goes by in a flash, you know? One day you wake up and you're sixty-two and still single. And maybe not as happy as you might have been.

"And you?" he asked. "How is it that you're still single?"

She grimaced and looked away. "I had a habit of picking bad guys when I was younger. And hurting the people I loved. I haven't been involved with anyone in a long time. It's just not worth it."

He jutted his chin forward. "You don't really mean that, do you? You don't mean that if the right person came along, you'd rather be alone?"

"I absolutely mean it," she told him. "And I'm not alone. I have Anna and her children to watch over and take care of. Why would I risk that?"

"Why would you think a relationship would put that at risk?" he said. "Hope, I hardly know you, and I know Anna even less. But even so, I can tell she adores you. Why would you think that she'd stop loving you if you ever let a man into your life? She can't possibly be that selfish."

"No, she's not selfish at all," Hope said. "It's just the opposite. The truth is…" She looked down into her lap. "The truth is, I haven't always deserved her love. And now that I have her back in my life, I'm never going to let that happen again." She stopped herself from explaining further. Yes, Keon was caring and sweet, but the conversation was getting way too personal. She pointed to the refrigerator. "Do you want more lemonade?"

He chuckled softly and shook his head. "No," he said. "No, I don't want any lemonade."

She laughed, too, at her obvious attempt to change the subject. "Look, Keon, it's not all that big a deal," she said, readying herself to tell the truth. "I fell for a married man once, and my heart was broken, and I was too caught up in my own silly disappointment to pay attention to Anna when she needed me. And that's all there is to it. I'm too old to fall in love again. All I want to do is be a good aunt to Anna and a good great-aunt to her kids."

She took another look at the kitchen. "Actually, I could use some lemonade. And did I hear you say before that there are brownies in that bag?"

They had a quick and mostly quiet dessert, and soon afterward, Keon left for the evening. Hope turned off the overhead light near the door and walked back to sit on the couch. The apartment was now lit only by a table lamp, its yellow light casting a small, lonely shadow on the floor. She had told Keon that her love affair was no big deal, but in fact it was huge, and he didn't know the half of it. He didn't know that she had fallen head over heels for Andre. He didn't know that she found him charming and witty and incredibly attractive, and that she had believed him when he said he'd leave his wife and marry her. He didn't know that right after she quit the ballet to live with Andre in Paris, he told her he'd decided to work things out with his wife. He didn't know that a few days after Andre dumped her, she found out she was pregnant.

And he didn't know she'd planned to stay in Paris and keep the baby, even though she had no job and no money. He didn't know that she returned to New York, intending to ask her brother for help. He didn't know that when she got there, she couldn't bring herself to admit to Anna and David that she was pregnant, or that she had walked away from her dance career. He didn't know that she ultimately lost the baby, and had been so overwhelmed by her own grief and shame that she stayed away from her family for years.

Hope turned off the lamp and went to get ready for bed. She was sorry she had ended the evening so abruptly. She liked Keon, and she admired him, and if she were ever going to get involved with someone, he was the kind of person she'd like to get involved with. But she was too ashamed to tell him her story, and she couldn't start a relationship with him if she was unwilling to be truthful. Her only choice was to push him away and try to forget that she ever thought she could have feelings for him.

In bed, she reached over to set her alarm for six-thirty. Anna and the kids were expecting her to bring bagels the next morning, and she wanted to be first on line at Pearl's. She had to make sure she got the cinnamon raisin ones Evie loved, which always sold out quickly.

CHAPTER SIXTEEN

Finally it was Saturday.

The five days since the hot dogs had felt so strange. Anna had barely paid attention to the everyday routines of her life—getting the kids up and out in the morning, helping customers during the day, making dinner at night. When the realtor came by to view the house and go over a printout of comparable prices, she couldn't even concentrate. Her mind seemed always to be on Aidan. She often imagined how it would be to feel his warm presence next to her as they entered Sogni di Lago. She'd never been there, but she knew it was fancy and elegant, with lots of rooms where small, candlelit tables nestled. Her stomach jumped when she thought about how it would feel to see him across the table from her, his jaw covered by that neat layer of stubble he wore so well.

The idea of abandoning herself to the evening made her chest rise with anticipation. She never would have imagined even a month ago that she could be drawn to another man. Was this how things were supposed to go? That suddenly, in the middle of so much grief and loss, she'd start thinking about someone new?

"Maybe it's too soon," she told Hope on Friday, as they created a Caribbean-themed display for an upcoming library fundraiser in the studio. Her kids had walked to the store after camp to help out—Evie was working with Melanie near the shoe armoire to untangle a string of tropical-themed lights, while Liam and Zac were in the office, creating a mass email and some social media publicity for the event. Anna was pleased at how comfortable her kids were with Melanie and Liam. She longed for the moment she would know for sure that they had finally turned the corner and were emerging from their grief. But deep inside, she worried that moment was still very far away. Zac had started getting up nearly every night, and she could hear him turning the bathroom faucet on and off, and then saying he was fine and it was nothing when she got up to ask what was wrong. And Evie was so attached to those plastic sunglasses in her backpack. She never let Anna open the backpack to retrieve her wet bathing suit and pool towel, but instead insisted on pulling them out herself.

"Too much is happening too fast for them," she said.

Hope set up a ladder by the window. "Why do you say that? They seem pretty happy."

"Sometimes they do, but other times… it's hard to tell if this is all just normal growing up or if they're still not okay. Anyway, I don't think they're ready. I don't think *I'm* ready either."

"Ready for what?" Hope said. "Sweetheart, I think you're overreacting. It's only dinner."

"*Sssh*," Anna said, gesturing with her chin toward Evie and Melanie. She reached inside a carton atop one of the ottomans and began pulling out Margarita glasses with *Born to Salsa* imprinted in red. "I don't want them to know," she said, her voice low. "They have no idea why they're spending tomorrow evening with you."

Hope tilted her head. "Anna, you're allowed to go out to dinner. You know Greg wouldn't have wanted you to be sad for the rest of your life."

"I guess. I mean, I know you're right, and Aidan's a very sweet guy—"

"And the reason the kids are spending tomorrow night with me is because I want them," she said. "I've been wanting to take them to the county fair ever since you got back in town. The ferris wheel is open, and there are carnival games, and they have a band playing, too. We'll have a ball." She motioned to Evie, who came running across the room with a freshly untangled string of lights. "Isn't that right, peanut?" she said, and gave the little girl a loud kiss on the cheek. "I was just telling Mom that we're going to have so much fun tomorrow night, right?"

"Yup!" Evie said and trotted back to Melanie.

Anna smiled, glad that her kids loved Hope as much as she did. "And Keon doesn't mind spending Saturday night with them?"

Hope started up the ladder. "I'm not seeing him this weekend. I cancelled."

"What? No, you shouldn't cancel your plans for me."

"It's okay. I'll see him another time."

Anna leaned on the carton and shook her head. "This all feels wrong. And it's not just about the kids, it's everything." She held up a hand to pause the conversation as Liam and Zac emerged from the office to say they were hungry and would go get a table down the block at Sal's. Anna called over to Evie and Melanie to join them.

"What feels so wrong?" Hope asked once the kids were all gone.

Anna picked up the string of lights that Evie had brought over, and handed it to Hope at the top of the ladder. "It's just that Aidan hasn't been alone for that long either, and I don't really know him. He said the other night that the jewelry store he owned was near the beach. But it was Rochester, a few hours west of here, and that's not near a beach. And when I asked him about it, he said he meant to say the lake."

"So? You can call the area around a lake a beach."

"No, but he also mentioned the waves. And when I asked him about it, he got nervous, as if I caught him on something. And when I googled him last night—"

Hope's eyes widened. "You googled him?"

"I wanted to know more. But I couldn't find a thing about a jewelry store in Rochester owned by an Aidan Lawrence."

"Maybe it wasn't exactly in Rochester. Maybe it was outside of Rochester."

"And then he said there were millions of reasons he shouldn't have dinner with me again. Why would he say that? It all feels like a mistake."

Hope finished arranging the lights and tugged on the end of the cord.

"Sweetheart, the problem is you're coming at this from a very unusual angle. You met Greg when he was just starting out. Of course he was squeaky clean. But Aidan's… what, twenty-five years older than that? His life is more complicated. Everyone's life gets messy. I know you like things to be all clean and perfect, but they aren't. Nothing is."

"I don't think Greg was perfect. I don't need things to be clean and perfect—"

"Of course you do. It runs in the family. I'm like that, too. So was your dad." She stepped down from the ladder. "Look at the ballet solo you and I love so much. It's no secret why: sixteen counts in one direction, sixteen counts in the other direction. Perfectly clean steps, repeated over and over."

"All ballets have repeating steps."

"Maybe so, but the Lilac Variation *really* repeats. The opening combination repeats *four times*. Four times, to get it perfect."

Anna shook her head teasingly. "Aidan tells me that's not what the ballet's about. He tells me that in the video, you were doing the steps differently, not better."

"You showed him my YouTube video?"

"He wanted to see it."

"You found a man who wanted to watch ballet on the first night you went out with him? And who really thought about it? Hang onto him, sweetheart, he's a keeper—"

"Hellooo!" Trey said from the doorway, carrying two little cups. "I toned down the smell but bumped up the pink. Lavender-infused smoothie with a pinch of tangy hibiscus crystals. Give it a try."

Anna took a sip, and couldn't stop her lips from descending at the corners.

Hope was more direct. "Ugh! Tastes like soap!"

Trey sighed. "Oh, no. That's what Stan said. Back to the drawing board, I guess."

"Wait, I'm leaving, too," Hope said. "This cord isn't long enough, I want to run down to the hardware store before it closes to pick up another." She took Trey's arm and looked back at Anna. "Do you mind closing up?"

"No, I have to wait for the kids to get back from dinner anyway," she said as she waved them off, and began stuffing the tissue paper from the glasses back into the carton. Maybe Hope was right, she thought. Maybe she was feeling guilty because this second dinner felt so much more like a date than the hot dogs did. Maybe her guilt was making her paranoid. Maybe some people used the terms "beach" and "lake" interchangeably.

But still, she thought. There was something strange about the way he'd said it.

*

"Aunt Hope's here!" Anna called, and gave each of her kids a kiss as they headed out the door. She was glad that Zac had finally cheered up. He'd been scowling all morning about spending a Saturday night with his sister and aunt. But then it turned out that two of Zac's friends were also going to the fair, and the band was a local group the boys all liked. Anna had agreed that Zac could sit with his friends.

"But only if there's always a grown-up around, either Aunt Hope or somebody's parent," she said. "And Aunt Hope always has to know exactly where you are. Got it?"

He'd nodded, and so with mixed feelings, she got them ready to go.

"You're going to be okay, Mom, right?" Evie called back as she scampered toward Hope's car.

Anna gave a thumbs up and watched them drive away. Then she closed the door and went upstairs to get ready. Her footsteps echoed loudly in the empty house, and she told herself to stop thinking so much—as Hope had said, she was doing nothing wrong. She took a cool shower and focused on how good the soft spray of the water felt on her skin, which helped her to relax. Wrapped in a towel, she reached inside the middle drawer of the vanity for her brush and her hair dryer. But when she took them out, something felt wrong. Greg's hairbrush was missing. It was one of those wooden oval ones made in England, which he thought it was cool to use. And he liked how it made his hair, which could be unruly when he came home from the lake or when he woke up, look smoother and neater. She thought he kept one here and one back home. She thought she'd seen the one here a few times this summer. But maybe not. She told herself to put the matter out of her mind; it didn't make sense to worry about it. But that made her feel even worse: if she made herself forget about the brush, was that the same as making herself forget about Greg?

She shook her head to push the thought away, and went into her closet for the black, spaghetti-strap dress she'd worn to the gala for the mental health center in Syracuse last summer. It was maybe a little too formal, but the restaurant was fancy, and she didn't have anything else that was appropriate. She slipped the dress on, but her fingers felt so clumsy and her arms lacked muscle tone, so she couldn't get it zipped. Her heart raced: she didn't know if she could reach Hope on her cell phone and ask her to come back and help, and she couldn't answer the door in a half-zipped dress. Thankfully she finally got the zipper up—although the effort left her so sweaty that she had to sit down and cool off.

Her make-up was another disaster, as her shaky fingers created eyeliner smudges that looked like massive storm clouds, and twice she had to wipe her eyelids clean and start again. And she had such a hard time working the clasp on her good necklace that she eventually decided to go without jewelry.

But finally she was ready, with ten minutes to spare. Pulling the straps of her dressy sandals over her heels, she tried to calm down by repeating in her head what Hope had said—that Greg wouldn't want her to be sad for the rest of her life. The problem was, she wasn't sure Hope was right. Greg had always been devoted to her and the kids, and he might not have wanted to believe she'd ever care for someone else, even after he was gone. He had decided to drive home from the Metropolitan New York Business Awards dinner just as the storm hit, instead of waiting it out or even taking a room at the hotel, as other attendees were doing. She'd begged him on the phone to stay put—the TV said the winds could be gale force, and driving would be treacherous. But he was tired and he wanted to come home to keep them all safe. Why else would he have gotten on those roads?

The doorbell rang, and she took one last look at herself in her mirror, feeling like a sixteen-year-old going on a date for the first time. Then she went downstairs and opened the door.

And there Aidan was. He had on a gray sport coat and slacks over a slightly darker gray-green shirt that was open at the neck. The colors of his clothing complemented him, bringing out the gray in his eyes and the sun-kissed tone of his skin. He looked handsome, but also a little out of his element, like a boy whose mother had cleaned him up for church.

"Hey," he said. "You look beautiful." He held out a bouquet of lilacs wrapped in cellophane. "I couldn't get them out of my mind after watching the ballet," he said.

She took it and breathed in the sweet fragrance. "Thank you," she said. "That's so nice of you." Greg had never bought her lilacs, which was kind of funny, since the house was called Lilac House. But his mother had loved hydrangeas, so hydrangeas had always been his default choice. She'd come to love them, too. She'd carried white ones in her bridal bouquet.

"But how did you find them?" she asked. "We never even see our lilac bushes in bloom here. They only bloom in the spring."

"So I discovered," he said. "But the florist in town knows shrubs. He researched a few species that bloom in the summer, and was able to get me some cuttings."

She backed up from the door and went to put the flowers in a vase, glad that he was perceptive enough to wait in the hallway while she went to the kitchen. It was awfully romantic, the lilacs, and she wasn't ready for it. If the rest of the night was this intense, she didn't know how she'd cope. Her hands were shaking as she pulled out a vase from the cabinet, so that it clinked repeatedly against the other glass objects around it. Luckily nothing fell and shattered. Walking back, she set the vase on the entranceway table. Then they left, and Aidan led her to his car, a weathered Audi sedan. He opened the door, and she folded herself into the passenger seat.

The restaurant was darker and even more romantic than Anna had anticipated. The tea lights—on tables covered in starched white tablecloths—flickered a warm golden-orange. The maître d' led them to a room with a wall of floor-to-ceiling windows, and sat them at a table overlooking the lake, which shimmered dark blue against the dusky sky. He held her chair for her, and Aidan waited until she was seated before he sat down opposite her. She was struck by his gallantry, but it also unsettled her. Greg had been a much more casual person. He'd never even suggested once that they go to this restaurant, even though they'd been coming to Lake Summers every year since they met.

The waiter put the wine list on the table, and Aidan offered it to her. She instinctively chose a California Chardonnay, because that was what Greg had always liked. Actually, she thought, he was more partial to reds, Cabernets especially. Although in the summer he chose whites, unless there was a good selection of craft beers…

"Anna?" Aidan was leaning toward her, his eyebrows raised.

"I'm sorry… what?"

"I was just asking you how your day was."

"It was good, it… was good," she said, forcing herself to pay better attention. "Melanie came in to help Hope, so I took the kids out to brunch and to the lake—and then we stopped at the store and Melanie was showing Evie how to use some of the new hair clips… and you? Did you have a good day?"

He nodded. "Watched Liam's swim practice this morning—he's looking good. Especially his backstroke. Then I got an email from the head of the village board. They're willing to install a few more benches on Main Street. Seems like it's turning out to be a good summer for business. Which maybe isn't so great, since I was brought in to help the retailers. Things get too good around here, I'll be out of a job." He smiled at his joke.

"Oh?" she asked. "And what would you do in that case? Maybe go back to the beach… I mean, Rochester? Would you maybe do that?" The words came out of her mouth before she had time to think them through, and she regretted them immediately. It was just that she'd started to feel claustrophobic, as though she'd climbed into one of the boxes that the salsa merchandise came in.

He looked confused. "No. We're not going back."

"That's good," she said. "I'm glad. But maybe you might want to… open a store again? Or something?" She knew she was sounding unhinged, but it was challenging trying to keep the conversation going. She picked up her water glass and took a large gulp. Aidan was studying her.

The waiter returned and poured Anna a sip of wine. It was delicious, cold and citrusy, and she nodded. He filled their glasses, and she watched the wine shimmer, anxious to drink more and relax. She looked at Aidan, who was so handsome in his gray-green shirt. She felt the air conditioning kick in, and was aware of just how bare her shoulders were. Suddenly she remembered that the dress she was wearing was also the one she'd had on the night she and Greg went into the backyard after the Syracuse gala. She hadn't made the connection earlier, but she grasped it now, and the thought made her feel sick. She recalled taking the dress to the dry cleaner, hoping he wouldn't ask about the spots where the mud had caked. She laughed with Greg about it later that night…

"What do you think?" Aidan was asking.

She blinked. "Excuse me?"

"I was just asking what we should drink to," he said.

She lifted her shoulders. She didn't know what to say. Happiness? Good times? The future? They all sounded way too suggestive.

"Let's drink to… your store," he said. "A long, prosperous future for The Lilac Pointe."

It was sweet and thoughtful, just as she would have expected if someone had asked her what kind of a toast Aidan would propose. They were the words that were coming to define him in her mind, and she felt more scared than pleased about it. She lifted her glass to clink it with his.

He went on to talk about Liam and some delivery mix-up at Pearl's, and while it seemed like a funny story, Anna had trouble following it. She forced a few laughs in what she hoped were appropriate places. A silence followed, and she reached again for her water. The draft from the air conditioning had stopped, and now she was burning, as though the tea lights were searing her skin. Her dress was so tight she could barely breathe. The waiter reeled off specials, but the only one she heard was branzino. Yes, she thought, branzino, a simple fish, easy to eat, and the sooner it arrived, the sooner she could go home. The restaurant's front door seemed far away. There had to be a back door, maybe through the kitchen…

"Anna, are you okay?" Aidan asked.

"I'm fine," she said. She didn't want to run out. It would be too mean to do to this very nice man. "It's… I'm sorry, but I'm feeling very strange. You're such a nice person, Aidan. But I don't think I'm ready for an evening like this."

He nodded. "I knew this was a quiet place, I guess I didn't realize it would be so dark and… anyway, I'm sorry. I don't think I'm ready, either. Let's just think of this as a friendly dinner. Nothing more. Okay?"

She nodded. That would be perfect.

"So after you mentioned that Greg was in politics, I looked up a few articles about him," he said. "He sounds pretty impressive. One of those unusual politicians that people actually like."

"Everyone loved him," she said. "He had a way of always doing the right thing. And he was a great dad, too. I remember one time around Christmas, Evie was seven, and she wanted a stick horse—you know, one of those toys that kids pretend they're riding on? She saw it at the store, and it was beautiful, with this snow-white mane and royal-blue reins. And I thought, that's crazy—it's a baby toy.

"But then one night Greg was working late, and I went to pick him up from the train station, and it was cold and starting to snow, and he came to the car carrying—of course—the stick horse. He didn't care if she was too old for it, he just saw that it meant something to her. She has it still. She never rode it, she never played with it like a toddler. She just had it and loved it. He was right. I was wrong."

They were quiet for a minute, as the story lingered. Then Aidan spoke. "I read about that train derailment. Sounds like he saved a lot of people."

"That was an unbelievable night," she told him. "The train derailed and Greg went there to help, and right then I went into labor with Zac. I got myself to the hospital, and I had no idea where he was. Zac was a few hours old by the time he made it over to us. I guess he knew we'd be okay. He always went where he was needed most."

She looked at him. "Tell me about your wife," she said.

"Emilia lit up any room she was in," he said, shaking his head as he knew what an unlikely couple they were, with him tending toward the serious and brooding. "Her father was one of my dad's best customers—that's how we met. He sent her east to college, thinking she'd become an investment banker or corporate lawyer. And she was smart enough, for sure. But she didn't want all that. She wanted to be a gym teacher. She worked at Liam's elementary school. We had a quiet life. It was a great life."

He took a sip of water, and she saw his hand shaking just a bit. He put the glass down and stroked the side of his jaw. She felt sad for him. He deserved that quiet, great life he once had.

"And then, out of nowhere, she gets cancer," he said. "We tried to make the best of the time we had left together. We went to Alaska for two weeks, the three of us. It was amazing. But I guess I ignored other parts of my life. Like my father, and our store. I knew my dad's memory was failing, but I didn't know how bad it was until after Emilia died. Turns out he… screwed up the business pretty bad. Really bad. We had to close down."

"I'm so, so sorry," she said.

"A few years ago, I never could have imagined where Liam and I would be now. I guess you feel the same." He twirled his wine glass. "But we like the town, we like the people. And lately things seem a little better. I've even gotten to learn a few new things about lilacs. I think there's something positive about that."

"And I got to learn about hot dogs," she said.

The waiter took their plates a short time later, and brought the check.

*

Back in town, Aidan parked in front of her house. He walked her to her door, and she took out her key.

"Thanks for coming out with me tonight," he said. "It was a great dinner, even though neither of us ate much. Hopefully it will taste good warmed over." He held out the plastic bag with their packed-up meals. They'd been too immersed in their memories to eat.

"Are you sure you don't want it?" she said.

"You take it," he said. "You have more mouths to feed than I do."

She smiled and accepted the bag. "I should go in, Hope will be bringing the kids home soon," she said. "Thanks, Aidan. I had a nice time."

He nodded and took a step back, and she knew he was giving her an opportunity to walk right into the house. She thought she should do just that. But her feet didn't turn. After a moment he moved closer, and when she still didn't step away, he reached out and lifted her chin with his hand. Then he brought his mouth down to hers. It was a sweet kiss, warm but restrained, longer than a friend's kiss but shorter than a lover's. His lips were full and firm. They felt good against hers, and she was sorry when it was over.

In the house, she waited a beat, and then went to the kitchen and looked out the front window. In the darkness, she watched him get back into his car and drive off. Soon she couldn't see any sign of him.

All she could see were glistening circles of light shining from the lampposts onto the street. Then a fine, silky rain started to fall.

CHAPTER SEVENTEEN

"Cute picture," Maxine said, gesturing with her chin toward the copy of the *Lake Summers Press* on the bar. She slid her pencil back into her hair. "I'll put this right in for you. Looks like Lonny did a nice job on that deck of his."

"What picture?" Aidan asked, but she was already on her way to the kitchen with his sandwich order. He'd been in meetings with town officials and bankers all day, so he hadn't had a chance to read the issue that came out this morning. He pulled the paper over and paged through it for photos, not knowing what he was looking for. Then he came upon a photo spread with a headline that spanned both pages: SUMMER FEVER HITS LAKE SUMMERS! He scanned the spread, which carried assorted pictures of people sunning by the lake, shopping on Main Street, and setting up blankets to watch an evening concert on the green. And then he found it: they were at the table in the corner, looking at each other and smiling, with a tray of five varieties lined up between them. "*Anna Harris, co-owner of dance shop The Lilac Pointe, and Aidan Lawrence, Lake Summers' retail consultant, sample a range of Lonny's choices*," the caption read.

"Oh boy," he mumbled, as he loosened his tie and unfastened the top button of his dress shirt. He wasn't comfortable in suits to begin with—he'd only worn one today because of the meetings—and now he felt like he was choking. It had been a week and a half since their dinner at Sogni. He'd seen Anna several times since then, stopping to say hello when he spotted her on Main

Street, or dropping by the store and pretending he was looking for Liam. He wanted to ask her out again. But he held back. It was better to go slowly. He thought she probably felt that way as well. Things felt comfortable, and safe, the way they were. Being with Anna at Sogni had been like dipping his toe into the ocean and realizing it wasn't nearly as cold as he'd anticipated. He'd felt as if he'd been holding his breath for months, and finally he could begin to let it go.

But now, right at this moment, it was as though that little spot in the ocean had been warmed by the sun, and had given him false comfort. The truth was, the water was still ice-cold.

He hadn't noticed the photographer, because his eyes had been on Anna. He could see it in the photo, the way he was looking. Like he didn't have a care in the world, other than her.

He took a sip of his Scotch, and then leaned on his elbows on the bar and rubbed his jaw with one hand, trying to predict the possible consequences of this photo. He wasn't worried about the physical newspaper. It was only sold locally. There was little danger of any private investigator from California coming across it. But would his picture now be on the paper's website? Would his name be searchable? It had seemed a good idea to use his middle name—Lawrence—as his last name. He'd thought it might be helpful when he tried to do official things, like sign the lease on the house, or register Liam for school. But now he realized he should have used an entirely different name and finessed his way through any questions that arose. Because an online search for Aidan Lawrence Block could potentially turn up Aidan Lawrence, pictured here, having hot dogs at Lonny's.

He didn't regret going to Lonny's with Anna. Or going to Sogni. What he regretted was not noticing the photographer at Lonny's aiming his camera at their table. He regretted being too drawn to her.

A few moments later, Maxine returned. "Two Chicken Cutlet Heroes, one with onions and hot sauce," she said. "Say hi to your boy for me." She looked over his shoulder at the photo spread. "She's a sweetie, that Mrs. Harris," she added. "You guys make a cute couple."

He looked at the picture again, as it occurred to him that anyone searching for *her*, for Anna, could come across the photo, too. And she was a public figure, the widow of a real important guy. She likely came up in searches all the time. The question was whether anyone searching for her might have reason to want to discover *him* as well.

Closing the newspaper, he drained his drink and pulled out his wallet. It was a mistake to let this go any further. He couldn't ignore the facts. The problem wasn't even so much that someone would be searching for her to find him; it was simply that his face was out there now, his name was out there, and the more people searched for her, the more widespread his face would be. He shouldn't be getting involved with anyone, least of all someone like her. He'd come east with the intention of spending the next three years lying low.

And he had to do that. It was the only way he would be sure to keep Liam. That's what he'd promised Liam the night before they left California, when he explained what was happening. He'd kept it all from his son for as long as he could—the closing of the store, the sale of the house, the goodbye to his dad—so there was no chance of Liam accidentally revealing anything to anyone. He'd enlisted one of Emilia's sorority sisters to sell all the furniture and keep the photos and other mementos in the basement of her house. He refused to tell her the whole story, because he didn't want her to have to lie if anyone ever questioned her.

That night, Liam had looked at him, his eyes wide like the little boy he used to be.

"What?" he'd said. "What?" Aidan himself could hear how crazy the whole escape sounded. But he'd made his voice firm and unwavering, so Liam wouldn't be scared. "Three years is not such a long time," he'd said. "It's the only way to make sure we stay together. And then we come back to our regular life."

In the car the next day, he'd listed all the new rules—how they had a new last name and a new home city, Rochester; how they'd never been to California. "I'm doing this for us," he'd said. "Because if we stayed, they might take you away." He'd hoped to see love in Liam's eyes, or at least acceptance. But Liam had looked at him like he didn't even recognize him anymore.

Picking up his suit jacket from the next stool, Aidan dropped some money on the bar and headed down to the street. Within a few weeks, Liam had adjusted and accepted everything—maybe not happily, but he'd accepted it. And he was the most important thing in Aidan's life. So whatever Aidan had—or almost had—with Anna, was over. He'd press reset, go back to the way he was when he first came to Lake Summers, and think only of work and Liam. He liked Anna. Hearing her talk about Greg and her kids had somehow made him calmer about his own losses. To him, she was exactly the way she'd described ballet—seemingly delicate, but in reality rooted in strength. Maybe she was that way by nature, and maybe also because of all she'd been through—but whatever the cause, he wanted to be with someone like that now. Because of all that *he'd* been through. Because of how torn and fearful he had become.

But none of that mattered. All they had had together were two dinners, and they hadn't even eaten anything at the last one. There was no relationship yet, just the possibility of one. Now was the time to call it quits, before anyone got hurt. It was still early in the game; he probably didn't even have to provide much of an explanation…

His phone beeped, and he took it out of his pocket. Liam had texted: *Getting dinner with some of the guys after practice.* Aidan looked down at the plastic bag in his hand. Oh well, the extra sandwich could keep until tomorrow. Across the street he saw

Anna's store, the setting orange sun bursting out from either side of the building. Through the window, he could see her there, standing behind the counter. It didn't look like Hope was around. He figured now was as good a time as any to talk to her.

He crossed the street and went up to the entrance. Even though it was past closing time, the door was unlocked. He opened it, and the chime above sang. Anna was studying the screen of the laptop.

"Hey," he said.

She looked both surprised and happy to see him, a mixture he found almost intoxicating. As was her appearance. She was wearing an airy kind of dress, white with a floral print, thin shoulder straps—what did they call those, spaghetti straps?—and a full skirt. When did she start wearing dresses to work? She'd also started wearing her hair a little more casual—not as close to her head as when she first got here. Longer and wavier.

"Hi," she said. "What are you doing here?"

He wanted nothing more than to touch her hair. Or touch the smooth curve of her shoulder. For a moment, a tiny moment, he thought about what their life could be like. How it would be to come home to that strong, lovely person, every evening.

"I was just leaving the Grill, and I thought I'd say hello," he said. "Am I interrupting anything?"

"Not at all," she said. "I was just going over our sales numbers. Glad to take a break." She closed the laptop.

"Something wrong?"

"I don't know. The beginning of July was good, but I think that's because of the promotions. Things are slowing down. Ballet gear isn't like bread and milk, you don't need to buy it every week. And bookings are good for a few more weeks, but it really drops off after mid-August."

"Sometimes there's a lull. That's normal. But I suspect things will pick up when you bring in the new fall merchandise."

"I was hoping things would stay good through the summer. At least, that was the original plan." She shook her head. "Let's change the subject. You look dressed up."

"I had a few meetings with bankers, to try to help some of the merchants get loans." He smiled. "They take you more seriously if you're in a suit."

"It looks good on you. Very professional."

"And you… look beautiful," he said. "I like your hair."

"Oh." She reached for the ends with her fingers. "Just my relaxed Lake Summers look, I guess."

He hadn't meant to embarrass her. "Did you ever eat the branzino?" he asked.

"I did, the next night. I shared it with my kids. It was delicious." She pointed to the bag in his hand. "Is that dinner for you and Liam tonight?"

"It was supposed to be. But he just texted that he's eating with his buddies. So I guess I'm on my own. How about you? Heading home to the kids?"

"It's barbecue night at camp, so I'm on my own, too. I told Hope I'd close up. I have to go get them in a bit. I was just thinking about what to eat."

"I have an extra sandwich—can I interest you in that?" he said. "Nothing as exotic as Lonny's hot dogs. Just chicken cutlets with marinara or hot sauce."

He waited, hoping she'd say yes. He didn't want to spend this time doing anything other than being with her. Yes, he had planned to tell her he couldn't see her anymore, but being here, so close to her, he couldn't bring himself to say those words.

"I don't know where we would eat, the desk back there is a mess, and… wait, I have an idea," she said.

She went into the office and came back with two bottles of water. Then she locked the front door, grabbed a roll of paper towels from behind the counter, and led him down the hallway.

They took off their shoes and stepped into the studio, and she went to turn on the sound system. An orchestra began playing a waltz. She pulled some yoga blankets from a cabinet, and together they spread them out. She sat down cross-legged, and he did, too. He felt large and awkward at first, but then he felt okay.

"A picnic on the million-dollar floor," he said. "Too bad Hope's not here to enjoy."

She pointed a finger at him. "You are never to tell her we did this," she said.

He laughed and offered up the sandwiches. She couldn't decide which one to take, so they agreed to split them both. "Mmmm," she said, as she bit off a chunk of one, and then wiped her mouth with a paper towel. "So much better than the salad I was thinking of. Hot dogs, and now this. You are opening up a whole world to me."

"It's good, right?" He looked around the studio as he chewed. The orange and pink sunset glowed through the skylights above.

"So, tell me more about dancing," he said.

"Like what?" she asked.

"Like... what happened after your ankle was better. Did you ever dance that dance again?"

"The Lilac Variation? No. I was done with dancing."

"Never? But it healed. You walk fine now."

"I know, but... there were other reasons." She looked down. "Fear, mostly."

"Fear of what? Getting hurt again?"

She shook her head. "The thing is, ballet is a lot about fear. You always start out scared—that you won't make it up onto your pointe shoes, that you'll fall over and look like a fool, that you're a fraud and don't deserve to be dancing at all. But then..."

She paused, and he held his breath. The air was sweet with the silence.

"Then one time, you find that spot where you're up on your toes, and suddenly you're there—in a moment that's completely in between all the fears. And it's incredible. It's as though you're not even human anymore, you're not even a body. You're just pure white energy in space. And you feel you can stay there until the end of time."

He watched the smooth, taut skin rise and fall above the neckline of her dress.

"I was scared of never feeling that again," she said. "Of trying and trying and never getting there. I didn't think I could bear that."

Aidan let this thought weave and tumble in his mind. "You know, you have another ankle," he finally said.

She shook her head. "It doesn't matter. I needed both."

"But you can still have that feeling with the other foot."

"It doesn't work that way. The choreography calls for you to go up on both feet. One and then the other. Anyway, it was a long time ago."

"But I'm not talking about the choreography," he said. "I'm talking about you. Now. And *you* have another ankle."

She tilted her head and smiled. "That is such an Aidan thing to say."

He raised his eyebrows. "Was I just insulted?"

"No, not at all," she said. "It's good. You're all about fixing things. Like our store, back when we had no customers. And Lonny's grill—"

"Well, I'm not so sure I fixed that. I'm a little concerned I made it worse—"

"And now you're helping the merchants with their loans—"

"I'm not so sure I'll be successful there, either—"

"But you try. You're all about quietly making things work, without any fanfare, without any ego. You're just like your father when you were growing up, the way you described him to me. You make people feel important. I so admire that."

They continued to chat and eat their sandwiches, Anna recounting Stan and Trey's earnest attempts at ballet-themed smoothies, and Aidan assuring her that they'd eventually get it right—after all, their gingerbread smoothie, which they'd invented for the Build-a-Snowman charity fundraiser on the green last December, had also taken a long time but turned out delicious. Listening to her laugh, he thought for a moment how crazy it was that he was sitting here, cross-legged on a yoga blanket in a dance studio. Six weeks ago, he never could have imagined himself like this. But even though his back was starting to hurt and his leg was falling asleep, he didn't want the evening to end.

She glanced at the clock on the wall. "Oh, no, look at the time. It's late. I've got to get my kids."

They gathered the garbage, and Anna turned off the sound system. He picked up his suit jacket from the floor, and they left the studio, put on their shoes, and went back down the hall.

At the doorway, he held her hand and gently kissed her twice, once on the forehead and once on the lips, a little more deeply than the last time in front of her house. He would have liked to kiss her longer, but he knew she had to leave. So he opened the screen door and held it as she closed and locked the main door. Then he watched her get into her car and take off.

Walking down Main Street toward home, he thought about what she'd said in the studio—how she admired him, how she saw in him the very qualities he'd seen in his father back when his father was whole. It might have been the best compliment he'd ever received, and he loved that she had felt strongly enough about it to say it. She saw things in him, and said things to him, that helped him. That gave him hope, confidence that there was still a future to be had.

And that's when he decided. He wouldn't stop seeing her. He would make this work. He would be careful and discreet. They would take it slow. But he couldn't give up. He was falling in love with her. He was starting to believe that he could build a life with her, a life that could extend beyond these next hard years.

His phone beeped. It was another text from Liam. He read it, then dropped down on one of the new town benches.

Tag broke his elbow, it said. *The coach says I may be going to Atlanta.*

CHAPTER EIGHTEEN

Everything was different.

That's what Anna kept thinking in the days following the picnic in the studio. The quiet shush of her shoes on the front walk that led to the store, the patches of coolness on Main Street that formed beneath the canopy of shade trees, and the penetrating heat from the unimpeded sun by the lake were familiar as always, but the sensations were richer, calling out with more gusto. The scenery, too, was more intense than usual—the varied hues of green in the leaves, the almond tone of the sand that caught her eye as she brought Evie to camp; even the clarity of the atmosphere. Was that what always happened in the second half of the summer? She thought it could be, but then changed her mind. There was another reason why everything was so pretty and inviting. It was because of Aidan.

She had so enjoyed their sunset picnic. How he had teased her about the "million-dollar floor" and what Hope would say. How he'd asked her about dancing. How he saw her injury as something that didn't have to define her. There were even moments now when she thought she no longer wanted to sell Lilac House. She hadn't yet begun to pack Greg's things in those two empty suitcases she'd brought from home. The realtor had phoned her twice last week to ask about her plans, and she hadn't returned the calls.

Stopping at Pearl's one morning soon after their picnic, she got on line and studied Liam's face behind the counter, recognizing the hint of a smile in his predominantly matter-of-fact expression.

She knew Aidan hadn't told him about their dinners together—it was still early, and they both seemed to have tacitly agreed not to say anything about one another to their kids just yet. Liam's smile was an everyday one. But she felt a new appreciation for it anyway.

Walking up Main Street with her coffee in hand, she found herself daydreaming about a wonderful new life with Aidan. She imagined Zac and Liam heading out to high school together in the mornings, Evie walking with friends to Lake Summers Elementary. She imagined preparing for Thanksgiving with Aidan here in town, maybe in a home they'd chosen together. They'd invite Hope and Keon, Stan and Trey, maybe some of Aidan's co-workers at Village Hall. It would be so different from last year, when she'd dragged herself out of bed to go to her mother-in-law's in New Jersey for Thanksgiving, and everyone tried to be cheerful for her kids' sakes. She imagined decorating the store for the holidays, having Aidan and the kids string ballet-pink lights along the porch, and setting up a menorah with candle holders in the shape of ballet slippers. Maybe they'd host a town holiday party in the studio.

It was a silly, unrealistic fantasy. She'd be mortified if anyone knew about it. And yet deep within those musings, she sensed resilience and a capacity for change—things she hadn't recognized in herself in a long time. Ahead of her, three young mothers from Hope's ballet fundamentals class were comparing their turnouts, using the handles on their baby strollers as ballet barres. And yesterday when she passed by the green, there were kids practicing hip-hop moves they'd learned at the studio. One customer left a comment on the website's "About" page: *Thanks so much for bringing dance to Lake Summers!* She felt proud that she was doing what Aidan had urged her to do that first day they spoke at Village Hall. She was using her passion for dance to help people love their lives a little more.

The store was quiet when she got there, although Trey had already made his way over. He was holding out a platter with purplish drink samples to Hope, and he looked at Anna as she stepped in, a twinkle in his eye. "Stan was telling me that he saw Aidan come in here a couple of nights ago," he teased.

Anna looked down. The mention of that night with Aidan was sweet, and she was embarrassed by how it made her smile.

Evidently she wasn't able to fully hide her emotions. "So you guys *are* a thing? Hallelujah!" he sang out. He gestured toward an open newspaper on the counter. "The whole town's been waiting for you and Aidan to get together!"

"What?" Anna felt her smile disappear, as she went to the counter and her eyes zeroed in on the photo in the newspaper spread. How had that happened? She hadn't noticed anyone taking their picture. She only remembered Aidan asking *not* to be photographed. She looked back at Hope and Trey, feeling as though her silly fantasy had been played on a giant TV for the whole town to see. She hated the idea that she was the subject of gossip. It was one thing to spend time with a nice guy, but a whole other thing for people to conclude they were a couple. What if her children found out? How betrayed and confused would they feel if they heard people saying their mom was in love? They knew Aidan from around town, and they knew Liam from the store, but that was the extent of it. They didn't know about her dinners with Aidan, or the way he'd kissed her. And she didn't want them to know. Not now, and not for a long time to come. Not when it could hurt them so badly.

She looked at Hope. "People are watching us?"

"No, Trey's just teasing you. Trey, stop—you're upsetting her."

"But this isn't good. I don't want any attention—"

"And you're not getting any," Hope said. "Nobody's watching you, sweetheart. Everyone in town has their own life to worry about."

"Yeah, I'm just playing with you, Anna," Trey said. "I'm sorry, I didn't mean to freak you out. Anyway, back to the smoothies.

See, it's purple, which is a ballet color—ish—and it's made with thyme, like a play on words, you know, 'Hey, everyone! Time for dance class!' Well?"

Anna walked into the office, only half listening to Hope comparing the flavor to burnt metal. She leaned her back against the closed door and took in a shaky breath. It wasn't so much that she feared people watching her and Aidan. Hope was right—people had their own lives to worry about. And Trey probably was just having some fun. But thinking back now on what Trey said, she suddenly saw herself from the outside, and she didn't like the view at all. Should she really have gone out to a fancy dinner with Aidan? Or strolled along Main Street at night with him? Should she have put herself in a position to be photographed alongside him, or kissed him right there on her front walk? She started to regret that she had ever let any of that happen.

Yes, she liked Aidan. Very much. She had found in him a connection, a warmth and comfort she hadn't known since Greg had died. Maybe even before that, since the last months before the crash had been marked by how stressed and unsettled Greg had seemed. And she was attracted to Aidan. Very. Both times they'd kissed, she'd felt herself wanting more. But even though she was drawn to Aidan, that didn't give her license to act like a lovesick teenager. She was a parent. Other things were more important than her feelings. Her children were more important.

She sat down at the desk and peeked through the office blinds out on to the sidewalk. She feared she would see Aidan walking in the direction of the store, as he sometimes did at this time of the morning. She feared he would stop in to say hello. But he wasn't there, and she was relieved. She couldn't talk to him right now. Not when she felt this exposed and this guilty.

She wondered for a moment if it would ever feel completely okay to date again. To kiss someone again. To fall in love again. When would that be? In a year? Five? Ten? She thought now that she might never feel completely good about being with someone new. That even when he was gone, Greg was simply too important to belong anywhere but center stage in her life.

*

Hope was right, she repeated to herself in the days that followed, as July flowed toward August. Nobody was paying attention to her and Aidan; people had their own lives to deal with. But sitting in bed each night, she would think of Aidan and feel uneasy all over again. She hadn't seen him in a few days; Stan said that he was working all hours, trying like crazy to help some merchants secure loans they desperately needed to stay in business. It was good that they stay apart for a little while, she thought. She needed time to sort out her feelings.

Leaning against the headboard one night, she looked at the nightstand, where she'd moved the lilac cuttings Aidan had brought her, and had kept them as long as they lasted. Everything had been so much less complicated with Greg. When she'd met him, he'd been young, and his life had been simple. *You get what you see, I'm an open book*—that's what he'd told her. And he loved that idea—he always used that line when he was campaigning. When Crystal arranged family photo shoots for his campaign brochures and TV commercials, he'd always insisted on settings that were so predictable, they were practically a cliché: the four of them in front of their picket-fence house in Silver Plains; Evie playing lacrosse on the school field; Zac doing his math homework at his desk at home, with Greg standing nearby, presumably helping him. Greg and her in their running shoes, starting out on one of the trails in Silver Plains Park. No matter that she never ran because she was scared of injuring her ankle again.

Greg avoided thorny situations. That's what she'd seen so clearly a few years ago, when he'd encouraged her to start up that volunteer program for Asian immigrants who wanted to improve their English. He had advised her on the morning of her first class to be kind but always professional.

"Help them as much as you can, but don't get personally involved," he'd said.

It had sounded like a helpful tip, but a few weeks into the term, one of her students, a woman named Kim who had trained as a concert pianist in Korea, mentioned in stilted English that she was hoping to continue her music studies. She had recently located a former teacher now living in the Bronx, but she didn't know how she could get to his apartment, because she wasn't skilled enough to drive in heavy city traffic. Other options were unworkable as well: a bus would take too long, cabs were expensive and unreliable, and she couldn't park her car at the station and take a train, because the town issued parking permits only to legal residents, and she was living in an illegal sublet.

As Kim spoke, Anna reached into her bag and grasped her wallet, where her own parking permit lay. She didn't use it often, and wouldn't have missed it if Kim borrowed it once a week. But permits were not transferable, a fact Greg had reminded her of a few months earlier when she'd mentioned she was thinking of lending hers to a neighbor.

"The police don't check the permit numbers against the license plates that carefully," she said. "It's not like we're going to get caught, and even if we did, the fine can't be all that big."

"It's not the penalty, it's the principle," he'd told her. "State senators and their wives can't break the rules."

She'd studied Kim that morning, taking in her round face framed by chin-length hair, her bangs clipped back with a bobby pin. She longed to help her out. But she heard Greg's parking permit argument in her head, along with his admonition not to get personally involved with her students, and that trumped Kim's quivering chin and lowered eyes. She let go of her wallet, and it sank back to the bottom of her bag. The subject never came up again, and eventually the term ended.

Anna pictured Kim's face now, and she deeply regretted not just handing over the stupid parking permit and telling her to hightail it over to her teacher's apartment. Kim had always looked so homesick and lonely, and this little skirting of the municipal code could have made a big difference in her life. And if Anna had been caught, she'd have apologized and paid the fine. Simplicity sounded good, but nobody's life was simple. She wouldn't have been seen as a criminal; she'd have been seen as human.

And there were other times when she'd gone along with the simple route to avoid having to face painful thoughts. That's exactly what she'd done after her father died and she shattered her ankle. Without even thinking about it, she had pushed dance to the recesses of her mind, except for those occasional private moments when she was feeling lost. But she had never shown her kids any of her dance recital pictures. She had never shown them the video of Hope dancing—Hope had shown them that herself. She had never shown them the album she'd made with photos of Hope's performances, which she knew was somewhere in the attic of the Silver Plains house. She had never even taken them to see *The Nutcracker* at Lincoln Center at Christmas. She had convinced herself that she no longer cared.

And that's when she admitted to herself that her life with Greg had never been simple, no matter how many happy family photos he'd made Crystal take. If it had been so simple, then why was a reporter coming up to talk to her in a couple of weeks about how anxious Greg had been? Why had Hope said he looked so tired when he spoke to her about co-owning the store? Why had he driven home the night of the storm, when she and the kids were perfectly safe at home, and nobody was risking such a trip? What was simple about any of that?

Kicking off the covers, she climbed out of bed and went up to Evie's room, even though it was almost midnight.

"Mommy?" Evie said, pulling her head up and squinting from the hallway light.

Anna sat on the bed and pulled her daughter close. She stroked Evie's hair away from her eyes.

"Honey, did you ever want to take ballet classes?" she asked.

"I don't know," Evie murmured. "Maybe."

"Why didn't you?"

She yawned. "Because you didn't want me to."

"Did you ever ask me?"

"You made me take gymnastics. You hated ballet."

"You thought I hated ballet? But I danced ballet. You knew that, right?"

"I don't know. Maybe."

"And I've been working with Aunt Hope…"

"I know," she said. "I didn't get it, either."

"Honey, I'm so sorry," Anna said. "But you're not too old to start now. Lots of kids start dancing at your age."

"Would you be happy if I did?"

"Yes, of course. If it's what you want."

Evie sighed and smacked her lips. "Mommy, can we talk about this tomorrow?"

Anna kissed the top of Evie's head and settled her on the mattress. She closed the door behind her and went back down the hall, noticing the light in Zac's room coming from under the door. She thought about knocking, but decided not to. When she asked him what was wrong, it only seemed to annoy him.

Back in her room, she turned off the lamp, feeling cold even though the window was open and the night was warm and still. This was the life of a single parent—grappling alone not only with the major ruptures, but with the little cracks that stung, like paper cuts on your fingers that could become infected if you weren't vigilant.

It was good that she'd gone upstairs to talk to Evie about ballet, she thought. But somehow she suspected the work wasn't done. As she began to fall asleep, she had the disturbing feeling that more such cracks were in her future. She wondered how many more cracks would emerge here in Lake Summers—and what cracks would be waiting when they returned in a few weeks to Silver Plains.

CHAPTER NINETEEN

The school bus pulled up for the first time on a sunny Wednesday morning, and the kids filed into the building, sporting leotards, tights, skirts, tee shirts, and hip-hop pants, all donated by Lake Summers residents. The lakeside yoga class had even purchased drawstring bags, paying extra to have the store's logo imprinted on them on a rush basis. Standing in the hallway alongside Anna and Keon, Hope watched as the kids, who ranged from age six to eleven, took off their sneakers or flip-flops and put on their dance shoes.

She followed them into the studio, with Keon behind her. The younger ones stared wide-eyed at the unfamiliar surroundings, while the preteens mostly seemed to be trying to appear cool and unmoved. The exception was one of the girls, who stood out thanks to her gold-flecked cornrow braids, long legs, and open-mouthed expression.

"That's Clarisse," Keon told her. "She took ballet in her church's basement until there was a flood and they had to stop the program. Apparently she's a standout."

He put his hands on Hope's shoulders. "Some of the Jayson trustees want to come next week to see the classes. And Dara Steen's coming by in a little while to watch you with the kids. You're okay with that, right?"

"Why would I not be okay?" Hope said as she squirmed away from under his hand. She'd gotten used to Keon bringing over Jayson people. Dara, the chair of the dance department, had been there twice before to see her teach the college students.

"No reason, just checking," he said.

She went into the studio, not wanting to talk with him more. She had been avoiding him for almost two weeks now.

She proceeded to the center of the studio and asked Melanie and the other Jayson students to divide the kids into a younger and an older group. The plan was to separate the studio in half, and have Maz, the hip-hop teacher, work with the younger kids, while she taught the older ones ballet. Thirty minutes in, they'd switch groups. Hope would use the studio's sound system on her side of the studio, and Maz, a pair of portable speakers connected wirelessly to his phone. Anna had set up a large, sound-muffling screen to help keep the two groups from distracting one another. It wasn't the same as having two private studios, but it was the best they could do.

When the groups were set and the older kids had spread out at the barre, Hope started the warm-up. Immediately she could see that Keon was right: Clarisse was exquisite. Her legs were strong, her leg extensions high, and her back and feet remarkably flexible. Her face was expressive, too, her joyfulness contagious. The last time Hope had seen this kind of talent and effort was with Anna.

The groups switched sides, and Hope wiped her face with a towel and glanced toward the doorway. Keon was still there, now speaking with Dara. She was an older woman with cherry-red lips and jet-black hair piled high on her head, and when Hope looked over, she smiled widely.

Hope bowed her head and pressed her palm to her chest in response. It was flattering that Dara liked how she taught. She owed Keon so much. He had made all this happen—the Jayson classes, the Kids Club classes, the visits from important Jayson people—and thinking about that, she felt even worse about shutting herself off that night in her apartment. But she'd been scared that he would judge her harshly and reject her if he knew everything about her. So she kept her story to herself. Life was easier on her own, she told herself. And she didn't deserve a nice guy in her life anyway. He was better off without her.

The younger kids were flexible and energetic, with both boys and girls leaping high into the air and spinning with abandon. The time sped by, and when the class was over, Keon led the kids back out of the store. Hope came outside and waved as they boarded the bus. She started for the outside stairs to go up to her apartment, when Keon caught her elbow.

"Hope, got a minute?"

"Now's not a good time," she said. "I have to change out of my dance clothes, and then I have to get back to work. Anna's been looking at some of the sales numbers, and she wants to show me some things—"

"But I don't think it can wait. Believe me, you're going to be thrilled when you hear what I have to tell you."

He looked so earnest that she couldn't say no. She nodded and led him back to the store and into the office.

He shut the office door and stood opposite her with the desk between them. Leaning forward, he tapped his fingertips on the desk's surface, evidently so full of adrenaline that he couldn't keep still.

"Dara *loves* you!" he said. "She thinks you're exceptional. And she needs new instructors this fall, since the dance department is set to expand. Hope, she wants to talk to you about joining the Jayson faculty!"

"She… *what?*" Hope said, putting a hand to her mouth. A month ago she couldn't even attract enough people to form one dance class at her studio. She plopped down in her chair, feeling her heart pumping up to her ears. After so many years away from the dance world, somebody important had actually noticed her. Somebody important in the dance world actually thought she still had worth!

"But how would I do it?" she said. "What about the store?"

"Well, I've been thinking… there are a few ways," he said. "You could keep the store and do both. That would work, but you'd have to hire some staff and step back from the day-to-day. Or maybe it makes more sense to move over to Jayson full-time and sell the business. Anna's going back to Silver Plains at the end of the summer, isn't she? You've built something pretty great here. Maybe you both could make a nice little bundle."

"I don't want to sell my store," she said. "I built it from nothing. Anna loves it, too. I would never propose we sell so I could walk off and do something else. I would never let her down that way."

"But her kids have to go back to school, don't they?"

"Maybe they'll go to school here. Maybe she's going to stay. Maybe she's thinking that Lake Summers is where she and the kids belong. That was the original plan Greg had—that we'd both own the store for… you know. Forever."

"Then don't sell it," he said. "Like I said, you can do both."

He walked around to her side of the desk and sat down on the edge. "But teaching—it's not the same crazy hours as owning a store," he said. "No weekends, more flexibility. Maybe that would sound good to Anna, too. You'd both have more time for yourselves. And it would be nice to have you on campus, to see you every day."

She looked at him, speechless. It all sounded reasonable, and the part about wanting to work with her and see her every day affected her deeply. She had to admit, she liked him. Just seeing him interact with his students and his colleagues and the people at the Kids Club, she knew he was a straight shooter, utterly incapable of being sly or deceitful, or of hurting anyone.

And yet, what would it mean if she remade her life simply because this man suggested she do so? She had twisted herself into a pretzel for a man before, and she had ended up all but destroyed. Not to mention that along the way, she had lost the people she loved and desperately wanted in her life: her baby;

her brother; her niece. It had taken years, but finally, when she was well into her forties, she had picked herself up and begun to build a good, new life for herself, and this one had to be the one that stuck. With Anna and the kids in her life, and a store that felt just like home, she had everything she needed.

He raised his eyebrows, evidently noticing her anger intensifying. "What?" he said. "What did I say?"

"Keon, stop pushing me, will you?" she said.

He stood up. "Pushing you?"

"You're trying to run my life. You're trying to fix me. And I won't have it. I'm not one of your students. I don't need you to make my decisions."

"But I'm not… I don't understand," he said, lines of confusion forming across his forehead. "I thought this was something you'd want."

"Why do you think you know what I want?" she said, standing up and leaning into him, refusing to let him control the space in the room. "You don't know everything about me. You hardly know anything about me! I have everyone I need—I have Anna and her kids, and they love me as I am. I'm happy with the life I have, and I'm done. I'm done!"

"But…" Keon said. "I thought…"

"No, don't think any more, okay?" Hope said. "Because it's my life! And I don't want you fielding job offers for me or telling me what to do with my store. I'm almost sixty years old, and I'm fully capable of making my own decisions, thank you very much."

She stared at him, hard, her face still, her lips zipped together. She was scared that if she moved even a tiny bit, the truth would all come pouring out.

He kept his eyes locked on hers for a moment, and then dropped them down.

He nodded as though he agreed with her, as though she'd exposed him. She thought back on that day outside the smoothie shop, how excited he'd been to share his idea about the Kids Club, how he could be so earnest because he thought he understood who she was. He probably knew that people as earnest as he was ran the risk of seeming foolish. He probably never thought that she'd be the one to make him feel like a fool.

He pushed himself away from the desk and went to the door, and she followed behind. "Keon, I'm sorry," she said. "I didn't mean to sound like that. You don't know everything I've been through. Keon, please, don't leave like this—"

He turned and raised his palm in her direction. "Stop," he said, his voice quiet and firm. "You don't need to apologize. I misunderstood what you wanted, that's all. There's no need to make this into a big deal."

"But wait," she said. He wasn't listening. He was gone.

Standing by her desk, she closed her eyes and tried to tell herself that it didn't matter that he had left, or that she had treated him so badly. If she hadn't lost him now, she'd have lost him eventually.

She blew her nose with a tissue and walked out of the office. The sales floor was empty except for Anna, who was at the jewelry counter, and Stan, who was sitting on one of the ottomans, his belly pressing against his Smoothie Dudes apron, making the letters in the words spread apart.

"The card store, too?" Anna was saying.

"The card store what?" Hope asked.

"The copy place put up a closing notice," Stan said. "And the card store may be closing, too."

"I feel awful about this," Anna said. "My kids love going into the card store, checking out all the quirky things they carry, like the big, stuffed pillows with the funny sayings. And the copy guy, he helped us with our fliers when we were just getting started.

Everyone's so nice around here. What will the town become, without them?"

"And we're also hearing rumblings about the hair salon." Stan shivered. "Three shuttered storefronts in one town? What do they say in politics? The optics aren't good."

"But Aidan's been talking to the bank about loans," Anna said. "Won't that help?"

"Hope so," Stan said. "Yeah, I feel bad for the ones that are closing. But it's bad for the ones that are left, too. Retailers need synergy, you know? Like the hair place—their customers always come to us for smoothies, and they shop at the dress store, and go to lunch at the Grill. If they're not coming here to get their hair done… shit, that's gonna suck."

He pulled himself up from the ottoman with a groan. "Sorry to be the bearer of bad news," he said. "I probably should go. Trey's working on the lilac thing, and it still smells like a chemical waste dump."

He left, and Hope walked around the counter and took his place on the ottoman. Anna looked at her. "Are you okay?"

"I'm fine, sweetheart."

"Are you sure? You don't look fine."

"I'm fine. Was there something you wanted to show me? You said something earlier about sales numbers…"

Anna retrieved her tote bag from behind the counter, then pulled out her laptop. "I made some notes last night—can you believe I've been dragging this thing around all summer?" She opened the laptop on the counter. "Stan said all those things about those other stores, and I'm kind of worried about *our* store as well."

"Our store? We've been doing so well."

"July was good, yes, but I think that was because of the grand opening promotions."

"But it's been crowded—"

"Yes, but it's deceptive. The store *looks* busy, with the kids coming in today, and the Jayson dancers taking classes here.

But see this?" She pointed to the computer screen, and Hope walked over to get a closer look. "We have no studio bookings from mid-August on—no parties, no events, nothing. And the early-bird pricing for the fall classes has been up for a week, and the rosters are empty."

Hope studied the calendar page. She had to admit, it made sense that things were slowing down. Half the people in the regular, non-Jayson classes were summer people who'd be leaving soon, and others were teachers who'd be going back to work in the fall, or parents whose kids were coming back from sleep-away camp. The Jayson dancers would be going back to campus for the fall semester. The Kids Club kids could be staying—but that didn't bring in any income. And there was the problem of synergy, like Stan said. If people weren't coming into town for lunch or smoothies, then they weren't going to be around for dance classes or to buy dance clothes or accessories or yoga mats or anything.

She looked at Anna. "So we're going to have to try something else. Another promotion, a new idea. Maybe SummerFest will turn things around. Maybe we can come up with some good ideas to make the most of it."

Anna slowly shook her head. "I don't think I have any more ideas."

Hope went to say something encouraging, but then stopped herself. The look on Anna's face told her that this was bigger than inventing some new sales scheme. She sighed. "So what are you thinking, sweetheart?" she said. "What is it you think we should do?"

"I think… Aunt Hope, I hate to say this. But I think we should start to look at selling. Or even closing down."

"You mean now? Before the end of the summer? But you've been so happy here. What about Aidan?"

"What about Aidan?"

"I thought you might be thinking of staying in town, so you can spend more time with him."

"This has nothing to do with Aidan. This is about us. I can see the writing on the wall, and I know you can, too. Maybe the sooner we get out, the more of our investment we'll be able to salvage."

Hope folded her arms over her chest and walked to the window. Her window, overlooking her beautiful deck and onto Main Street, which glowed in the sunshine. She didn't want to cry. But it seemed that the one good thing, the one solid thing she'd ever accomplished in her life was coming to an end.

Anna came up behind her. "I'm sorry, Aunt Hope. I don't want to hurt you. But this has all become too much for me to handle. Zac still has these outbursts that I don't understand at all, and Evie's so closed and guarded—and I'm losing things, too. I haven't been able to find Greg's iPad all summer, and it's driving me crazy, and there are other things—his hairbrush, his toothbrush—I know that sounds so dumb, but where could they have gone? And the key I leave under the planter in case the kids get home before me—it's gone, and the water valves for the washing machine have been fiddled with, and for the life of me I don't remember moving or touching any of these things. I'm confused, and I'm scared, and I think my feelings for Aidan are making things worse. It's not good for me to be this way…"

Hope turned around and wrapped Anna in her arms, wishing that she could protect her from all this hurt, just as she'd wished to protect her that final night in New York City when she said goodbye, thinking it was the last time she'd ever see her niece. "Oh, Anna," she said. "We'll do whatever you want us to do about the store. I'm just so sorry for what I did to put you in this position in the first place. I feel so terrible—"

The door chime sounded, and a mother and two daughters appeared in the doorway. Anna nodded to let Hope know she'd help them, and Hope nodded back and went outside to the wicker sofa, numbed by all that had happened in the last little while.

A few minutes later Anna came out. "They're trying on leotards," she said and sat down on the rocker. She leaned forward. "Do you want to talk about what happened with Keon? You both looked very upset when he left."

Hope waved off the subject with her hand. Why burden Anna even more? "It's nothing. It was nice, getting to know him. But it's not going anywhere. He's all into family and community and helping others—and I'm too much of a loner. I belong alone, that's all there is to it."

"Alone?" Anna said. "What are you talking about? What about all you've done for the Jayson kids and the Kids Club kids? And how you've been so good to my kids and me this summer, and how you came down to be with us when Greg died? And how you were such a good aunt to me when I was a little girl and dreamed of being just like you… You and Keon are exactly alike. You look out for people, just like he does."

Hope leaned forward and squeezed Anna's hand. "You're being kind, and I love you for that. But I wasn't there for you. I wasn't there when your father got sick and died, and you were alone—"

"But that wasn't your fault. You were far away, and there was no way to reach you, there was no email or text back then. You had no idea what was going on—"

"No, that's not true—Anna, that's not true!" she said and dropped her forehead into the heels of her hands. She couldn't do it anymore, she couldn't let Anna go on thinking she was a better person than she was. It was bad enough to hide the truth from Keon, but it was even worse to do that to Anna, her own niece. "That was a lie, a big lie that I told, and you believed me. But the truth was, I was here."

Anna's shoulders tensed. "What do you mean?" she said. "You were—what?"

Hope lifted her head. "I was here in New York, I was living in Poughkeepsie when your father died."

"What? No, you weren't. You were in Europe. I was trying to find you. But nobody knew where you were, nobody could give me any information."

"And the reason was that I wasn't there anymore. Oh, Anna, how can I explain it? I had been dancing for so much of my life, and I was so tired, and my knee was starting to give out, and there were all these younger, stronger dancers coming up behind me. I wasn't even aware of it, but I guess subconsciously I was looking for a way out."

She went on, explaining about Andre and how she decided to quit the ballet to be with him, and how he rejected her. "And I was pregnant," she said.

"Pregnant?" Anna asked. "You… had a baby?"

Hope shook her head and described how she came back to New York intending to be with David and Anna, but changed her mind because she was too ashamed to admit the truth. "I decided that I should never see the two of you again, that you shouldn't be saddled with me and my baby," she said. "I told you that I was going back to Europe, but I wasn't. I tried to make a new life. But… but in the end…"

Anna pressed her palm against her chest. "Oh my God," she said. "Aunt Hope, what happened?"

"I carried her almost full term," she said. "Then she stopped moving. They said she'd died a few days earlier. Something about the umbilical cord." She looked down at her hands, clenched together on her lap.

"Oh, Aunt Hope," Anna said. "I'm so sorry. What you went through—I can't even imagine…"

"It was devastating," Hope said. "I didn't think I'd ever get through it."

"Then why didn't you come home to us?" Anna said. "We would have taken care of you."

Hope lifted her shoulders. "I couldn't," she said. "I couldn't think of anything but just making it through it each day. It went on for months. Oh Anna, I wanted that baby so much!" She wiped the corner of her eye. "I don't even know how much time passed. I thought about reaching out to you. But I was just so consumed with my own loss. My own grief. I never even knew that your father had died. I was right there in Poughkeepsie, just a train ride away. I never even knew that you were alone."

Anna folded her arms over her chest and looked skyward. "I was so scared when he died," she said. "I called all the dance companies you worked for, all the places you stayed, all the numbers I had. I was sure you'd want to know. I wanted so much to have you with me, or even just to hear your voice."

"I wish I did know, Anna," Hope said. "I wish that now. But I was overwhelmed and ashamed. There were times I thought I deserved to lose my daughter, because of all the bad decisions I made. I hated myself. I thought you'd hate me, too."

"Hate you?" Anna stood and faced her aunt. "How could you think that? I loved you. I cried when you left after each visit, I missed you so much. And Dad, he wanted to see you before he died. He wouldn't say it, he was so proud, but I knew he felt it. And we'd have wanted to help you with whatever you were going through if you'd just given us the chance. Aunt Hope—we're family."

Family. It was the word that meant so much to her now, the word that hurt so much that she tried to keep it out of her head for so many years. "I know, I know," she said. "And I didn't want to stay away so long, not at first. But the longer I stayed, the harder it got to even consider coming back. I know that sounds awful, but that was how it was. I thought you'd be happier without me."

Anna grasped her hands together below her chin. "So what did you do all that time?" she asked softly.

"I jumped from job to job, teaching ballet at local colleges. I liked teaching at the college level, and I was good at it. But sooner or later the school would find out I didn't have a degree, and they'd let me go. I'd get a temp job until I could find another school that I hoped wouldn't check my credentials." She closed her eyes and pressed her fingertips against her forehead, thinking of all those miserable years she bounced around. "Then came the train derailment, and I saw pictures of you in the paper, with your wonderful, brave husband and your newborn son. And that's when I realized I was through grieving. I had come to terms with the loss of my daughter. I wanted to be with you again."

Anna shook her head. "I don't even know what to say," she said. "I was so lost without you."

"But you found yourself, isn't that what matters?" Hope said. "You were strong and smart and you made a great life for yourself, don't you see? You probably ended up much better than you would have if I were around."

Anna looked at her as though baffled by that logic, and even though Hope meant it, she knew it sounded like a lame attempt to win forgiveness. Anna looked toward Main Street. "I have to go," she said, sounding like she was on the verge of tears. "I need to process all this before the kids get home. Can you manage the store alone? I'll see you tomorrow."

"Anna… please, Anna," Hope said, getting up from the sofa. But Anna was already down the steps.

"Uh, miss?" someone called from inside the store. "Can you help us? We're ready to check out."

Hope massaged her bad knee for a moment, and then went back inside. The bell above the door chimed as she stepped in. But it didn't sound tuneful and magical anymore.

CHAPTER TWENTY

Liam took the steps down from his bedroom two at a time. "Dad, get this! I'm going to Atlanta next week!"

Aidan handed some bills to the delivery guy and took the pizza box to the table. "Well, what do you know?" he said, trying to sound pleased. "How'd this all happen?"

"The coach just emailed me. Tag's gonna be in a sling for another couple of weeks."

"Poor guy."

"Yeah, I feel bad for him. But we told him the rocks by the lake were slippery." He hooked his drawstring bag over his chair and then went into the kitchen for plates and glasses. "There's an extra practice tonight for the guys who are going. So I can't eat much now. I'll take a slice when I get back."

Aidan put napkins on the table. He'd been hoping this wouldn't be the outcome ever since he'd gotten Liam's text outside of Anna's store almost two weeks ago. And at first he thought he'd dodged the bullet. When the details came out, the injury didn't seem as serious as it could have been. It wasn't Tag's elbow, it was his forearm, and it wasn't badly broken, it was a simple fracture. Aidan thought the kid would maybe just miss a few practices, but not lose his Atlanta spot. Now he had to have the conversation with Liam he'd so desperately wanted to avoid.

Liam pulled a slice out of the box. "Can you believe it? I'm the next fastest after Tag. I'm the only sophomore going. What do you think Mom would say?"

Aidan had been about to get a slice, but he changed his mind and let the box top go. The mention of Emilia was so unexpected. It was the first time since they'd moved here that Liam had spoken about her so casually, so happily. "She'd be very proud of you," he said.

Liam took a couple of bites, slurping up the hot, gooey cheese. He wiped his mouth with the back of his hand. "So I'll get all the information tonight—the hotel and flight and all that stuff. The only thing we have to pay for is the plane ticket."

He finished his first slice and took another, evidently too excited to remember he'd said he didn't want to eat too much. "And Dad, I can pay for the plane with the money I made this summer. It could be expensive because it's so last minute. You owe me some money anyway for the dance store website, right? Ha, right? Dad, you okay?"

Aidan handed him a napkin. Liam was thoughtful and unselfish, just like his mom. But the cost didn't matter; he was not going to Atlanta. There was no way Aidan could let him be in a live-streamed ESPN event, with people from all over the country able to watch. If anyone were to recognize Liam, it would be easy to find out what school he went to and where they were living.

Or what if the competition officials looked closely at his school records, what if they realized there was something fishy about his last name? What if they tried to reconcile his records in Lake Summers with records in Rochester—records that didn't exist? Aidan had been lucky; Lake Summers was a small community, and when he brought Liam here, the school secretary had casually accepted all the forms he'd filled out. But maybe the officials at this tournament were more sophisticated. What if they saw the discrepancies? What if they came to the wrong conclusion, and thought Liam was kidnapped or something? What if they brought him to the police to get everything straightened out?

Or what if Liam let his guard down, being away for four days with a bunch of guys and a coach who had lived in California? What if he accidentally admitted where he'd grown up, that he'd never lived a day of his life in Rochester? Hell, Aidan himself had slipped up. It was just so easy to do.

"You have to make sure we get the ESPN live-streaming," Liam said. "I think we subscribe to that already, don't we? What is it? Dad, what's up?"

Aidan looked at his son. "Liam. I can't do this."

Liam's face became blank. "You can't do what?"

"You can't go to Atlanta. It's too dangerous. Someone could recognize you and ask questions, or they could question the paperwork... I'm sorry. We can't take this chance."

"Dad, no. No, please, don't do this." Aidan watched his son shrink before his eyes. His chest and shoulders, which had become so strong this summer from all the swimming he'd done, now collapsed. His back hunched over, as though Aidan were sucking the life out of him. "I'm the only sophomore going. The coach says he thinks I could make the finals—"

"I know, I know you're good, just like your mom was an athlete," he said. A part of him wanted to go crazy, shake his fists and scream, *What is the matter with me? I'm destroying my son—the one person I still have!* But he knew the only way he'd get through this moment was to stay in his comfort zone. Firm. Calm. Quiet.

"But that's not important now," he continued. "I should have said something as soon as you told me about Tag. But I didn't expect it to turn out this way. And I didn't want to have this discussion. And I'm sorry, but you can't go."

"But this doesn't make sense," Liam said. "I'll keep my goggles on, I'll stay away from the cameras, okay? And I won't say anything I shouldn't—you know I can do that, I've been doing it so long already." He was hyperventilating now, his upper lip trembling. "Dad, what am I supposed to tell the coach?"

"We'll tell him we're busy. We have a family commitment. I'll make the call if you don't want to."

"I'm going, you can't stop me—"

"Yes, I can. I won't give my permission. There's no way the coach will take you."

"But… but…" Liam froze for a moment, then stood up and kicked his chair so it toppled over, making a snap that sounded like wood in a campfire. "Fuck the swim team!" he said. "Fuck Atlanta! I don't give a shit about it. I just don't want to live like this anymore. When are we going home, already? We don't belong here—"

"I've answered this," Aidan said, still working to keep his voice low and controlled. "Three years. Then you'll be eighteen, and you can get back in touch with your grandparents and write me off completely if you want. You'll never have to see me again, if that's what you decide. But for now, we have to make sacrifices—"

"Oh, yeah? What kind of sacrifices are you making, Dad? I don't see you making any sacrifices when it comes to taking out your little girlfriend for hot dogs—yeah, I saw that stupid picture in the newspaper—"

"Stop, Liam," he said. "Don't start this."

"Does she know why we're here? Does she know about your fake name and all?"

"Liam, enough. Calm down. Email the coach, and tell him you can't go. You'll still be on the team. You still can swim this fall."

"I don't want to swim this fall!" He grabbed his drawstring bag from off the fallen chair and whipped it across the table. Their plates and glasses crashed to the floor.

"You're a liar, Dad," he added as he ran upstairs. "A liar and a loser! I should just leave you alone, you know that? I should just leave, and let everyone know where the fuck you are!"

Aidan stood still in the silence that followed Liam's slamming of his bedroom door, the sound reverberating in his ears. Then he righted Liam's chair and went into the kitchen for some paper towels and a trash bag. How had he turned a smart, well-behaved teenager into this furious young man? How had he gotten to the point where his son, his boy, called him a loser? He thought about Emilia, how heartbroken she'd be if she could see what he had done to their son. "I'm sorry," he said, even though no one was there to hear it.

He put the large pieces of the broken plates into the trash bag. What a jerk he had been these last few months, to think things were going well. What a jerk he had been to let himself start to feel something for a woman. He'd actually foreseen keeping Anna in his life. He thought she could be good for Liam, and he could be good for her kids, once she was comfortable enough to let him get to know them. He thought they could be a family.

Now he knew that none of that could happen. Liam was right—if he couldn't go to Atlanta, then Aidan couldn't have Anna. They had to go back to the original plan. Two loners, with no ties to anyone. Cool, arm's-length acquaintances only. He would stay close to home this weekend, being with Liam as much as Liam would allow. Maybe if Liam settled down, they could do something fun, like go hiking or fishing, to get their minds off the Atlanta trip that Liam would miss next week. And then he would go talk to Anna and say he couldn't see her anymore. He would tell her everything. He owed her that.

He finished cleaning and went upstairs, thinking he'd kill some time working in the little bedroom. But it was too hard to concentrate on the wire swimmers, and he didn't stay very long. He left the room and paused outside of Liam's bedroom, then went in. Liam was still in his clothes, but was asleep in his bed, even though it wasn't even nine o'clock.

Aidan sat down on the edge of the mattress. Sleeping on his side with his mouth open, Liam looked like a little boy. On his night table was a bunch of soggy tissues.

The weight of Aidan's body evidently woke him up. "I'm sorry, Dad," he mumbled. "I shouldn't have said that."

"I'm sorry, too," Aidan said.

"I don't want them to take me from you. If you think that could happen, then I shouldn't go to Atlanta."

"I don't want to lose you either."

Liam sighed. "I miss Mom so much."

Aidan nodded.

"I'm so tired, Dad. I just want to sleep."

"Okay, bud," Aidan said. "I'll see you in the morning."

He left Liam's room and went back to the swimming sculpture. He still hadn't figured out how to affix the swimmers so they would appear to be suspended above the platform mid-dive. He decided that he never would. There had to be an anchoring wire. Chokingly thick, to keep them forever tied down.

CHAPTER TWENTY-ONE

The following Monday Aidan went to the store first thing. Anna looked up from the counter.

"Hey," she said. "I didn't know you'd be stopping by. I almost wasn't even here. I have a reporter from Silver Plains meeting me at the house a little later—"

"We have to talk," he said.

Her smiled disappeared, and her back stiffened. He understood why—good news never followed an opener like that. He hesitated, unused to being in this position. He hadn't had many relationships in his life, and of those he'd had, he'd never been the one to end them.

He could hear music playing. Hope must be in the studio. He knew that ordinarily Anna wouldn't leave the sales floor while Hope was teaching and before Melanie arrived, but there were no customers, and she clearly realized he had something important to say. She gestured to him, and he followed her into the office.

He closed the door behind them and stood facing her. His plan was to tell her that he couldn't see her anymore, that Liam was still struggling with the loss of Emilia, and he thought he should devote himself entirely to his son. His plan was to say their relationship was getting too serious, but he couldn't commit to her at this point, and he didn't want to hurt her by allowing both of them to get closer. After all, he had demanded that Liam keep their secret. He couldn't ask any less of himself.

And yet, looking at Anna, whose eyes were so wide and trusting, who had been so open and vulnerable with him, he knew he had to tell her the whole truth.

"I haven't… I wasn't completely honest with you about my past," he said.

"Oh?" she asked.

"When I told you at Sogni that my father made some bad business decisions, I meant… they were more than bad."

He went on to tell her how he'd gotten a visit at his jewelry store late one night soon after Emilia had died. It was Mitch, one of his dad's oldest and best customers, who had left his wife's diamond ring at the store a few weeks earlier for cleaning, and now realized the stone had been replaced with a fake.

"My father had started putting fake stones into jewelry brought in for cleaning or repairs, and then selling the real diamonds," he said. "I don't know what he was thinking. I know he'd never have stolen them intentionally. It's hard to say. His mind was going, and maybe he thought the diamonds were his to sell. But by the time I found out about it, he had full-blown dementia. He was too far gone to ask."

Anna looked stunned. Her eyes were wide, her mouth open, her body still. He thought she'd probably expected him to say something predictable, like Liam had found out about their relationship and was having trouble adjusting. He was sure she'd never expected to hear something so serious.

He went on, describing how he contacted all his customers who'd dropped off jewelry in recent months to see if they'd been cheated, too. How he'd depleted his savings and taken out new loans to make the customers whole. How he decided it was best to close down the business.

"Then, on my final day, Emilia's father stops by," he said. "He never liked me. I was just a shopkeeper's son, and he wanted Emilia to marry an Ivy League guy, someone who was going to a top law school and would one day be a partner in a fancy law firm. Like he was. Boy, how he regretted bringing her into the store to help choose a birthday present for her mother that summer. I showed her this vintage silver charm bracelet, and I think we both fell in love that very minute. I didn't care that in the fall, she would be going back to college all the way across the country. I just wanted to see her, again and again. But she wasn't even allowed to date me. She would say she was going out with her girlfriends, and then come meet me at the store.

"When she finally graduated, and moved back to California and into an apartment with some friends, that's when we got serious. She wanted nothing to do with her father because of how he felt about me, and nothing to do with her mother, for going along with it. But I told her to be patient. I thought they'd come around. And they did, when Liam was born. They started visiting us, inviting us over on the holidays. I was relieved. I knew she missed them. And I wanted Liam to have a big family.

"Anyway, he shows up out of the blue after Emilia had passed, because he heard the store was closing and I was in debt. He starts talking about Liam—how am I going to take care of him, what if I can't pay off the loans, how am I going to keep a roof over his head and food in his belly? And I didn't have any answers. And suddenly I realized that he and Emilia's mother wanted to take Liam away from me. That they were planning to have me declared an unfit parent so they could become Liam's legal guardians. And her dad's a big shot, too—very wealthy, a big donor to local politicians. He has a lot of influence. He's the kind of guy who gets what he wants."

He paused. "We come from L.A. That's why I said that night that our store was near the beach. It's true, it was near the ocean. We never lived in Rochester. We changed our last name, too. It's Block, not Lawrence. We're hiding out here."

She folded her arms over her chest, as though she were feeling cold. "I… I don't know what to say—"

"You don't have to say anything," he said. "I just want you to know the truth. I know Emilia's parents, and when they want something they don't give up. It's true, I let the business fail, and they'll use that to convince a judge that Liam would be better off without me. And they'd put Liam in the middle and make him answer a lot of hard questions about me, maybe even about Emilia. I can't let that happen. I can't cause Liam any more pain. He's my son."

He looked at her, and she looked so beautiful to him, in another one of those pretty dresses she'd started wearing, and her hair so soft and wavy. And he thought about the first day he met her, how he'd wanted to see her embrace the business, even to love it. He had wanted to help her. Instead, he was hurting her, making her life more difficult, and he felt terrible for that.

"As soon as Liam turns eighteen, we'll go back and straighten everything out," he said. "But for now, this is the way we have to live. They're rich, Emilia's parents, and I have no doubt they've hired a private investigator to try to track us down. All I can do is make it hard for them to find us and try to let the clock run out."

He looked at her, hating to reveal where all this was leading. "I wanted this to work out, between you and me," he said. "But then the picture at Lonny's showed up in the paper, and I need to stay hidden—"

"No, don't," she said, putting up her hand to stop him from continuing. "Of course you have to put Liam first. Honestly, Aidan, this was moving too fast for me, too. And now that you've told me this… I mean…"

She trailed off, but he knew exactly what she meant. It would be hard enough to bring a new man into their lives. He couldn't be someone who was hiding. Who might need to flee at a moment's notice, if he thought he'd been tracked down. Who could end up in court in an ugly and public custody battle.

"I should get back out on the floor," she said, her voice thin and shaky. She smoothed the skirt of her dress. "I enjoyed being with you, Aidan."

He took her hands in his. Was it only a few weeks ago that he'd gone to the florist shop and asked for lilac cuttings? He thought about the ballet, the solo, that person—no, not a person, a good witch, a magician? No, it was a fairy, a lilac fairy. No wonder Anna liked that ballet so much. What was there not to like about a story where somebody can dance right over and save the day?

"Me, too," he said. "Greg Harris was a lucky man—"

Just then the office door opened. Aidan was too surprised to let go of Anna's hands.

"Oh, I'm sorry," Hope said. Behind her was a slim man with a shock of blond hair, black-rimmed glasses and a messenger bag slung over his shoulder. "But Anna, this gentleman says you're expecting him today—"

"Anna! Great to see you," the man said. "Sorry I'm early, but I wanted to check out the store." He turned to Aidan. "And you look familiar. Aidan Lawrence, right? I saw your picture in the local paper. I'm Dan Groner, from the *Silver Plains Inquirer*."

CHAPTER TWENTY-TWO

She hadn't expected him to show up at the store. Nobody knew about it—not even Crystal. She wondered if he'd learned about it from that picture of her and Aidan in the newspaper—the caption had mentioned The Lilac Pointe. But why would he read the *Lake Summers Press?* What would he make of finding her here with the very same man she was photographed with?

He apologized for surprising her and said he'd wait if she had things to do, and she said no, she could get back to business later. She didn't like being alone with reporters to begin with, and his showing up like that made her even more uncomfortable. She wanted to be done with him as soon as she could. She'd taken her car to work that morning, so she said he could follow behind. Driving down Main Street, she had the sense that he was staying close behind her. She knew it was her nerves getting the best of her, but she felt he was expecting her to try to lose him.

She reached the green and turned, wishing she had more time to herself than just this quick trip home. She hadn't even fully processed what Hope had told her a few days ago; hadn't even really spoken to her aunt since then, other than to update her on merchandise shipments, or to say "Excuse me," when she had to squeeze past her around the counter or in the hallway. And now came this totally unexpected revelation from Aidan. But it made sense. Her instincts had been right. Of course, she completely understood why he had changed his name and the city where they came from: to keep and protect Liam. She'd do anything to keep and protect her children, too. But still, he was different now from the person she'd believed he was. She pictured scenes from the times they'd had: the first meeting in Village Hall, the hot dogs at Lonny's, the dinner at Sogni. They scrolled through her mind like flashbacks in a cheesy TV show.

Except that here in the car, picturing those scenes wasn't cheesy. It was the first step in saying goodbye. It was just as she had started to tell him: she couldn't bring another man into her children's lives right now, let alone one who was lying about his name and his whereabouts, one who was enmeshed in a serious feud with his dead wife's parents, a feud over custody that could end up in court. She couldn't risk being seen one more time with him, and having their names linked together in another newspaper article or even on the lips of townspeople. There was no way to erase what people had seen in the past, but at least she could stop the damage now. At least it was finally clear. She had to put him out of her life for good.

Pulling into the driveway, she saw the house the way Dan Groner would see it as he parked alongside the curb—charming and welcoming, the perfect look for an image-conscious politician and his family. But now she also saw things she hadn't noticed this summer, the little signs of neglect. Like the overgrown, out-of-bloom lilac bushes leading to the front step. And the little tear in the screen door. And the crabapple tree on the side of the house, the one Greg joked about using to haul luggage straight up to the second floor—now the big branch was so long, its leaves were scraping Zac's window. She figured Dan would notice them—he was a reporter, after all. Would he think Greg had done all the minor repairs in the past, and see these flaws as a sad sign of Greg's absence? Or would he conclude that she'd become lax or distracted this summer?

The thought made her aware that her appearance also had changed. She was no longer so buttoned up, the way she'd been in Silver Plains. She was wearing one of her new sundresses, and she'd let her hair dry naturally, the way she'd been doing for most of the last month, instead of blow-drying it straight. It had become her regular appearance here, but seeing Dan now made her realize how different it was from the way she always looked when she was Mrs. Harris, wife of the state senator. Would Dan mention that in his article?

She unlocked the front door, feeling him come up right behind her. She stepped inside and walked briskly down into the hallway, to put some distance between them. When she reached the living room, she turned and gestured toward the sofa.

"Please sit down," she said, trying for her most welcoming voice, the one she'd use when she and Greg hosted cocktail parties for donors. "Would you like something to drink?"

"Sure, thanks, but don't go to any trouble." He sat and placed his pad and pen on the coffee table, and his messenger bag on the rug next to him.

The living room wasn't as neat as she'd have wanted. She'd planned to come home to straighten up before the interview. She picked up the juice glass that Zac had left this morning on the coffee table and straightened the throw pillows on the sofa. In the middle of the floor was Evie's backpack—the shoulder strap had broken that morning, and the zipper wouldn't close all the way, so Anna had folded a bathing suit and towel into a shopping bag and given her that to take. Now she picked it up by the good strap to get it out of the way. It was no wonder the thing was falling apart—it was ridiculously heavy. What had Evie stuffed in there anyway?

She set it down against the wall near the writing desk, and went into the kitchen. She came out a moment later with two glasses of iced tea, then went back into the kitchen and returned with some lemon wedges and a sugar bowl.

"So when did you get into town?" she asked.

"Yesterday afternoon."

"Traffic?"

"Not too bad."

She watched him stir sugar into his glass. "I'm sorry I wasn't on the sales floor to greet you when you arrived," she said. "I had no idea you were coming there."

"I saw the store mentioned in the local paper, and I stepped in to take a look," he said. "I didn't even know you'd be there. And anyway, you looked like you were in the middle of something important. My uncle was in retail. I know it can be stressful."

She nodded, wondering what exactly he'd seen or heard when he walked in on her and Aidan. The timing couldn't have been worse: when the door opened, Aidan had been holding her hands, and she'd been on the verge of tears. She would have to find a way to dismiss any assumptions he might be making. The last thing she needed was an article in the Silver Plains paper that suggested she had a new boyfriend. Her kids would feel so betrayed. Actually, all of Silver Plains would feel betrayed. It was possible that nobody would understand how there could ever be a new romance in her life. Greg had been just so loved.

She reminded herself to stay cool and calm, a devoted and polished politician's wife. That shouldn't be difficult. She had done it for so many years. She was good at it.

"Did you like the store?" she said. "Did my aunt show you around?"

He nodded, adding that Hope had also given him the history of the place—how Greg had bought it for Anna as a surprise, how she and Anna had been working so hard to make it a success, knowing this is what Greg would have wanted. Evidently Hope had been able to convince Dan that everything was right as rain between her and Anna. Listening to him, however, Anna realized another thing her kids didn't know—that she wasn't merely helping her aunt out. It was a revelation to her, that she had kept two very important secrets from her children this summer: that she owned the store and that she'd been falling for Aidan. No—there were three, if you counted her intention to sell the house. It hadn't been strategic or deliberate; she'd just held back on new information because she hadn't wanted to confuse them. She hadn't wanted to upset them.

But now she questioned her judgment. Was keeping secrets really the way to help them feel normal again? Or had she been creating a false sense of stability that was bound to end? Did they truly believe that nothing was changing, or did they know that life didn't work that way? By denying that anything new was going on, had she simply been making them even more insecure?

"So I think I'm up to date with the business side of things." He adjusted his glasses. "And Anna, I just want to say, I'm sorry about Greg. I didn't know him very well, but he was always fair and honest with me. And I hope my being here, my doing this story… I hope it doesn't make things harder for you. I have some tough questions. I hope you understand that's my job."

She watched him adjust his glasses again and then take a sip of his drink. What on earth was he going to ask her? She remembered what Crystal had told her on the phone a few weeks ago: *You can be tough, too. If you don't like a question, don't answer it.* Whatever he was planning, she was going to protect her husband's legacy. She decided to lay down her own agenda.

"Thank you for saying that," she said. "I appreciate your concern. And I should tell you that I'm very pleased to do this profile about Greg. I want to leave the community with a final picture of the wonderful person he was. I think it will be good for my children. And I think it will be good for Willow Center."

He unzipped his messenger bag and reached inside. She saw him start to pull out a digital recorder, then push it aside and pull out a folder instead. She wondered why he'd decided against recording her. He combed a lock of his hair between the second and third fingers of his hand. Then he picked up his pad and pen from the table.

"So, let's get started," he said. "Anna, how would you say Greg was last fall? After the summer... after you got back to Silver Plains?"

She pursed her lips. She had expected him to start with softballs: what kind of a husband was Greg, what kind of father? He clearly had a plan in mind.

"He was great," she said. "Glad to get home, glad to go back to his office, be with his staff. I think he was very anxious to get back to work on Willow Center."

"Anxious?" Dan said. "Like... nervous?"

Shit. Why had she said that? She supposed the word had been in the back of her mind all summer, because Crystal had said people described Greg that way to Dan. "No, that's the wrong word," she said. "Not anxious. More like... charged up."

He nodded, made a note with his pen, and then looked at one of the documents on his lap. "Okay, but was there anything for him to be nervous about? Because, to be honest, some people I spoke to for this story said he was acting a little unusual last fall."

"Oh?" She tried to sound surprised, feeling as if she was on the edge of a high dive. Something sharp and cold and shocking was potentially ahead.

"Not a big deal, just a little... well, anxious," Dan said. "And there was some talk that he looked tired. Like he wasn't sleeping well."

"Oh?" she repeated. "Who said that?"

"Sorry, it was on background. But generally speaking, it was people who knew him. And not just one, or I wouldn't have brought it up."

She pressed her hand against her chest to steady herself. "He was working hard. The talk about running for governor—it was getting more serious. And he was trying to rally support for

Willow Center. I don't even know what's going on with it now, I've lost track being up here—"

"A majority of council members may be leaning toward no. They're discussing it at the city council meeting tomorrow."

"I'm sorry to hear that. It's a good project. I hope they'll reverse themselves when they remember why Greg fought so hard for it."

"Why do you think he cared so much?"

"About Willow Center? Because he thought it would help people."

"Yeah, but why a mental health center? If he wanted to help people, why not… I don't know… a soup kitchen? Or a senior center?"

"He supported all of those things. He was a great supporter of all social services, you know that. Willow Center—it was timing, really. A project whose time had come, with that nonprofit group buying that empty building."

Dan nodded, so she went on.

"Plus, Greg felt deeply about people who were stigmatized for one reason or another. He thought people were objecting because they feared mental illness. And he wanted to show there was nothing to be afraid of—"

"Was the pressure to run for governor too much for him?"

"Not at all. He wanted to run—"

"Anna, why did Greg drive home during the storm?"

Anna was taken aback. "Because he wanted to come home," she said. "Dan, what's going on? I've been feeling something strange ever since you showed up. I thought this was going to be a profile about Greg and our life together, but it feels like you're going in a very different direction. What kind of article is this?"

He closed the folder and put it on the sofa. "It's an honest article," he said. "I wish I could write another puff piece like every other reporter wrote after he died. But that's not where the story's going. I have to follow the story."

"And where is the story going?"

"People were worried about Greg last fall," he said. "They saw things in him that weren't right. They thought he wasn't sleeping, they said he didn't look well. And some people said it reminded them of the way he acted after the train derailment. So I have to wonder: was *he* battling mental illness? Was he trying to hide it? Was he going to run for governor and keep this from the voters?

"Was the pressure too much for him?" he added. "And did that make him choose to go behind the wheel on a night when it was way too dangerous to drive? At least for anyone who wanted to make it home alive?"

She stopped breathing, as his words reverberated in her head. The interview wasn't nearly as casual as Crystal had led her to expect. And yet, she had to admit that the questions weren't as shocking and outrageous as perhaps they should have been. She felt as though she'd been waiting for someone to ask her these things. For a long, long time.

"It was a sharp bend, and the visibility was bad," she said. "That's what the investigation revealed. It's not like he wanted to kill himself."

"I'm not saying he did. I'm saying a lot of concerns have come up. And you confirmed it. You said he was nervous."

"I said he was charged up—"

"You said he was anxious—I can't pretend you didn't."

"But I also said it was the wrong word." She swallowed hard. "Dan, you're a good reporter, and you have a job to do. I get that. And I won't lie—I have questions about Greg myself. That's normal when someone dies—you're always left with questions that can't be answered. But why go down this route? It can't change anything. All it can do is cause hurt. For the people who loved him. For my kids."

"That doesn't mean the questions shouldn't be asked."

She folded her hands over her chest. No matter what Crystal wanted, no matter how much the people supporting Willow

Center were depending on this story, she was done. Enough was enough. She would deal with the consequences later. She would explain to Crystal that she had no choice.

"My children have been through so much," she said. "Their dad is their hero, the guy who saved people from the train crash, the guy who was always helping others. That's all they have. I can't let you take that away from them. The investigators made their report, and they stand by it. I can't let you write this story. I'd like you to leave—"

"With all due respect, it's not your decision whether I write it or not."

"If you publish that I said he was anxious, or anything else I said that could be seen as negative, I'll deny it," she told him. "I'll call you a liar."

"But *you'd* be lying—"

"No, I corrected myself, that's different from lying."

He combed his hair with his fingers again. "Anna, come on. I'm not trying to trap you. That's why I'm not recording this. I'm willing to work with you—"

"But I don't need you to. People loved Greg, and they'll believe me, not you. Your editor will never publish this story, not without even one source on the record. You're going to look bad if you submit it. I think you'd better think twice—"

"My editor wants a new angle, not another fluff piece about what a 'great guy'"—he put the words in air quotes—"Greg Harris was. I said I'd deliver it, and I intend to."

"So write about the store. That's new. About how Greg bought it for me. I can talk about that all day—"

"More fluff about how much he loved you?"

"If that's not good enough, then you have no story. Not from anyone on the record, and not from me." She stood up. "We're finished. You need to leave."

He looked at her, and she knew he knew she was right—the story wasn't going to fly with just a few unnamed sources. She really did understand the media, more than she'd realized. He'd evidently been hoping she'd reveal *something*, and that once he had something from her on the record, he could go back and get his other sources to go on the record, too. He looked let down, and for a moment she felt regretful. Greg had never let an interview deteriorate to the point that he had to throw the reporter out. How had she made such a mess of this? But that didn't matter now. It was done.

He gathered his things together and started for the door, his messenger bag under his arm. But he stopped before he got there. He wasn't ready to give up.

"Look, I can play hardball, too," he said. "What's up with that guy who was in your office today?"

"Nothing's up," she said. "He works for the town, and we had some business to discuss."

"You guys were pretty close in that picture at the hot dog place. How come he ran out of your office when I got there? And how come when I asked about him at Village Hall, the nice receptionist said he used to own a jewelry store in Rochester—but I couldn't find any record of a Rochester jewelry store owned by a guy named Aidan Lawrence? And how come when I searched further, I stumbled upon an Aidan Lawrence *Block* who owned a jewelry store near L.A. and looks an awful lot like this guy?"

She raised her palms. "I have no idea what you're talking about."

"Your friend's on the run, and I can easily find out why," he said. "So here's the deal. You own up to what you know about Greg, and you tell his colleagues they can talk on the record about him. Because if you don't, I'll expose whatever your pal is hiding. If he ends up in deep shit, it'll be on you."

He opened the door. "I'll be at the city council meeting tomorrow night, and then I'm writing up my story. You have until tomorrow night to make up your mind."

He dropped his business card on the hall table. "That's where to reach me," he said as he walked out the door. "The ball is in your court."

CHAPTER TWENTY-THREE

She closed the door and watched it blur, and then refocused her eyes to try to get ahold of herself. She couldn't fall apart now, just like she couldn't fall apart all these months when she thought about Greg or saw her children struggling without him. She had about one day—thirty hours? A little more?—to figure out what she was going to do.

She sat down on the sofa, pressing the fingers of both hands against her lips. It was true, Dan's reporting, even though it came from unnamed sources. And she was face to face with it now. She had come close to the truth many times since last December. She had grazed it. And then she had glided right by it. She had pushed it away, just as she'd pushed away the yellow flashlight she found in the closet on the morning two months ago when she and the kids left Silver Plains.

But she couldn't push it aside anymore, because Dan wouldn't push it aside. It was true: Greg had been overtired, stressed, distracted. He'd been… anxious, the word she'd used before she took it back. But she shouldn't have taken it back. It wasn't wrong. If anything, it was too mild.

Because now she saw it anew—the half-empty bed she would wake to in the middle of the night. And the bathroom light switching on and off. Over and over, sometimes for more than an hour. Greg would eventually stumble back to bed, claiming he was simply restless. So she would go back to sleep, and maybe there'd be two or three nights of peace. But then it would start again. Sometimes he'd unlock and relock the front door. Or open bathroom cabinets and then close them, hissing *Damn!* Or *Stop! Gotta STOP!* Or check, multiple times, that that damn yellow flashlight worked. She'd see his pale face the morning after a bad night, and she'd look away and finish fixing breakfast. Why hadn't she said she knew something was wrong, and they had to get him help? It had been hard work, convincing herself constantly that he was fine.

And it had felt safe, to accept the assessment that poor visibility had caused Greg's car to hit the rail and flip over the embankment. To believe it was an accident. That he had simply not understood how bad the roads would be, that he had wanted to get home to her and the kids. It would have been unbearable to let herself think about that night any other way. And the toxicology report had come back entirely clean. But now she wondered what she'd been too frightened to ever wonder before: had the road really been to blame? Or had Greg decided he couldn't live inside his own tortured head anymore?

No, *no*—she didn't believe he'd chosen to leave them. She would never believe that. And equally important at this moment, she could never let Dan Groner write that, or even suggest it. She could never let him publish a salacious story for the world to see. It wasn't fair to Greg, and it wasn't fair to Zac or Evie. She'd been right when she said Greg was their hero. That's all they had of Greg now—their belief in who he was. How could she let this reporter take that away from them? How could she shatter them like that?

But what was the alternative? To refuse to let Dan quote her? And throw Aidan under the bus? How could she do that, when Aidan had confided in her this very morning, had told her about the decision he made to leave and how he did it so he and Liam could stay together? And she admired him for it. She agreed that he was doing the right thing by putting his son first, by refusing to let Liam's grandparents come between them. If Dan uncovered the truth about what had happened in California—and he seemed pretty sure he could do it—Aidan could end up in a horrendous court battle that could damage Liam forever. Aidan and Liam were innocent bystanders in this horrible situation she'd created. How could she ruin their lives?

Too upset to sit still, she started to rise. But her knee bumped the coffee table, and both of the iced tea glasses flew into the air. One came crashing back down and shattered on the table, but the other soared higher. She went to grab it, but could only manage to strike it with her fingers. It careened toward the front hallway and smashed onto the floor, as her ankle caught the leg of the table and she landed flat on her chest.

She lay there for a few moments, feeling the shock of the wind knocked out of her. Then she pushed the floor away and lifted herself to her hands and knees. Glass was everywhere. Grasping the edge of the coffee table, she started to stand, but a thick bolt of pain shot skyward from her foot. She feared she'd injured her bad ankle again. Using the sofa arm for leverage, she pulled herself up onto her good leg and hobbled over to the chair by the writing desk, hoping that a few minutes of rest was all her ankle needed. Lowering herself down, she stretched her leg out alongside Evie's broken backpack and took a few deep breaths. Her arms were trembling, and her forehead was sweaty. She needed to calm down, and that's when her eyes rested on the computer in front of her, the one Zac used to stream baseball games.

She found the video, clicked on the arrow, and expanded it to full screen. It started up with the glorious orchestra. Aunt Hope—so graceful and strong, the dancer she still worshipped back then—emerged from the corner. She lifted her leg high into the air, starting that gorgeous sequence of steps that she would repeat three more times. And suddenly, sitting there at the desk, with glass shards showered behind her and her ankle throbbing, Anna realized that Aidan was right after all. The steps *didn't* get better with every repetition. They simply changed ever so slightly. Now Hope tilted her head more, now she held the extension of her leg a fraction of a beat longer. It was the essential lesson of ballet, the lesson Hope evidently had drawn upon as she performed the piece, the lesson Anna had been missing all along: that infinitesimal revisions could create something new. Not necessarily better—just new.

Sitting back, she seized upon the idea that she could use that lesson now. Did she have to expose either Greg or Aidan? Might there be another possibility, another approach? According to the ballet, there was always a chance to do something different. A tiny bit different. And change the world.

She clicked out of the video, thinking that she would give herself a few more seconds of stillness before getting up again.

That's when she saw something strange on the computer's desktop screen. She hadn't noticed it before, since Zac was the only one who'd used this computer this summer. But sitting here, she saw it beside Greg's work folder icons. Another folder on the screen. It was named "For Anna."

She hovered her hand above the keyboard, torn between wanting to know what was inside and wishing she'd never sat down. But she had to open it, now that she knew it was there. She lowered her fingers and tapped the key. There was a video inside. *ForAnna.mov.* She clicked and up popped an image of Greg, sitting right in this room, on the living room sofa.

She caught her breath, and the pressure in her chest spread as the seconds went by. But her body refused to breathe. It was as though she didn't know how to anymore, that her muscles had forgotten what they were designed to do, and would only allow her tiny gasps. For so long, she had wished she could talk to Greg one last time. To ask him everything she wanted to know: why had he given Hope their savings? Why had he bought her a dance store? Why had he driven home during that storm? What had he been going through last fall? She'd never imagined that she'd be able to see him and hear him again. Speaking here in this place they loved. Speaking to her.

She clicked on the arrow.

He was in a pair of gym shorts and his old gray Binghamton University tee shirt, the words faded and the neckline frayed. He was wearing his reading glasses, she assumed because he'd been reading directions on how to make a video.

He was leaning forward, his hands clasped, his elbows on his spread knees, his head lowered so it could be seen on the screen in front of him. The computer had been on the coffee table, which was now covered in iced tea and shards.

He took off his glasses, reached forward to set them down on the table, and then let out a big, self-deprecating sigh.

Hmmm, I guess this is working. Okay, Anna. Here goes.

And that's when she started breathing again, long, deep, loud breaths. Her head tilted and her eyes filled as the sour ache of all that was lost rose up from deep in her stomach. She fought against the urge to close her eyes and drop her head and fold into herself. Her Greg. Her beautiful Greg.

She watched him speak to her.

So, where I am right now, it's summer, and you're out picking the kids up from the lake so we can head back home tomorrow. But where you are right now—if I've done this right—it's New Year's Eve, four months into the future for me. And you're wondering why I wanted to spend New Year's in Lake Summers when we've never done that before, and why the empty building that we just passed has a sign that says 'Future Home of The Lilac Pointe,' whether Hope bought the place after all, and why, if she did, she hasn't told you yet.

And although you're by yourself at the Lake Summers house watching this video, and I'm at Pearl's right now with the kids getting hot chocolate—he raised his pointer finger—*through the miracle of technology, I'm going to answer your questions.*

She smiled. He had always been funny. She remembered how he'd squint when he tried to figure out how to do something new on the computer, how he'd look at her and feign a scream before reaching out and gingerly pressing a key. He'd never had any problem making fun of himself.

Yes, Hope bought the building. But so did we. I used my grandfather's money to go in halves. I bought'cha a dance store.

She watched him sigh and rub his eyes with the thumb and third finger of one hand. She knew that meant he'd be getting more serious.

So you're wondering why I did that. And I have to back up to explain. You know how I've been having trouble sleeping? Of course you do. And I've said it's stress, but it's not just that. It's also how I find myself checking everything… the lights, the locks. It's like… something let out of a box. I think I've felt it all my life, but I used to be able to keep the box closed.
But then came the train accident, and something inside of me changed, and I wasn't able to control it. Turning that damn flashlight on and off, worrying that every time I turned it off, I wouldn't be able to turn it back on, and you and Zac would be in danger. Did you notice? I don't know if you did. I was mostly able to keep it together. Except for the flashlight. Remember the flashlight?

Oh yes, she remembered the flashlight. The way he'd turn it on and off all those months after Zac was born. It was why she hated it. Feared it. Which was why she could never bring herself to throw it. She didn't know what Greg might do if he couldn't find it.

Then everything was fine again. Until... I don't know, about a year ago, suddenly the thing came out of the box again. And I can't put it back in. It's taken over. I didn't want you to worry. So I went to a doctor and he sent me to a specialist, who diagnosed me with OCD. Obsessive-compulsive disorder. Which, after hearing all this, you probably figured out.

And the thing is, I can't hide it anymore. It's making me sicker, the secrecy. So I want to go public with it. And I'm going to resign. I'm so sorry, Anna. I'm so sorry we built this great life together, and now I have to take it away from you. But I see the opposition to Willow Center, I know a lot of people might not have voted for me if they knew about this. At least, I know it would be an issue, and I don't want to stir up any more controversy. I want to get past this. And then I can go back to helping others. Maybe not as a politician. Maybe as a person.

And then you told me about Hope and the store. And I thought, what a great way to make up for the life I was taking away from you, by giving you a new life that you might love even more. So I went in halves with your aunt. I'm hoping we'll move to Lake Summers for a while, and the kids can go to school up here, and I can get the treatment I need—and we can try living in the slow lane for a while. I know you gave up a lot so I could go into politics. You made my life more important than your own. And I wanted to be your hero, like that story... that fairy person in that ballet of yours. The person who saves the day. But now I'm the one who needs saving.

So I hope it's okay if I'm not your hero. Just your husband. Is that okay?

She found herself mouthing the words: *of course*. How could he think otherwise?

So there you are. Now I gotta figure out how to turn this thing off. I think—

Just then there was a clamor off-screen. Anna heard herself telling the kids to put their wet bathing suits in the washing machine. Greg looked to the side, then turned back to the camera and leaned in close.

Oops, you're home, he said, chuckling as he lowered his voice, as though even with all he was dealing with, he could still understand how surreal it was to be making a video for the future her. He lowered his voice. *I just need to keep you away from this computer, so you won't see this until we come back up here on New Year's Eve. So for now, I'm going to… Okay, okay!* he called toward the doorway. *The Grill sounds good, burgers for all, I'm coming I'm—*

The video stopped.

She covered her face with her hands. It had started the night of the train derailment, he'd said. She remembered that night so well. She'd been nine months pregnant, huge and uncomfortable, watching TV to pass the time, when the breaking news about the accident appeared. Greg was just starting in politics back then, as a Silver Plains City Council member, and he'd called to say he was going to see if he could help. A little while later she'd gone into labor. New to the area and without any close friends yet, she'd left multiple panicked messages on Greg's cell phone, and finally called a taxi to take her to the hospital.

In the delivery room, with the contractions growing more intense, she begged the nurses to check for Greg. But he wasn't anywhere in the hospital, and because cell service had gone down near the crash site, nobody on the floor could reach him. After six intense hours of breathing and pushing, she welcomed Zac into the world by herself. Later in her hospital bed, she'd cried hot, angry tears, wondering how Greg could have missed his son's birth.

It was almost dawn when a gigantic white basket arrived at her door, filled with blue balloons, yellow roses, teddy bears, a bottle of champagne, a box of gourmet cupcakes, and a tin of fine chocolates. It was from the City of Silver Plains firefighters, who had tracked down some of the best retailers in the area and asked them to come out in the middle of the night to help create the gift. Not long after, one of the nurses came to see if she was awake for a call from the fire chief, who described how extraordinary Greg had been that night, keeping up the spirits of the first responders and victims with stories about his impending fatherhood and updates on Zac's progress, which he learned from ambulance drivers traveling back and forth to the hospital.

"He was making jokes, telling us what a clumsy excuse for a father he'd be," the chief said. "He knew just what to say to keep everyone strong. I truly think he saved lives tonight, Mrs. Harris. You can tell your new son that his daddy's a hero."

Finally Greg showed up at her room, exhausted and pale, with streaks of soot on his cheeks and forehead. The nurses cleaned him up and wrapped him in paper gowns, and she handed Zac to him. He broke down and cried as he wiggled his pinky inside Zac's fist. Immediately her anger dissolved, and she hugged him and cried, too.

Sitting here now, with her swollen leg outstretched in the direction of the lamp table with that old Sleeping Beauty doll, Anna realized just how badly she'd misread their marriage all these years. Yes, Greg wanted to be a hero—for her, for the kids, for everyone. But she had wanted him to be that, too. She had needed to be saved when he found her that day in the woods, Happy Meal in hand. She had needed a hero, so she didn't have to think about her father or her future. She had turned her back on dance and bought into the life of a devoted politician's wife not begrudgingly, but because it suited her. And she had turned a blind eye when Greg had been suffering so much, after the train derailment and again this past year, because—like everyone else—she'd bought into the myth of the invincible Greg Harris.

He had been ready to come forward and tell the truth about his illness. He was planning to announce it to the public, and to resign from office. And he wasn't even scared or regretful about it. His only fear was how *she* would take it. He felt bad for letting her down. And he had bought her the store to make it up to her.

She thought now about how selfish she had been. Why had she assumed she was entitled to a hero? She had given up dance so long ago—why had she never realized until now that although you can dance in a fairy tale, it's wrong to think you can live in one? Greg hadn't let her down; she'd let him down, by not speaking up when she noticed him struggling with the locks and the lights and everything else.

But then, as she sat there, she realized there was a way she could begin to forgive herself. A way that would show her children, for the final and most important time, how wonderful their father had been. A way to teach them an exquisite lesson about love. She would follow his lead and speak out, the way he'd intended but hadn't lived long enough to do.

If only she wasn't too late.

With her ankle feeling better, she nudged her chair closer to the desk, and started to Google airline information. But the chair leg grazed Evie's backpack and made it topple, and something thin and weighty slid out. She leaned over to look closer.

It was Greg's iPad, the one that had gone missing a couple of weeks ago, the one both kids had denied seeing. She picked it up, and then picked up the backpack and looked inside. That's when she saw Greg's toothbrush and hairbrush, as well as other things she hadn't noticed missing yet: Greg's headphones; a biography of Alexander Hamilton, which he'd received as a gift but never read, just kept in his top drawer; a polo shirt; the bow tie to his tuxedo.

She pushed the items around in the backpack, trying to make sense of why Evie took them. But before she could reach any conclusions, there was a loud crack from outside and then a scream. She rushed to the back door and onto the patio.

By the side of the house, a branch from the crabapple tree lay flat across the lawn. And a few feet away was Zac, sprawled on his back, one hand clutching the opposite arm.

CHAPTER TWENTY-FOUR

Hope would never forget the way Anna's voice had sounded on the phone—steady and firm and urgent—when she'd said she needed her to come to the house *now*. She'd never heard Anna so forceful; she almost had to ask who was on the phone. Melanie wasn't working that afternoon, and Hope had a class to teach in a few moments, but Anna was insistent. Hope had shooed all the customers and students out and locked the front door—the first time she'd ever closed during business hours.

And now here she was, a day and a half later, walking with Evie into Village Hall alongside what looked like nearly everyone in town. It all felt strangely calm to her, considering the frenzy of yesterday. How had they crammed all that had happened into six or seven hours—the trip to the hospital; the x-rays of Zac's arm; the discussion about Dan Groner; the quick stop back at the house so Anna could pack; and then the harried ride to the airport so Anna could catch her flight? Hope knew they'd never have been able to do it all if Anna hadn't stayed so strong and focused. She was truly remarkable. And Hope was glad she'd been there to see it. And to help.

She squeezed Evie's hand as they moved into the lobby. "Wow, look at all they did," Hope said. The sofas and tables had been pushed aside to make room for at least a dozen long rows of folding chairs, all facing a large monitor on a stand. People filed in all around them and began filling the seats in preparation for the seven o'clock streamed meeting of the Silver Plains City Council.

"And this is all for Mom," she added. "Come on, let's get a good spot."

She led Evie toward the front of the room. Near the monitor, she spotted Aidan conferring with Village Hall's tech staff, and around her, she saw many people she'd come to know so well this summer: Stan and Trey from the smoothie shop. Mrs. Pearl. Lonny from the hot dog place. The owners of the copy place and the card store. The couple that ran the hair salon. Maxine and the bartender from the Grill. The photographer from the *Lake Summers Press*. Anna had asked her to call all their fellow Main Street merchants, and to post about the meeting on Facebook, because Greg loved Lake Summers, and she knew he would have wanted the whole town to hear her. Hope complied and was elated by the response. Nobody she called had needed any convincing to show up. They'd all spent so much time with Anna this summer, and had come to love her. They all said they wanted to be here for her tonight.

As they moved closer to the front, Evie tugged on her arm and pointed across the aisle. "That's Nicole," she whispered. Hope looked to where Evie was pointing and saw Zac sitting beside a girl with a long ponytail that draped down the front of her tee shirt. Hope caught Zac's eye and motioned to his right arm, which was bent across his chest and supported in a sling. She gave a thumbs up and raised her eyebrows, to ask if the Advil was working. He nodded and returned her thumbs up. He was feeling okay.

She and Evie found two seats in the front row, and she scanned the place once more before sitting down. There, across the room, was Keon. The sight of his Jayson-logoed polo shirt almost made Hope cry. He was so reliable, so much the determined and devoted supporter of people he cared about. To his side were Melanie and the other dancers from Jayson, and behind him, she recognized Dara Steen and some of the trustees who had peeked in when she taught the kids from the Kids Club. Then she noticed that Keon had also brought some of the older kids from the club, including the beautiful dancer Clarisse, as well as a few people who were probably parents of those kids.

Her eyes caught Keon's, and he raised his hand and waved. She gave a small wave back and then turned away. She didn't blame him for keeping his distance. She hadn't seen him since that day at the store when she had told him to leave her alone. He had complied with her demand and had found a way to manage the program and be in touch with the Jayson dancers while staying out of her sight. It was probably for the best. It would have been too painful to keep seeing him every day.

The lights lowered and the screen came alive with the words "Silver Plains Council Meeting," along with the city's seal and today's date. The words dissolved, and a stage appeared, with seven people in business suits sitting behind a long table. There was a lectern facing the stage, with a microphone poised on top. The camera, positioned in a back corner of the auditorium, also revealed a number of filled rows in the audience, as well as several photographers lining the walls and kneeling in front.

The man seated at the center of the table introduced himself as Mayor Johnson Reeves of Silver Plains, and went on to make some announcements about street closures, water main repairs, personnel changes, and the planting of a red maple as the first step in creating the highway memorial to State Senator Harris. Then he opened the floor for public comments regarding the proposed Willow Center development plans. He explained that the council would consider the comments and vote on the project next week. A long line formed behind the lectern.

Hope spotted Anna on line and squeezed Evie's hand again. "There she is!"

"She looks different," Evie whispered. It was true—different, but only because she had changed so much this summer. Now she was back in the clothes she'd always worn as a politician's wife—a button-down blouse, tailored pants, and close-toed heels. But her hair was casually wavy, instead of blow-dried into an obedient, close-to-the-neck style. Hope wondered if she hadn't had time to do her hair in the old way, or if she'd decided intentionally on a blend of the old and new.

"A little different," Hope whispered back. "But it's still her."

The people on line each stepped to the microphone, one by one, to speak. Some predicted that the opening of Willow Center would depress property values and bring violence and homelessness to the city, while others disputed that. Some spoke fondly about Greg and his passion for the project, while others insisted that passion for the dead state senator shouldn't influence the discussion about such a risk-filled facility. At times Evie appeared fidgety, and then she looked sleepy, so Hope gave her some money to get water and chips from the vending machine. Then they counted down the number of speakers left. Six... three... one. And then Anna stepped up.

"Here we go," Hope whispered.

The camera showed Anna's profile, as she opened an iPad and placed it on the lectern. She dipped her eyes toward it for a few moments, and Hope tapped her lip with her fingers, wondering if Anna was nervous, and trying to send courage through the screen. But in the end, Anna didn't need help. She raised her eyes and began speaking.

"Good evening, Mayor, council members, and friends," she said. "My name is Anna Harris, and as most of you know, my husband, State Senator Greg Harris, was a huge supporter of Willow Center before he died in a car accident eleven months ago. Many shared his enthusiasm, and I've often wondered what he'd say if he knew the project was on the brink of failing. I think he would be heartbroken.

"And I'm heartbroken, too. You see, Willow Center is personal to me, and mental illness is personal. And that's why I'm here tonight. I recently found out that somebody that I loved, and many of you loved, was suffering from mental illness. My husband. And he was planning to tell you all about it. But since he's not able to, I'll do it for him."

Hope looked down at Evie. She wasn't fidgety anymore. She was mesmerized. Hope squeezed her hand.

CHAPTER TWENTY-FIVE

Standing by the wall next to the tech guy, Aidan watched the large screen. He hadn't seen or talked to Anna since early yesterday when he told her his story, right before that reporter showed up at the shop. It was Hope who had called him last night to tell him that Anna had flown down to Silver Plains, and to ask him to help her arrange the live-streaming. Now he saw the cast on Zac's arm, and the limp in Anna's walk, and he heard the resolve in her voice, and he knew that the past thirty-six hours or so must have been difficult. He was sorry that he hadn't been there to help.

"My husband was diagnosed with obsessive-compulsive disorder last year," she said. "The truth is, he'd had it for a while. It flared up after he helped with the train derailment years ago. It flared up again more recently, and more severely, too. He intended to go public with this news. He thought people should know the truth.

"Before he died, Greg was looking forward to getting treatment, spending time with his family, and continuing to serve the community and people he loved. He still had so much to accomplish, and that included cutting the ribbon at the opening of Willow Center. He understood how important Willow Center would be, because he knew firsthand how it felt to need this kind of facility. And there was more. He also knew that Willow Center would reflect our values as a community—values like compassion, and altruism. He knew it would do honor to all of us who live here.

"My husband had a favorite saying—you can't change everything but you can do what you can do. And the truth is, sometimes you *do* change everything. So I ask you all tonight—Mayor Reeves, council members, and everyone here—to do what you can do. Support Willow Center. In memory of my husband, and with compassion for all the people that truly need it."

The audience applauded, and those who could be seen on the screen rose up, as did the mayor and most of the council members. Applause also broke out right in the Village Hall. Aidan watched, feeling his chest expand with emotion. He had known from the time he met Anna that she was strong, but he hadn't realized just how strong. Hope had said on the phone last night that the local reporter had come up with some serious findings about Greg. But rather than hide and wait for the damaging article, Anna had gotten out in front of this story. She had told it herself, on her own terms. And now she was a hero in her own right.

Aidan thought he'd never known anyone else who'd ever acted so courageously. But then he changed his mind. Emilia had been brave, too. She'd been brave when she lost her hair. She'd been brave when the three of them went to Alaska, and she knew it would be her last vacation. She'd been brave especially toward the end, when she started to say her goodbyes, telling him and Liam that they'd never be without her, never spend a moment without her love. He suspected he knew what Emilia would want him to do. And he knew she'd want him to do it right now.

CHAPTER TWENTY-SIX

The Silver Plains mayor called for a fifteen-minute recess, and Hope stood and stretched her legs. She was in awe of her niece, how directly and honestly she'd talked about such difficult and personal things. Anna looked relaxed and proud up there on the screen, soaking in the audience's support. It made Hope think about her own behavior. She couldn't rewrite history. She couldn't go back to the last time she visited David and Anna in New York and tell them the truth about what she'd done. She couldn't change the fact that she'd run away, ashamed and scared of how they might react. She couldn't give them the opportunity they deserved back then to show her that they were her family, and they would love her no matter what. But like Greg used to say, she could do what she could do.

Next to her, Evie was looking up and down the rows, clearly ecstatic at all the people applauding her mom. Still, it was getting late. Hope looked over at Zac and his girlfriend, who were deep in conversation. She didn't want to interrupt them, but she knew Zac must be exhausted, and she was anxious to bring him back to her apartment, give him another dose of Advil, and get him settled for the night. Against the far wall she saw Aidan, talking to Mrs. Pearl and a man in a Lake Summers High School jacket. And sitting a short distance away from them was Keon.

She motioned to Evie that she'd be right back, and then walked over to him. He stood when she approached. She looked straight into his eyes—or as close to straight as she could, considering how much taller he was than her.

"Can I talk to you for a moment?" she asked.

He nodded, stone-faced. "I'm listening."

"I never should have said the things I said in my office," she said. "I'm sorry."

Keon took a deep breath as though he needed a moment to pull his thoughts together. "Hope… you accused me of wanting to control you and run your life," he said. "When all I was doing was talking out some options that I thought might help if you wanted to take the job."

"I know. It was a terrible thing to say. It's just that I've let people into my life before, and they were people I shouldn't have trusted. It's been safer to be on my own. Not to let anyone in."

"That's what you think of me, that I shouldn't be trusted? Hope, I realize we haven't known each other that long, but I've been nothing but open with you. You've met the people I work with, you've met the students I advise. And that night at your apartment—"

"I know," she said. "You've been so open, but it's different for me. There are things that are hard to talk about, things I'm not ready to share with you yet. And we were getting awfully close to that territory that night. So I felt I had to push you away for a while. Can you understand that?"

Keon put his hands in his pockets and looked down, and she could tell he was processing what she'd revealed. "I guess it's my fault, too," he said. "I have a tendency to get personal pretty fast. And I should have paid more attention. I should have seen that you weren't ready."

She smiled, touched that he would take responsibility like that. "Do you think we can start over again?" she asked.

He gestured with his chin toward the front of the room. "Looks like Evie's trying to get your attention," he said. "Why don't we go there together and see what she wants?"

Hope nodded and started to walk with him, then paused behind Zac's and Nicole's seats. She leaned down to rub her knee—not because it was hurting, but because the kids looked so darling together, and she wanted to eavesdrop a bit on their conversation.

"Does it hurt?" Nicole was saying, putting her head on his shoulder and gently touching his sling.

"Not too bad," Zac said.

Nicole lifted her head and looked at him. "I didn't know your dad died. He sounds awesome."

"He was," Zac said. "So is my mom."

Hope continued on with Keon toward Evie, feeling warmed by the kids' sweet exchange. She couldn't wait to tell Anna what she'd just heard.

CHAPTER TWENTY-SEVEN

Aidan looked at his watch. He wanted to be back in time to see what the city council would do next. He still had seven minutes. If he hurried, he could make it.

He rushed out the door and down the walk, then crossed the street and went into Pearl's.

Liam was behind the counter. "What?" he said.

"I came here to tell you that I just spoke to Mrs. Pearl. She's sending one of the other employees to take over for you. You've got to hightail it home. Your plane leaves in a few hours."

Liam looked at Aidan, expressionless. "What plane?"

"You're going to Atlanta."

Liam's eyes widened. "What? But why—"

"We'll talk about this later. All you need to know is that you gotta come home and pack."

"I told the coach I couldn't come."

"And I just talked to him. And now you're going."

Liam took off his apron and came out from behind the counter. Aidan grasped his shoulder. "And one more thing, bud. After Atlanta, we're going back."

"Back… here?"

"No, back for real," he said. "California. You were right. This is no way to live. We're going home."

"But what about all you said about what could happen…?"

"Don't worry, bud," he said. "We'll work it out. I'll keep you safe. I'm your dad."

CHAPTER TWENTY-EIGHT

It would have been nice, she mused as she waited to board her flight, if after the mayor announced he'd decided to hold the vote right then, the council members had been unanimous in favor of Willow Center. But in the end, it didn't matter. Only one member voted to challenge the development. The others, along with the mayor, decided that Willow Center deserved their support.

Anna had returned to her seat after the break, with Crystal next to her. When the mayor announced the vote, the council members were polled one by one. There were gasps of surprise that grew in volume as it became clear how the majority was swinging. Crystal grasped Anna's hand as the members weighed in and most of the audience erupted in cheers and applause. Crystal threw her arms around her.

And then the whirlwind started. Dozens of people pushed through the crowd to shake her hand. Two Willow Center board members asked if she'd consider joining the board. Mayor Reeves came off the stage to congratulate her. He said he planned to propose that Willow Center name the lobby or a conference room in the new space after Greg.

"You spoke beautifully, Anna," he said. "Have you ever considered a career in politics yourself?"

Then Crystal tapped her shoulder and held up her phone. "Look at this—the media's going crazy, and not just the local outlets. I'm getting calls from the *New York Times* and ABC News and even the *Today* show. I'll start scheduling interviews tomorrow, and—"

"No," Anna said. "I'm going back Lake Summers. My flight leaves at eleven o'clock. I need to call an Uber—"

"You're going back *tonight?* But your kids are staying with your aunt, aren't they? There's so much to do—"

"I want to be there for my kids in the morning," she said. "I'll be in touch as soon as things settle down. I promise." Then she wove her way through the crowd and out of the auditorium.

Near the front doors of the building, Dan Groner was waiting.

He sauntered over, chin down. "Congratulations," he said. "You were great out there."

She wasn't sure what she wanted to say. After all the good that had resulted from what he'd done, she wasn't nearly so angry with him anymore.

"I'm sorry about what I did yesterday," he said. "It was indefensible."

"I shouldn't have threatened you, either," she said. "It would have been wrong for me to call you a liar."

He nodded. "You know, you scooped me. After weeks of working on this, I have no story. And this was an important assignment. I may lose my job. Guess I got what I deserved."

She reached out her hand. "I've got to run and catch my plane. Good luck. I hope things work out for you."

It was an unexpected ending to what might very well have been the most unexpected day of her life.

When she'd found Zac flat out on the lawn, moaning and clutching his elbow, she'd rushed him to the emergency room.

Then they sat side by side on a curtained-off hospital bed, waiting for the results of the x-rays to come back and letting the painkillers start to work. Anna wrapped her arm around Zac, her hand stroking his good shoulder.

"So what was all this about?" she asked.

He looked into his lap. "I had to get home to dry up the water on the bathroom floor," he said. "And make sure the basement floor wasn't flooded."

"What?" she said. "You had to get home for… what?"

His beautiful long lashes glistened with tears. "There's always water, from the sink and the bathtub," he said. "And the toilet, it's always running, and in the basement, the water drips near the washing machine. And you or Evie could slip on it and fall or even die. I've been coming home every day to double-check the floors. But I'm never sure, I can never be sure I dried up all the water…" He sighed and dropped his forehead into the palm of his good hand.

She repeated what he said to make sure she'd heard it right. "You've been coming home during the day? You've been… leaving camp?" she asked.

He nodded. "It didn't take much time if I ran, and I had the key from under the planter," he said. "But today I saw you through the window, and I didn't want you to know, so I climbed up the tree… the branch was close to my window, and I didn't think it would break…"

He shook his head, his breath growing shallow and loud. "Mom, I can't take it anymore," he said.

She guided his body closer to hers, moving slowly and gently so as not to disturb his bad arm. So this was it, she thought. This was why he was always using so many towels, why he was always yelling about Evie making a mess on the floor, why the washing machine valves were turned off, why the key to the house wasn't under the planter where she'd left it. Nothing had made sense before, but now it all added up. Greg's video had explained everything. She didn't know if OCD was genetic or not; but whether Zac had inherited OCD, learned Greg's behaviors or internalized the same demons that had haunted his father, he was most definitely his father's son.

And though she hadn't understood what Greg was going through, she did understand now about Zac. Greg had given her the information she needed. So now she could help their son.

"So this is what you've been going through all this time," she said. "I didn't know. And I didn't know with Daddy, either. And I'm so, so sorry you've been suffering alone."

And that's when she felt him break down and cry—huge, noisy gasps that started in his belly and shook his upper body. She eased him even closer, and as he leaned his head on her chest, she rocked him slowly, hoping to envelop him in all the warmth and all the reassurance she could provide. He hadn't cried at Greg's funeral, he hadn't even cried when she took him and Evie to the hospital to say goodbye to him, as he lay there nearly lifeless in the ICU with countless monitors projecting incomprehensible readings. And it struck her as fitting for this strange, strange summer that Zac, who'd been trying so hard for so long to hold back the water, was now soaking her shirt with his tears.

But she didn't care. She would stay there on the hospital bed, rocking him and soothing him for as long as he needed, for as long as the sobbing lasted. Because sometimes flowing water was a good thing.

And now, as she waited by the boarding gate and remembered how good it felt to finally comfort her son, she found herself thinking about her father. *People plan, and God laughs*, that's what he used to say. He wasn't a religious man, but he loved irony, and he always found it amusing how life would kick people in the teeth at the very moment they put on their brightest smile. He would have appreciated that he had died the night before he was to see his daughter dance her first solo. And that she'd broken her ankle that same night and never made it to the performance. And that his sister had disappeared at the very moment his daughter needed her most. And that when his sister had finally resurfaced, she went on to hand her niece a financial mess.

But then she wondered if he'd have appreciated the reverse irony of the last day and a half, how some things that should have gone wrong went right. Hope had come rushing over when she got Anna's call, Zac had suffered only a broken wrist and some scrapes, and her ankle was merely bruised. Stumbling upon Greg's video had enabled her to understand what Zac had been suffering from, and carry out Greg's plans to go public with his diagnosis after all. Dan's malicious threat had put all this in motion.

In the end, she had written and delivered her own speech—something she'd never wanted to do before. It had been easier, safer, staying quiet or giving speeches Crystal had written. Just like it had been safe dancing for so many years in the *corps*. Yes, her one and only attempt at a solo had ended in sadness and hurt. But that didn't mean she should never again try to soar. She had hesitated only twice in the last day—once before telling Hope to alert the Lake Summers community about the live-streaming, and then again just before she'd stepped up to the lectern. But she had muscled through both times. It was what her husband would have wanted. She wished he could have seen her.

She opened her iPad to watch the Lilac Variation before she boarded. Then she watched it again. And again. Hope's smile on the screen now seemed to confirm what Aidan had noticed weeks ago: a ballerina wasn't joyful for having multiple chances to get the beautiful steps right. No; a ballerina was joyful because she got to do the beautiful steps multiple times.

*

It was after two in the morning when the Uber that picked her up from Syracuse Airport crossed the drawbridge into Lake Summers. She was foggy from having slept in the car, but had enough presence of mind to ask the driver to drop her off at the store instead of going on to the house. The weather was sticky, and rain was falling as she unlocked the door and heard the welcoming chime. She turned on the lights. In the silence of the night, the store felt so much more intimate.

She went to the armoire and pulled out a pair of shoes she'd had her eye on for a while, the soft Chacott style with the pale pink finish. She cut some strips of ribbon and elastic, and then pulled out a needle and thread from the drawer and sewed the strips in place. Although she worked quickly, her stitches were still neat and even. She had never lost her touch. Then she grabbed two gel toe pads and some hairpins from the drawer, and pulled out a black camisole-top leotard, a floral wraparound skirt, and a pair of tights from the floor displays, just as she had planned out when she was on the plane.

She walked into the studio and flipped on the lights. She went into the dressing room and put on the dance clothes, then pinned up her hair. Back in the studio, she sat down on the floor and ran her finger over the tip of one shoe. She'd always loved the combination of materials in a pointe shoe: the hardness of the toe box, the silky softness of the fabric. Ballet was full of contradictions. She'd always loved the mysteries that a dance shoe contained.

She pointed the toes of her right foot—the healthy one—and put the toe pad on, then slipped the shoe over it. It hugged her arch, her toes, and her heel, as though her foot and the shoe were one and the same. She adjusted the elastic so it lay flat over the top of her foot, and laid one stretch of ribbon over her ankle. It draped like a baby blanket on a newborn. She laid the other ribbon on top and then wound them both around the lower part of her leg, finding the familiar sense of tightness. Then she turned to her left foot, the one that was damaged long ago—and then again after she tripped on the coffee table. She slipped on the toe pad and put her foot in the shoe. The swelling had gone down a lot, and although her ankle was stiff and a little sore, it wasn't too bad. She straightened the elastic and tied the ribbons. She put her feet flat on the floor and stood.

Padding across the room, the toe boxes of her shoes tapping softly on the floor, she reached the sound system and attached her phone. The gorgeous melody of the Lilac Variation started to play. She warmed up at the barre with a few pliés and a few kicks, and then lifted her knees, one at a time, and rotated each leg in its hip socket. She raised her hands over her head, and then folded over to touch the floor.

It was time.

Standing in the center of the studio, she pointed her injured left foot—which had been the stronger one before she'd broken it—and lifted it off the ground as she bent her left knee. Then she sprang forward, trying to step cleanly onto her right toes with her left leg extended behind her, in arabesque. But her ankle complained with a sharp twinge, and she stumbled sideways.

I'm talking about you, Aidan had said. *You have another ankle.*

She walked to the barre to review her technique. Holding on with her right hand, she extended her right, healthy foot and then sprang forward onto it. She wobbled, grasping the barre, as she searched for the place where her weight should be. It was difficult because this wasn't her naturally strong ankle. But it would have to be the good one now. She repeated in her head all the lessons from teachers long ago: *Root down, shoot your energy through your extended leg, lift up, center your shoulders over your hips, eyes forward, chin raised.* She tried a few more times at the barre, getting more balanced and more confident each time.

She went back to the sound system and started the music over. Then she returned to the center of the studio. She waited in fifth position for the first note, legs crossed, heel against toe. Bold and strong, not letting any doubt enter her mind, she started the sequence from the beginning, and soon it was time for the arabesque. With a deep, determined breath, she sprang up onto her right leg, her left one extended behind her.

And there she was, back in a place that felt like home.

She was in that secret spot between the fears, just as she had described it to Aidan. And she felt like she never had to come down.

When she finally landed—she didn't know how long she'd been up there, maybe moments, maybe days—she heard the sound of someone applauding.

She looked toward the hallway. Aidan was leaning against the doorjamb.

She smiled. "What are you doing here?" she said.

"I've been waiting for you to come home," he said. "I was sitting outside your house, but it was taking you so long that I took a walk into town. And I noticed the lights on."

He came into the studio, and she ran to him and threw her arms around his neck, and he lifted her and spun her around. The Lilac Variation music played in the background, and a few stars twinkled through the skylights overhead.

And as she hugged him, it occurred to her that life was a lot like ballet. It was never perfect. But if you were lucky, it gave you several chances to muster your strength and leap toward your future.

CHAPTER TWENTY-NINE

The sunshine poured into her bedroom early the next morning. The humidity from last night had moved on. Anna got up to open the window wider. The air held just a hint of the weather from yesterday, carrying the fresh scent of moistened pine trees. It was the perfect day for SummerFest.

Down below, she heard the sound of car wheels on gravel as Aidan pulled out of the driveway. He opened the car window to wave. She waved back, keeping her smile fixed and her tears at bay. She didn't want him to see her cry. She didn't want to burden him with that. She watched him drive off, realizing that she barely remembered how he'd kissed her bare shoulder a little while ago before he left. It had been a gentle kiss, like a dream. She could barely remember it, but she'd never forget how it felt.

She did remember last night, and how she'd learned a whole new way to make love. With Greg, the lovemaking had been energetic and playful, defined by his boyishness and spontaneity. Aidan's approach was slower and more intentional, inviting her to take the lead and responding almost instantaneously, needing just a flash of a moment to see where she was going before shifting his body to complement hers. His attentiveness made her feel emboldened and she gave in to her impulses, finding an inventiveness she hadn't known was there.

"Your kids were so proud when they watched your speech," he told her afterward. "You should have seen their faces."

She hugged him, thinking those were the best words to fall asleep to.

Turning from the window now, she pulled on a tee shirt and a pair of leggings and started for the lake. It was the same walk she always took right before she got ready each summer to go back home. They had always felt bittersweet, those last few days before leaving. She would look out over the water, wondering how different she, Greg, and the kids would be when they returned. She had asked herself that very question a year ago, standing here, gazing across the water at Sogni di Lago, which looked very ordinary in the daylight, without the small lights glittering in the trees or the windows flicking orangey-gold from the tea lights inside. She had always assumed her kids would come back a little older and a little sassier, as preteens and teens did. That was the biggest change she'd ever envisioned. How clueless she had been.

But then again, standing here on this new morning, she had to admit that life still had the capacity to surprise her in good ways. She'd never have guessed she'd own a store this summer.

She'd never have guessed she'd meet someone who could make her see hot dogs in a whole new light.

She swung around toward Main Street and went back home, where she showered and changed. By then it was eight o'clock. Hopefully not too early to go to Hope's apartment. She couldn't wait to see her family.

*

Preparations were well underway at the Lake Summers Resort when she, Hope, and the kids came up the long driveway and pulled into the parking lot later that morning. They walked across the hilly lawn, weaving around workers who were offloading fixtures and tents from large vans, and merchants who were setting up their booths. As Aidan had promised, The Lilac Pointe had a central spot on the field, at the crest of a small swell, where a team of carpenters was now setting up a temporary stage and several folding tables. Nearby, Melanie, in black leggings and a gray pullover, was working on a poster on an easel, listing the free twenty-minute classes Hope would be teaching throughout the day. The poster also highlighted the studio's three featured performances: at noon, the kids were showcasing a hip-hop number; then Hope was leading the Jayson students in a demonstration of partnering techniques; and finally Clarisse was performing a solo that Melanie had choreographed.

Anna worried what the fall would bring. No matter how successful SummerFest was, she doubted it could turn their sales completely around. The sales numbers continued to look bleak, and building store traffic was going to get harder once the summer people left the town. She and Hope would need to decide what to do.

Near the stage, Keon was tinkering with the wireless speakers. Anna urged Zac to go on over and help. Liam was the expert when it came to all things technical, but they were going to have to make do without him. Aidan had told her last night that he'd sent Liam to Atlanta. And that when Liam returned, Aidan was planning to resign from his job, end the lease on his house, and move back to California so Liam could begin his junior year at his old high school.

"Your speech hit home," he said. "I can't keep running and hiding. What kind of lesson am I teaching him? It's hurting him more than it's helping him."

"But your in-laws…" she said.

"I'm going to reach out and talk to them as soon as we get back," he said. "And I'll ask them what their intentions are. I let my fear of a custody suit snowball for way too long. The truth is, I'm a good father, and they'd have a hard time making the case that Liam would be better off anywhere but with me."

She thought more about last night, as she tried to remember the dense warmth of Aidan's body, the touch of his fingers so gentle. She would have liked to have more time with him, even the rest of her life with him. He had been part of everything she was this summer. And if they were two different people—younger maybe, freer—she thought they might have had a happily-ever-after ending. But she knew that they'd had their last night together, at least for now. They both had things to take care of. She planned to leave Lake Summers and head home on Sunday. Camp ended Friday, and she wanted the kids to have a couple of weeks to settle back in Silver Plains before school started. The camp director had been very understanding when she'd called to explain what had happened, and the notion that Zac had fallen out of a tree trying to protect his mom and sister from slipping on wet tile had spread around camp and made him kind of a folk hero. Still, Anna knew there was no sugarcoating the situation. Zac needed help.

Turning away from the stage, Anna watched Hope show Evie where on the display tables to set up the price lists. Hope noticed her and pointed toward some boulders on the far end of the clearing. Anna followed her there. It seemed a good time for the two of them to sneak away alone and talk.

"Have I told you yet how beautifully you spoke last night?" Hope said, as she sat down on one of the rocks and proceeded to massage her bad knee. "I know I have, but I'll say it again. It was wonderful. People's lives are going to change in a good way, thanks to you and your courage."

Anna smiled, grateful for her aunt's praise. Then she looked away and shook her head. "The only thing I can really think about right now is Zac. I have to figure out what he needs. I still don't even know what he's going through. I mean, I understand it, I get it. But he's the one who knows how it feels."

"You'll work it out," Hope said. "You'll do exactly the right thing. And look at him," she added, pointing in the direction of the stage, where he and Keon were still fiddling with the speakers. "You can see it in his body language already. He's far more relaxed than I've seen him this summer. He knows you'll take care of him. It's making him feel better already."

"I think you're right," Anna said. Then she chuckled. "Although I think Nicole is also having a positive effect on his mood."

Hope laughed. "Maybe. Nothing quite like having someone in your life who thinks the sun rises and sets with you." She motioned to Anna to sit down next to her. "But seriously, sweetheart. Greg would be proud of you. Your dad would be, too." She sighed and squeezed Anna's hand. "I'm proud, too. I think you came into your own this summer. You became the person you were always destined to be. Starting from when you were a little girl, practicing the Lilac solo."

"But I never made it on stage."

"Sweetheart, dancing is nothing more than sharing a gift and making others' lives better for it," she said. "And that's exactly what you did last night. And what you'll keep doing. I have no doubt."

Anna reached over and hugged her aunt. Then she got up and walked a few steps to the maple tree shading the boulders, and ran her palm along the ragged bark. "I'm leaving this weekend for Silver Plains," she said. "It's time for the kids and me to go home."

"Of course it is," Hope said. "I'll miss you so much. But I know it's time for you to go."

"I know what the store means to you," Anna said, turning to face Hope. "Far more than I did when I got here. I don't want you to shut down. I'm going to talk to Greg's brother—he's finally back from India—to see how I can hold onto my share of the store for a little longer. So we'll have time to find an investor for my half, and you'll still be able to keep the place going."

Hope stood up and followed her to the tree. "I don't think that's going to work," she said gently.

"No? But I told you, I don't want you to lose it."

"And I love you for that," she said. "But I've also been coming into my own a little this summer. And I decided yesterday to do something bold and brave, too. Something that will have an impact on others. Most of all on you and your children, the three people I love most in the world."

She rested her back against the tree. "You know that Keon's been saying all summer that Jayson doesn't have enough studios for the dance programs. That's why he came to us in the first place." She paused. "So I asked him last night if he thought Jayson might want to buy our store and turn it into a satellite location for the dance school. And this morning he spoke informally to a few of the board members, and they sounded very interested in the idea."

"They want to *buy* the store?"

"Keon says they'll offer up a fair price."

"But this is *your* store, your life. What will you do?"

Hope shook her head. "This is the most unbelievable part. They want me to run the place, to teach and choreograph. I admitted that I never finished college, and it looks like it's not going to be a problem. They're going to help me finish my degree, and work toward a Master's, too. I can eventually have a title—Associate Professor. Can you imagine? Me—a professor."

"You'd be wonderful," Anna said. "But... is this what you want?"

Hope sat back down on a boulder. She picked up a stick and drew circles in the dirt. "At first I didn't want it at all," she said. "But it's sounding better and better."

Anna sat next to her. "I mean it—I don't want you to do this if you don't want to," she said. "I know how much you liked owning the place, having it as yours. And we can work it out, as I said. I'll talk to Ivan. There has to be another option—"

"No, sweetheart. Really. It's a good time for this to end. Making the store solvent would always be a battle. I'm a good teacher and a good choreographer. I should be spending my time with promising dancers like Melanie and Clarisse, not worrying about sales numbers or planning salsa parties. And by the way, I intend to insist they allow the Kids Club program to continue."

She tilted her head toward Anna. "But that doesn't mean I didn't love it. You came to love it, too—didn't you?"

Anna looked up at the sky. It was true, she did love the store. It had taught her that she was smart and creative and able. It had given her confidence and courage. She didn't know if she'd ever have seen Greg's video, if she'd ever have understood the true nature of his illness or Zac's illness, if she'd ever have reinterpreted her favorite dance solo and benefited from that new perspective, if she hadn't returned to Lake Summers this year. And partnered with Hope. And fallen in love with Aidan.

"I loved it," she said.

Hope put her arm around Anna's shoulder. "I'm sorry I wasn't the aunt you needed me to be. I'm sorry I left you alone for so long. I'll never forgive myself for that."

Anna thought about the aunt Hope was, the one who disappeared years ago. And she then wondered if she wasn't to blame for their separation, too. After all, she had idolized Hope for so long, wanting to see her only as a perfect ballerina, with a perfect career and a magical life. And nobody in the world could have lived up to expectations like that. Anna had had a rough life herself, and even as a teenager, she was wise enough to know that people were only human. Hope had experienced real loss, and Anna hadn't been there for her either. She wished she had given Hope that message, the last time Hope came back to visit. She wished she had let Hope know that she didn't have to be a star; that being Aunt Hope was way good enough.

And then Anna thought about the aunt Hope was today, the aunt who gave her space and time this summer to find herself. She thought about dancing in the studio last night, knowing she'd never have had the courage to start fresh if Hope hadn't been right there by her side. Now she realized that the person she'd become over these last two months had been inside her all along. Just waiting for a time like this summer, when she could emerge and start to soar again.

"You've been a fabulous aunt to me," Anna said. "I love you, Aunt Hope."

At that moment the bell tower on top of the resort sounded. It was eleven o'clock, and the first annual SummerFest had officially kicked off.

Before long, the lawn was overrun with parents pushing strollers, children holding balloons imprinted with the words "Lake Summers Realty," and packs of teenagers in tee shirts and cutoffs. Regular camp activities had been suspended for the day so that all the kids in town could take part in SummerFest, and soon Evie and Zac were with their friends. Despite how little sleep Anna had gotten the night before, she felt excited and motivated as she answered questions, rang up purchases, and packed merchandise in the store's signature pink bags. It amused her to think that one day in the not-too-distant future, people would be addressing Hope as Professor Burns.

The sample classes started, and Evie and her friends danced along, while Zac showed Nicole and the others how to operate the sound system and make sure Hope had the music she wanted. At noon, the performances started. The audience was huge—nearly everyone on the grounds looked up at the hill to watch. It was a wonderful celebration, by a community that until June had never cared about dance at all.

The day passed by much faster than Anna had expected, and before she knew it, the bell tower sounded four loud clangs, and the first SummerFest was history. Looking across the field, Anna saw Aidan shaking hands with some town officials. According to the smiles on their faces, the event had been a big success. Closer by, Hope and Keon were repacking shoes. Keon asked Hope if she'd like him to pick up some sandwiches from the Grill that they could eat for dinner at his place that night. Hope pressed up onto her toes and kissed his cheek.

Anna boxed up the last of the unsold tee shirts and, after gesturing to Hope that she'd be back soon, she ducked away from the big lawn. Passing the hotel's front entrance, she walked on to the hiking trail behind the building. She had avoided it all summer. But she was on the grounds of the resort today, and she was leaving town soon. She thought it was time to pay the place a visit.

She walked along the trail, looking for the spot where she had turned off that summer afternoon long ago. Remarkably, it was easy to find. Kids grew and people changed, but woods stayed the same. She left the trail and walked ahead until she found a sideways tree trunk. She didn't know if it was the same trunk—she didn't know how fast tree trunks decayed—but it could have been the same one. She sat down and remembered what had happened that day.

Looking around to be sure she was alone, she kicked off her shoes, hiked up her skirt, and pushed herself up on the toes of both feet. So far so good. Then she gingerly lifted her good leg to the back. But her bad foot was not cooperating, and she collapsed and tumbled down the woody slope toward the lake.

"Oh, God!" she groaned, pulling her legs together and scrambling to stand up. Grimacing from the pain, she slid her shoes on and limped back up the hill. There was no doubt about it—it was over. If she wasn't convinced before, she was now. She started to head back to the resort. And that's when she spotted him.

She had seen him around the hotel for a few days now. He had brown curls and a slim build, and was the best-looking and most popular of all the MBAs. She'd heard his name was Greg, Greg something.

And he was sitting on a tree stump, a McDonald's-wrapped hamburger in one hand and an envelope of French fries balanced on his knee.

The sounds of moving trucks drifted over from the lawn. Anna realized they were there to take the SummerFest displays back to town. Hope and the kids would be looking for her. Reaching into the pocket of her dress, she pulled out the Sleeping Beauty doll she had taken from the windowsill this morning, and placed it in the dirt near the tree trunk. Then she covered it up with brush and grass, so it wouldn't be easily spotted. It had taken her eight months, but she was finally ready to say goodbye—to the doll and to the life it represented. She hoped that one day another young couple would find it, and it would lead them to talk and to fall in love. Maybe the guy would be ready to make a change in his life. Maybe the girl would be grieving for her father and in need of a prince. Maybe they'd grow up together and even have a couple of children. And maybe the love they shared would endure forever, no matter how long their life as a couple was fated to last.

When she came back from the woods, Evie was sitting alone on one of the boulders alongside the booth that Hope, Keon, and Zac were now taking down. Her broken backpack was by her side. Anna walked over and sat down next to her. She put her arm around her daughter.

"Honey, can we talk for a minute?" she said. "About the things you've been carrying inside that backpack?"

Evie nodded.

"They're Daddy's things, right?"

She nodded again.

"Can you tell me why you started collecting them?"

Evie took out the oval hairbrush and ran it over the top of her hand. "Because I thought you wanted to forget about Daddy," she said.

"You thought I wanted to forget him? Why would you think that?"

"Because every time I said anything, you said you were fine. Back home, you said you were fine. When you took me to camp you were fine. When I asked if you would be lonely when we were at the fireworks, you were fine. You were fine, fine, fine, fine, fine. And then I saw the lady's card on the table about selling the house. And I didn't know how you could be so fine all the time."

She shook her head, and her face crumpled, and her eyelashes grew wet. "Unless it was because you didn't care about Daddy anymore."

Anna hugged her daughter and rocked her gently back and forth.

"I said I was fine all those times because I thought that's what you needed to hear," she said. "I thought it would help *you* to think I was fine. And when I talked to the lady about selling the house—it wasn't because I was forgetting Daddy. It was because I missed him so much that I didn't think I could be in Lilac House anymore."

She lifted Evie's chin and looked at her sweet hazel eyes, which looked so much like Greg's. "I'm not fine. I'll never be fine again. Because I'll never stop missing Daddy. But I'm strong, and I have you and Zac, who help me feel that I'm with Daddy, even though he's not with me. And I have a good life, because Daddy made it good. So you know what? I'll be okay.

"I'm not fine, sweetie," she added. "But I'm okay. Do you understand the difference?"

Evie nodded. "I'm not fine either, Mom," she said, wiping her eyes. "But I'm okay, too."

Then Anna waved Zac over, and the three of them sat on the boulder and talked about the ways Greg had made things better. They talked about the train derailment and the people he saved. They talked about Willow Center and all the people who would get the care they needed. And then she described how Greg had made Hope's life better, and Keon's, too, because the two of them now had one another in their lives. And how he'd made the lives of everyone in Lake Summers better, by helping bring dance to the community.

"He did all that," she told them, "when he bought me a store."

*

"So the renovation of the upstairs will start as soon as the deal is done," Hope said on Sunday, as Anna gathered up a few last things from the office and put them in a carton. "They want to convert my apartment into a small rehearsal space."

"You're welcome to stay in Lilac House for as long as you want," Anna told her.

"Or she may have another option, whenever she's ready," Keon said as he came in and kissed Hope on the cheek. He picked up the carton and took it outside.

Hope looked at Anna and grinned. "Anyway… it's still very early days, it's all being worked out. But they want to keep a portion of the shop for dance clothes and some Jayson logo merchandise. And we're hoping to have the big studio open throughout the construction."

Anna nodded. "And I spoke to Greg's brother yesterday," she said. "He said he'll be in touch with the Jayson people. And I'll come up as soon as it's time to sign the papers."

It had been a busy morning. She and the kids had woken up early to finish packing, and then loaded their bags into the trunk, reversing the process they'd begun in June. Before getting into the car, she'd stopped on the front walk to take one more look at Lilac House. It was a beautiful home. She didn't know what she was going to do with it now. It would depend on the outcome of the Jayson deal, and how much money that brought her. She no longer felt that she had to sell it, that she couldn't live in it anymore. She was okay, as she had told Evie. If Ivan felt it would be okay, the three of them could decide maybe to hold onto the house a little longer.

They'd climbed into the car, with Zac next to her and Evie in the back seat. The gravel crunched under her wheels as she pulled out of the driveway. She heard Greg in her head: *Goodbye house! See you next summer! Everyone, say it!* She decided it was right to continue the tradition.

"Everyone say it—goodbye, house!" she said. Unexpectedly, her voice cracked.

"Goodbye, house!" Evie said.

"Ugh, you can't say goodbye to a house," Zac groaned.

"I can do whatever I want," Evie said. "Don't miss us too much, house!"

With the office cleared of her things, she walked outside with Hope, hearing the door chime for what would be the last time in a long while. On the porch, Melanie was taking selfies of her and Evie, while Nicole was standing close to Zac, typing something into his phone. Anna had learned last night that Nicole's family was also here for the summer, and that they lived in Ardsley, not too far from Silver Plains. She had already invited Zac to the fall dance at her school.

Keon slammed the car trunk shut and came back up onto the porch. "Looks like you're all set," he said.

She reached over to hug him. "Take good care of my aunt," she said.

"I don't think your aunt needs anyone taking care of her," he said. "But I'll do what I can. Have a safe trip, Anna."

She nodded, just as Stan and Trey, in their Smoothie Dude aprons, came running over. "Here you go—the final rendition," Stan said, displaying a platter with those notorious paper cups.

Anna looked at Hope tentatively. What was this version going to taste like? Motor oil? Dishwashing liquid? Transmission fluid?

"Don't worry—we gave up on the ballet-themed infusions," Trey added. "We turned to ballet toppings instead. Behold—the Lilac Pointe Smoothie. Raspberry topped with candied lilacs."

Anna looked into her cup, savoring the amazing fragrance of the delicate, caramelized segments. Then she took a sip and one of the petals glided into her mouth. It was crunchy and rich and sweet, the perfect complement to the drink's tangy raspberry flavor.

"Oh my God," Hope said. "You did it! Yum!"

Anna nodded and hugged them both goodbye.

Then Hope walked her down the porch steps.

"Good luck, Professor Burns," she said.

"I miss you all already," Hope said, as she threw her arms around her.

Aidan was waiting by the car alongside Liam, who'd returned from Atlanta just an hour earlier. She was glad Liam had made in back in time to say goodbye. She gave him a hug, and then Aidan walked her around to the driver's side.

"So when do you leave?" she asked him.

"We start back for the West Coast on Tuesday," he said. "We're meeting Liam's grandparents for dinner next week.

"And what's next for you?" he said.

She told him she'd contacted the pediatrician who'd recommended a specialist for Zac with an excellent reputation for working with adolescents, and she was feeling optimistic.

"He'll be okay," he said.

"I think so," she said. "I think all three of our kids will."

He opened the car door, and then took her elbow and leaned down to kiss her on the cheek—the only type appropriate, with everyone around. His face lingered near hers for a beat. She closed her eyes and tried to memorize the way it felt. She didn't want to lose the feeling of being close to Aidan, the guy with the quiet voice and the subtle smile. He was the one who had gotten her back on her toes. Literally and figuratively.

"I'm not giving up on us, Anna," he whispered.

"Me either," she said. She believed in her heart that before too long, they'd be on Main Street together once again.

He took her hand. "Drive carefully. I'll call you."

She motioned to the kids that it was time to go, and a few minutes later they were off. It was hard to see all those people—Hope and Keon, Stan and Trey, Melanie, Nicole—waving to them from the porch. But it was the sight of Aidan and Liam in her rearview mirror that made the tears start. Aidan had one hand resting on Liam's shoulder. She remembered when she'd first met him in Village Hall, how he'd said that Liam was everything to him, the one thing that kept him going. It was the moment she'd started to fall in love with him.

She wiped the tears away, listening to the kids argue about whether they should stop at the Italian place on Highway 9, the sandwich place in New Hartford, or Big A's Diner on the Thruway. Evie called out to her: did she have an opinion?

No, she said. She didn't. It didn't matter to her where they stopped. So she let them continue to work it out, while she started toward the highway, listening in her head to the beautiful start of the Lilac Variation melody. She remembered how it had felt the other night when she'd finally gone up on her toes for the first time in forever. How she had risen up and it had felt like home.

The very place she'd be tonight. With her children. Finally, they'd be home.

A LETTER FROM BARBARA

I want to say a huge thank you for choosing to read *The Lilac House*. If you did enjoy it, and want to keep up to date with all my latest releases, just sign up at the following link. Your email address will never be shared and you can unsubscribe at any time.

www.bookouture.com/barbara-josselsohn

I hope you loved *The Lilac House*, and if you did, I would be very grateful if you could write a review. I'd love to hear what you think, and it makes such a difference helping new readers to discover one of my books for the first time.

I love hearing from my readers—you can get in touch on my Facebook page, through Twitter, Goodreads or my website.

Thanks,
Barbara

BarbaraSolomonJosselsohnAuthor

@BarbaraJoss

www.BarbaraSolomonJosselsohn.com

ACKNOWLEDGEMENTS

There are so many people who played a role in the creation of *The Lilac House*, and I am forever grateful to all of them.

First, thanks to my amazing agent, Cynthia Manson, and my extraordinary editor, Jennifer Hunt. There's no better feeling than knowing you are in good hands and the people who are guiding you are smart, visionary, and always have your back—and I have felt that every step of the way! Thanks, too, to the entire team at Bookouture—I am so glad to be part of the family!

I am incredibly lucky to have a writing community filled with generous and super-talented friends, colleagues, and mentors. Thanks to Caitlin Alexander, Jimin Han, Pat Dunn, Veera Hiranandani, Diane Cohen Schneider, Jamie Beck, Linda Avellar, Ginger McKnight-Chavers, Patricia Friedrich, Maggie Smith, Susan Schild, and Nancee Adams. Thanks, too, to everyone at the Women's Fiction Writers Association, the Writing Institute at Sarah Lawrence College, the Scarsdale Public Library, and the Scarsdale Library Writers Center.

I am indebted to everyone at the JCC-MidWestchester, and especially to Jayne Santoro, a wonderful and passionate dancer and teacher who inspired the character of Hope. Thanks, too, to Renee Laverdiere, whose beautiful store, Repertoire, was the model for The Lilac Pointe. Thanks to Dr. Kim Greene-Liebowitz and Dr. Leslie Blum for their expertise in answering my medical questions. I also want to give a shout-out to Laurel House, where I am privileged to volunteer. An exceptional organization, Laurel

House was the inspiration for Willow Center, the proposed mental health facility that plays a pivotal role in the book.

Finally, a huge thank you to my husband, Bennett; our children—David, Rachel, and Alyssa; and our indefatigable dog, Mosley. My characters' deep commitment to—and overwhelming love for—their families came directly from the five of you.

CPSIA information can be obtained
at www.ICGtesting.com
Printed in the USA
LVHW091050220520
656285LV00002B/476